This is a work of fiction. An events, and incidents are pro imagination or are used ficti construed as real. Any resen locales, organizations, or persons—living or dead—is entirely coincidental.

HEARTLESS PRINCE copyright @ 2021 by Brook Wilder and Scholae Palatina Inc. All rights reserved. No part of this book may be used or reproduced in any manner whatsoever without written permission except in the case of brief quotations embedded in critical articles or reviews.

# TABLE OF CONTENTS

HEARTLESS PRINCE .................................................................. 5

Chapter 1 ............................................................................. 6
Chapter 2 ........................................................................... 11
Chapter 3 ........................................................................... 16
Chapter 4 ........................................................................... 19
Chapter 5 ........................................................................... 26
Chapter 6 ........................................................................... 31
Chapter 7 ........................................................................... 35
Chapter 8 ........................................................................... 44
Chapter 9 ........................................................................... 49
Chapter 10 ......................................................................... 52
Chapter 11 ......................................................................... 56
Chapter 12 ......................................................................... 67
Chapter 13 ......................................................................... 73
Chapter 14 ......................................................................... 82
Chapter 15 ......................................................................... 88
Chapter 16 ......................................................................... 93
Chapter 17 ....................................................................... 100
Chapter 18 ....................................................................... 104
Chapter 19 ....................................................................... 113
Chapter 20 ....................................................................... 116
Chapter 21 ....................................................................... 122

Chapter 22 ................................................................. 129

Chapter 23 ................................................................. 134

Chapter 24 ................................................................. 140

Chapter 25 ................................................................. 147

Chapter 26 ................................................................. 154

Chapter 27 ................................................................. 157

Chapter 28 ................................................................. 164

Chapter 29 ................................................................. 172

Chapter 30 ................................................................. 177

Chapter 31 ................................................................. 184

Chapter 32 ................................................................. 188

Chapter 33 ................................................................. 191

Chapter 34 ................................................................. 195

Chapter 35 ................................................................. 201

Chapter 36 ................................................................. 210

Chapter 37 ................................................................. 217

Chapter 38 ................................................................. 222

Chapter 39 ................................................................. 224

Chapter 40 ................................................................. 229

Chapter 41 ................................................................. 240

Chapter 42 ................................................................. 247

Chapter 43 ................................................................. 253

Chapter 44 ................................................................. 258

Chapter 45 ................................................................. 263

| | |
|---|---|
| Chapter 46 | 268 |
| Chapter 47 | 272 |
| Chapter 48 | 276 |
| Chapter 49 | 285 |
| Chapter 50 | 288 |
| Chapter 51 | 300 |
| Chapter 52 | 308 |
| Chapter 53 | 312 |
| Chapter 54 | 321 |
| Chapter 55 | 326 |
| Chapter 56 | 335 |
| Chapter 57 | 338 |
| Chapter 58 | 348 |
| Chapter 59 | 359 |
| Chapter 60 | 371 |
| Epilogue | 375 |

# HEARTLESS PRINCE

## BOOK ONE OF THE *CAVAZZO MAFIA* TRILOGY

*I WAS FORCED TO PAY THE PRICE FOR MY FATHER'S SINS.*

I was sold to the highest bidder - a dangerous monster with a handsome face:

Lucas Valentino - Don of the Cavazzo Mafia
He made it clear from the moment he marched me off the auction block:

I can fight him, but I'll never win.
And the only way out is to pay the ultimate price.

Every inch of my body is his to ruin.
Every bit of my soul is his to defile.

In a golden cage he built for me, he intends to break me.

Make me do unspeakable things.
Humiliate me beyond my wildest imagination.
Make me beg and scream.

Until I accept his promise:

That even if he freed me, I'd *never* want to leave.

# Chapter 1
## Leda

The van bumped along the road, and I crashed against the metal wall, still not completely sure how everything had led up to this exact moment.

Less than an hour ago, I was summoned by my father, Carmine D'Agostino, to visit him in prison. And now, I was stuck in the back of a windowless van whose interior door handles were removed, going God knows where.

A particularly hard turn threw me against the wall of the van and a wave of nausea crept up in my gut. *Jesus, where did this guy learn to drive?*

I steadied myself against the jostle and tried kicking the door open again. Being a Mafia Don's daughter had some perks. One of which was the cheery knowledge that if they took you to a second spot, your odds of survival basically dropped down to zero.

Which meant that if I didn't get out of this van ASAP, my life was over.

Well, my life was probably already over, in all honesty. I thought the fact that my brother Nico had put our father in prison meant that we'd be free of his shitty influence.

But somehow, the man still found a way to keep us on his leash. That fucking bastard. Being locked up in prison for murdering a whole fucking family should mean you can't make demands anymore, least of all demand that your only daughter show up for a mandatory family visit.

Especially if the only thing you intended to do with the visit was to tell her that you've sold her to another Don for a favorable deal.

*Why couldn't you have just died when you had that stroke?!*

My mind whirled with the possibilities of the Don he would marry me off to. I'd met enough of them in my twenty-four years, and each one worse than the last. Most were old, fat, both, and almost every single one of them had already buried one wife already.

All of them wanted a wife who did what countless other women have already done: spread their legs for a man who disgusted them in every way, shape, and form. There would be no love, no devotion, and no hope in the future my father had chosen for me.

The van lurched to a stop.

I put my hands out to keep from being slammed against the doors.

I arrived.

I didn't know exactly where I arrived *to*, and something deep in my gut told me that I didn't want to be here. But after that nauseating ride, I welcomed the brief respite.

The doors opened suddenly, and I took two steps back as the cool night air filled the stifling vehicle. In an instant, I was rushing toward the man at the level of the van, nearly knocking him over in my attempt to escape.

I didn't get far before he grabbed my arm and hauled me against the cold steel door, the metal biting into my flimsy dress. "Nice try, bitch."

I stared at him defiantly, my eyes glittering with anger, not tears.

*Never tears. Tears were a sign of weakness. I was a D'Agostino, and we didn't cry.*

"Whatever my father has paid you," I said, lifting my lips into a cruel smile that my father would have been proud of. "I will double it if you let me go right now."

To my surprise, he laughed and shook his head. "Your father? You think Carmine is behind this?" He gave me a shove. "Get moving."

He acted like my father wasn't part of this at all, but I had heard his parting words in the prison before I was carted away. *Take her to her new husband.* I knew what was in store for me.

My sandals didn't provide any support for my feet as I was forced to walk over gravel, attempting to peer into the darkness to get some sense of where I was being taken. The air was crisp and cool, gently blowing at the sundress I had put on to visit my father earlier. Summer was coming to an end, and since it was my favorite time of year, I had way more of a summer wardrobe than I did for cold, harsh winter.

Right now, though, I would have killed for a light jacket.

Well, that, and a gun so I could shoot the asshole behind me.

We came to a door and my kidnapper twisted the handle, opening it up. "Down you go," he said, giving me a little push.

A set of stairs greeted me, and I swallowed as I descended, nothing but dim lighting ensuring I didn't fall down them. I hated the dark, the feeling of claustrophobia.

Nico used to tease me about my nightlights when we were children: the brighter the better. Even with the small lights around me, I felt the rise of panic in my throat. It was clear that we were moving underground.

But to where?

The anticipation of *something—anything—*was killing me.

The man urging me forward breathed down my neck as it were, but if I tried to hurry down the steep stairs, I could easily slip and fall.

Maybe it wouldn't be such a bad way to go…

My lips pursed. Well, it wasn't like my father would mourn my death. Nico and Rory would, but there was no one else.

No one who'd give a shit about me. I had a gaggle of friends, but all surface level. None of them was close to me like my brother and his little family. The people that I knew were haughty and rich. They snubbed their noses at anything that didn't fit in their little vapid world.

And unfortunately, I also knew for a fact they wouldn't give two shits about my death. Maybe there'd be a day of mourning. And that'd be it. Leda D'Agostino used to exist in their world. But no longer.

Steeling myself against the flare of hurt in my chest, I was relieved when the stairs ended, and we found ourselves at another door. The man gave three raps on the steel frame, the door opened immediately, and he shoved me through.

## Chapter 2
## Leda

A sapphire blue carpet greeted me as I was pushed forward, and I was surprised to see the bright lights of a chandelier above my head. Music floated from somewhere unseen, and I could hear faint laughter in the distance. The tantalizing smell of bread made my stomach rumble despite the predicament I was in. I hadn't eaten since lunch.

"This way," my kidnapper said and took me away from the carpet down a hallway before she shoved me into a room.

Inside, there was nothing but a rack of clothing and a single dour-faced woman giving me the up-and-down over her black-rimmed glasses.

"Thank you, you may leave."

My kidnapper snorted and walked off, shutting the door behind me and muttering something about not getting paid enough.

"I need help," I said immediately as the woman shuffled over to the clothing rack and riffled through the hangers. "Please."

She didn't acknowledge my presence and continued going through the rack, picking up different outfits—each skimpier than the last—and muttering to herself. I walked to the door, grabbed the handle, and gave it a turn.

The door didn't budge.

Tamping down my panic, I turned back to find the woman staring at me. "Take your clothes off," she said in a grating voice. "We don't have all night."

I blinked. "What?"

She waved at my dress. "Take it off, or I'll do it for you."

"I'm not taking off my dress," I said in a small voice. "Where am I? What is going on?"

The woman's mouth twisted in an unpleasant frown. "You're really going to make me do this the hard way?"

She advanced on me, and I pressed my back against the door, my mind racing. I could take her. I could knock her out easily enough. But that wouldn't get me anywhere. There were no windows in this room, no other way out except the door I was currently pressed against.

"Please," I begged. "I don't know what's going on."

She rolled her eyes. "Last chance to take it off willingly."

I glanced at her gnarled hands and decided that I would rather take my own clothing off. "Fine. Fine, just give me a moment."

"Be quick about it." The woman nodded and stepped back, a replacement dress with a plunging neckline in

12

her hand. "They have no problem dragging you out there naked."

My hands trembled as I reached for the straps of my sundress, shimmying it down my hips with tears in my eyes. I wasn't a prude by any means, having grown up around not only the Mafia but also the glittering world of high fashion.

I heard plenty of stories about the debauchery of the rich and powerful behind closed doors. Yet despite my best attempt at sneaking into those to get a look in person, my brother Nico and the reputation of my father's name always kept me out.

This felt different. More dangerous.

"Bra too," she stated. "It won't work with the dress."

Glad that I had put on a decent pair of panties this morning, I unclasped my bra and let it fall to the floor, the cool air causing my nipples to pucker. I'd honed my body in top form, regularly running and practicing yoga to keep up with my crazy lifestyle.

Still, my hips flared more than I cared for them to. And my boobs, well, they were on the slightly bigger-than-average side.

"Here," the woman stated, thrusting the dress at me. "Put this on, and put your hair down. They like that."

*They? I thought I was being taken to my husband?* I hurriedly put on the dress, finding the neckline plunging past the valley between my breasts to the top of my navel. The bottom hem barely covered my ass.

"Who are they? What's going on?" I asked, tugging on the ponytail holding my hair. Chestnut layers fell around my face, and I resisted the urge to run my fingers through them.

"Better," the woman said instead as a knock sounded on the door. "Time to go."

I drew in a breath as the door opened, and the same man from before was standing there, his bored eyes barely flickering over my lack of clothing. "Everybody ready?"

"She is." The woman nudged me with her arm. "Go on now. Don't keep them waiting."

I hesitated. The man sighed and grabbed for my arm. "Let's go, princess. Don't make me throw you over my shoulder."

His fingers bit into the upper flesh of my arm. I winced as his thumb rubbed my skin obscenely before he dragged me out of the room. My sandals slid on the hardwood floor.

"Try to run," he whispered in my ear. "And I will kill you. I don't care who the fuck you are."

The dark tone of his voice sent shivers down my spine, but before I could think about it, I was at a small set of stairs, the sounds of conversation louder now.

"Go on," he stated, pushing me toward the first step.

I didn't want to, but what choice did I have? I bit my lip until it hurt and walked up the stairs, finding myself on some sort of stage. The blue curtain blocked my view of what was waiting on the other side, but the noise was louder, and I briefly debated running the other way, not caring what happened to me.

I didn't know how far south my father's plans had gone, but I knew for a fact that my new husband was not on the other side of the curtain.

# Chapter 3
## Leda

A woman hurried toward me across the stage. "What are you waiting for?" she hissed. "Let's go."

There would be no escape today.

My feet moved of their own volition, and the lights blinded me as I moved from behind the curtain, the room growing quiet.

"Our next lot!" The woman announced. "Leda D'Agostino, daughter of Carmine and sister of Nico!"

There was a rumble through the crowd, and I felt goose bumps break out all over my body as I realized who I was standing before.

A crowd of Dons.

Most of them I recognized. Former friends and allies of my father. They had dined at our table, laughing and making conversation with me as I took over the hostess duties many times.

Now they leered at me like starving men staring at their first meal. Some even licked their lips in anticipation of what was about to happen next.

Dear God, what was their plan?

Frantically, I looked around the room as the woman clapped her hands. "Now, I know you all have been waiting for the moment that you can have her, but this is still an auction, after all." She looked at me, her lips pursing. "We have rules."

Despite my fear, I wanted to rip her hair out by its fake blonde roots.

She turned back to the crowd. "Remember the promises he's failed to keep and the price *you* paid. This is your chance to get back just a fraction of what he's taken from you."

*No. No. No. No. NO!*

My knees weakened as she spoke. Somewhere along the way, my father's plan had completely fallen apart.

I was never being taken to my husband. I was never being taken to a marriage.

I was being auctioned off.

This was all about revenge on my father. They couldn't take it out on him, so they'll do it to me.

The woman continued and listed the rules of bidding. I stood there in numb silence. It was as if I were a fly on the wall, watching some other girl get sold before a crowd.

Tears swam in my eyes and I blinked them away, thinking about my fate. These men weren't going to take me under their wing, to make sure that I would be taken care of.

They were going to throw me down on a bed and use me until I'm bloody. Until I begged them to stop.

Well, I wasn't going to show them that weakness. I was a D'Agostino, for God's sake. I was made of sterner stuff than that.

I lifted my chin and gazed about the room again as the woman droned on around me, meeting the eyes of any that dared look at me.

*Think I'm weak? That I'll just curl up and die? Think again.*

As I looked out into the sea of eyes, one particular pair caught my attention. They belonged to a man who stood in the back of the room, his arms crossed over his chest.

He was younger than the rest of the room, his dark hair raked off his forehead, matching the dark suit he was wearing. While I couldn't make out his features, I knew he wasn't here to help me.

No one was.

# Chapter 4
## Leda

"We will begin the bidding at five hundred thousand," the woman started. "The same rules apply as always. The club will not tolerate any fights or killings due to a bidding war."

I swallowed. How many times had they done something similar? What sort of club was this?

A half a million dollars. Opening bid.

A hand went up, and the woman acknowledged it. "Opening bid accepted. Do I hear one million?"

Another hand.

"Two million?"

Another hand. My own palms started to sweat at my sides, and I wanted to wrap my arms around my waist to provide some comfort. I wouldn't find any here, not among these assholes who thought it was okay to play with one's life.

"What about five?" the woman continued, clearly pleased at the bidding. "Is ruining Carmine D'Agostino worth five million?"

They wanted to ruin my father. I wasn't going to survive whoever won me. This kind of money wasn't going to give me the life I had been hoping for.

This was going to be my death.

My stomach roiled. I wouldn't see Nico or Rory again. They would wonder what happened to me, and after some time, I would be forgotten.

The bidding moved higher, almost to ten million, and my knees nearly gave out. Ten million dollars to ruin me and therefore have payback for whatever grievance they had with my father.

I hated this. I hated my last name. I hated my father.

"Twenty million."

Pulling myself back to reality, I saw the surprised looks on some of the dons' faces as they tried to figure out who had bid so high on me.

"Don Valentino," the woman said, clearing her throat. "Are you certain?"

I watched with bated breath as the man from the back of the room moved forward, his arms now loosely at his sides.

"Twenty million for Carmine's daughter." His voice was rich, like a fine wine that had been aged to perfection, and now I could see the sharp features of his face, the ice-blue shards of his eyes as he coolly assessed me. They had a practiced blankness to them. There was no warmth but I shivered regardless. This man was here with a *purpose*. I knew I wasn't just dealing with a horny middle-aged Don here.

The entire room went silent, and I noted that some of them were glaring at this Don Valentino with looks of disgust on their faces. It wasn't a name I recognized, and it was clear that he wasn't popular with the others.

"Well then," the woman replied after a moment. "Are there any takers for twenty-one million?"

Suddenly I wanted someone to outbid him. I could tell that he was dangerous. There was no expression on his face, not even the tic of his jaw as he waited for someone else to speak up.

When it was clear that no one was going to attempt to outbid him, the woman clapped her hands. "She's yours, Don Valentino."

I fully expected him to come on stage and throw me over his shoulder, but his lips curved into a cruel smile, and I felt fear trickling down my ribcage as he turned and walked away.

That was it. He bought me.

"Come," the woman stated as conversation started to buzz around us, grabbing my arm. "It's time to get you ready."

A laugh nearly escaped through my lips. Ready for what? Ready for my death? What were they going to do with me? Put me in another dress and lead me to whatever Valentino had planned for me?

She took me to the room where I had first gotten dressed, where the older woman was waiting.

"Valentino bought her," the woman said. "Make sure she's ready for him. He paid a hell of a lot of money for her."

"How much?" the older woman asked the moment the door was shut.

I couldn't speak, the events of the last hour barely sinking in. I had been bought. I had been purchased. For twenty million, but it was still a *purchase*.

I would rather have been married off as had been my father's original plan.

"Take that off," the woman sighed at my silence and pointed at my dress. "It's not his favorite color."

"What?" I asked. "What are you talking about?"

The woman shuffled through the rack of clothing. "Don Valentino, of course. He has a particular taste." She looked back at me, her eyes narrowing. "Are you a virgin?"

I blushed. I wasn't about to share my personal information with a complete stranger. "I—"

She turned back. "Never mind. It's written all over your face. That should make him happy. Makes all of them bastards happy."

My mouth opened, but no words came out. Make him happy?

"Here," she finally said, thrusting a black sheer negligee at me. It was sheer. Really? I might as well just go naked at this point.

"Put this on."

"I don't understand what's happening," I said instead, already slipping out of my sandals. "Please tell me what's going on."

"Are you dumb, girl? You were there. You saw it with your own two eyes and heard it with your own two ears," she said. "You've been *bought*, and they don't like to wait for what bought. Keep your head down and do what they say, and you might make it out of here with all your parts intact."

Her words didn't help me feel any better about this situation.

"Who is he? Don Valentino?" I asked as I stripped off the dress I was sold in.

There was no use in fighting, but wherever I was going after I got dressed, maybe I could escape from.

"Really?" she asked, arching a brow as I shimmied into the sheer negligee. In any other situation, it would have been cute, and I would have loved wearing it. But now... I felt dirty just being in it.

"You really don't know who he is?"

I shook my head. I had never heard of him before. Was he a new don or a son of one? I doubted it, considering how the woman on stage had addressed him.

"Can't hurt," the woman said after a moment. "You are better off not asking questions and accepting your fate." She took in my frantic expression. "He likes them quiet."

Before I could ask anything else, she was herding me out of the room and down the hall, away from the stage to a smaller room instead. There was a bed draped with sheer curtains and silk sheets, and nothing else. "What is this?" I asked.

"The sampling room," the woman replied. "Get on the bed."

"Wait, what?"

She looked around before leaning in. "Your buyer will come to examine his purchase. If you are a virgin, he has to leave you that way if he wants his money back. But everything else is fair game."

This was all too crazy. I wasn't really here. This was a bad dream because I had eaten some bad delivery or something. At any moment I was going to wake in my own bed in my penthouse and this nightmare will be just that: a nightmare.

This couldn't be my life. "Please, I don't belong here," I pleaded as she moved to the door. "This is all a mistake."

The woman looked back at me, and I saw what I hoped were pity in her eyes. "Blame your father for this one, Miss D'Agostino. He brought this down on your head when he fucked over those men in that room. You are the compensation."

She was gone before I could respond, the telltale sound of a lock letting me know that I wasn't getting out of this room.

My shoulders sagged, my skin prickling from the cool interior of the room and the lack of clothing on my body. I had fully expected to put up a fight against my future husband today, not be sold to the very devil himself! I wasn't lying when I said I didn't know Valentino, but given my brief instances with him, coupled with the warnings of the old woman, I knew I wasn't about to have a savior on my side.

## Chapter 5
## Leda

*You're the compensation.*

He paid twenty million for me.

He wasn't about to drink wine and laugh over this nonsense.

He was going to hurt me.

I wrapped my arms around my waist, ignoring the inviting bed in the corner. It was clear that this wasn't the first time that something like this auction had taken place, and I wondered how many times Valentino had attended these events. The staff knew his preferences well, which didn't bode well for me at all.

Was he one of those men that preyed on helpless women? Did he beat them?

Well, he wasn't going to get one over on me. I wasn't going down without a fight.

My father was going to blow his lid when he found out about this.

Even though it was my life that was being taken, I couldn't help but smile at the thought. All his carefully laid plans were going to go to shit, and if I died today, it would so be worth it to know that he wasn't in control of this.

A hysterical laugh escaped me. *I would pay twenty million just to see the look on his face, knowing that he* hadn't won. I hated him with every fiber of my being for what he had done to our family, what power he thought he had over both me and Nico.

The bastard still thought he was in control of my life and of his Mafia, but it was clear, given the words that had been said, that he wasn't. My father was going to get what was coming to him, and I hated that I wasn't going to be around to see it.

My smile died, and I felt a wave of despair well up in my chest. I didn't know what was going to happen tonight, but it wasn't going to be good. For twenty million, I was likely to be tortured before I was killed. Valentino was going to violate my body in ways that I couldn't even imagine, all because of my last name.

I would be shouldering the sins of my father, the very one that I hated.

Well, they weren't going to find a weak woman when it happened. I was going to claw and fight to my very last breath. They would know the name of Leda D'Agostino for far longer than my father's.

Realizing I had been wasting time, I hurried about the room, looking for anything that I could defend myself with. There was nothing save the sheets on the bed. I swallowed as I thought about them being wrapped around my neck, but quickly shook that thought out of my head.

My fingernails snagged on the silk, but I stripped the sheet from the mattress and wound it around my wrists like my brother had taught me long ago.

We had nothing else to do when we were younger other than learn how to fight, and he had taught me all sorts of tricks to protect myself.

A well-placed thumb, a good old knee in the crotch, and I might be able to escape. I was petite in a way that my size could be used for an advantage if I placed myself just right against my opponent.

Which was exactly what I was going to do.

When the door opened, I lost all train of thought, my body trembling as Valentino walked in alone. His blue stare never left mine as he shut the door behind him, barely acknowledging the sheet in my hands. Good Lord, he was gorgeous in a dangerous sort of way, exuding power just by standing there. He was tall, with wide shoulders and a flat waist under his open suit coat. His face was tanned, and my eyes strayed to the open vee of his dress shirt, noting the hint of tanned skin there as well.

My brother had taught me to size up my opponents immediately, to figure out what their weakness was and take in all the information I could gather.

At least, that was my excuse for ogling Valentino like I was doing now.

But hey, there wasn't anything else to look at.

My eyes came back to his face, and I saw an arrogance in his eyes and hated him immediately.

That was the problem with the company my father had kept over the years, the men I had been subjected to.

They were all arrogant, thinking that their money and titles made them irresistible to women.

I imagined Valentino was no different. He probably thought that the sun rose and set on his command and that I would do the same.

I wouldn't. I wasn't going to be the pet he expected me to be. I wasn't going to beg for my life, beg for him to let me go.

He wasn't in the business of mercy.

And I wasn't in the business of submission.

Still, it was a shame that this man standing before me was so gorgeous. Like straight off the runway, panty-melting gorgeous. His suit was expensive; the watch on his exposed wrist glittered in the dim lighting right along with his cufflinks on his white cuffs.

But his eyes and the way he looked at me scared me.

His gaze lingered here or there, not with lust but with blank practice, like a man looking at a horse he wanted to buy and counting up every dollar on every inch. How much did each part of Leda D'Agostino cost? Hair? Ten thousand. Hips? Twenty thousand.

When he spoke, I thought he was about to tell me to open my mouth so he could count my teeth.

But instead, he spoke in a voice that was hard and flat:

"Leda D'Agostino," he said. "What do you think you are going to do with that sheet in your hands? Choke me with it?"

His gaze drilled into mine and goaded me—daring me to do something.

I trembled, my bravado slipping. I didn't think that I could actually intimidate him. Somehow, it was a lot easier to intimidate him in my head. And now that he was in the room, I realized just how big he was. How he practically towered over me.

With each second he looked at me with that blank, practiced stare, I can hear his mind counting up the price on my body.

*A fighter?* Five hundred thousand.

*Needs to be taught a lesson?* Two million.

*A chance to ruin something beautiful?* I took a shuddering breath. *Stop it.*

But I couldn't fight reality anymore.

My fate was sealed. I could talk myself up that I might have a chance of getting out of here. But the truth was:

I didn't know what was going to happen, and I was afraid.

## Chapter 6
## Lucas

I watched the range of emotions flicker over her face when she realized that her efforts were futile. Her body betrayed her, and started shaking under the weight of realization at what she knew was about to happen.

Leda D'Agostino. The daughter of Carmine. Princess of the D'Agostino Mafia.

And all mine.

I could hardly believe that she came up for auction tonight. Guess that explained why there were so many dons here tonight. Everyone wanted a piece of Carmine D'Agostino, and what better way to make the old man fucking hurt than to ruin his little girl?

*All mine.*

I kept my smile to myself as I watched the fear flicker in her eyes. She was scared; whatever plans she had cooked up looked like they weren't going to work. She knows it, she knows I know it, and she knows that there's nothing stopping me from doing whatever I wanted.

I lived for moments of clarity like this—when someone knows exactly where they are with me. And they're looking at me like I was going to break out my favorite set of knives and play the worst game of *Operation* on them. For the most part, that was the best and most accurate guess.

And Leda…

Fuck, I could practically *smell* her fear. But there was still a sliver of defiance.

And that excited me even more. It made me want to do more than just scare her. It made me want to *toy* with her. And I felt my heartbeat rising at all the possibilities.

I savored the moment, letting it reverberate throughout my own body as I waited for her answer.

"Well?" I asked, nodding toward the sheet wound tightly in her hands. I'll admit, Leda had more spunk than I expected, which boded well for what I planned for her.

It meant that destroying her will be all the more fun.

"What are you going to do to me?" she asked finally, her voice hard.

*Good. Straight to the point.* I cocked my head and let my blank look slip to give her a hint.

I wanted to see the hope flicker out of her eyes, knowing that I held her life in my hands.

I wanted to watch the defiance slip away, become fear, and then ultimately transform into surrender.

Nothing would give me more pleasure.

I allowed my eyes to drift back over her body, feeling my cock stir as I drank in each and every curve. Up on that stage she had looked innocent enough. But now? Dressed in a negligee that hid nothing to the imagination?

She had no idea what a world of shit she just landed in.

I was going to enjoy ripping that band-aid off. Along with something else if I had to.

By the time I'd finish training her, she'd be nothing more than a shell of her former self. A princess no longer but my obedient pet.

Then I'd break her.

"Well? Are you going to answer me?" she asked. Her chin tilted with stubborn defiance. "Or do I have to ask it in asshole?"

I couldn't help arching an eyebrow at that. Okay, maybe Leda had more balls than I thought.

"You just bought a human being, you sick fuck!" she continued. But her voice wavered as I stepped forward and invaded her space. "Who do you think you are!"

My hand flexed at my side, not to hit her, but to grab her and bend her over that bed until she was screaming all sorts of obscenities at and about me.

*She thought I was an asshole?* Good. I wanted her to think that way. Because I could be the asshole of her nightmares.

"Your owner," I told her.

Her eyes hardened, and my cock throbbed painfully in response. It had been a while since I saw such defiance. If I were a less patient man, I'd have already buried myself in her tight warmth. "There are rules," I continued. "Rules that you will follow."

"Or what?" She challenged. "You'll kill me? I've already come to the conclusion and accepted that fate, asshole. I know I'm going to die. So, you know what? Why don't you take your best damn shot."

There it was—that last bit of defiance that I needed to stamp out. What I had planned for her was worse than death. "Drop the sheet," I growled.

Much to my excitement, she did the complete opposite. Her hands tightened around the silk. "Make me."

*Very poor choice of words.*

# Chapter 7
## Lucas

Blood rushed through my veins as I closed the distance between us and grabbed the back of her neck, my thumb pressing against the great vein that jumped under my touch.

She had no chance to react.

"Let me go!" Her eyes flared with panic as she struggled in my grip.

"Drop the sheet, and I'll let you go." I said softly, noting the green flecks in her eyes. Why in the hell was I noticing that particular part about her? "Can't have it both ways, Princess."

She struggled against my hold, and I had to bite my cheek to keep from pulling her body into mine. Hell, I knew I was fucked in the head. I enjoyed the fight, the way that it felt when someone was giving me a run for my money. After living for years being on the bottom, no way in hell was I about to give up my throne at the top.

I had been taught well.

"Let me go," she seethed as I allowed my hand to slide into her soft hair. Fuck, she smelled like fresh oranges, my favorite. And even though I knew that her clothes were hand-picked for my entertainment, I doubted her scent had been.

I released her abruptly and Leda stumbled.

She didn't see the knife until it was too late.

In one swipe, I had the sheet in half, hanging from her hands. Her belly was uncovered and my cock twitched.

"But I on the other hand," I murmured as I tucked the knife back into its hiding place in my coat as I drank in the view. "*Can* have it both ways."

Fear and rage flickered over her features. She let the silk sheets fall, and gave me my first unobstructed look at her breasts as they rose and fell under the flimsy material. The dusky color of her areolas pressed against the sheer material and I swallowed hard, my cock hard and painful inside my pants.

Her fear, coupled with the way her body looked, was driving me insane. Something I hadn't expected out of her. I knew the moment she walked onto that stage that I had to have her—that I *needed* to have her.

And I was right.

"There are rules, Princess." I repeated, pressing her up against the wall with my body. Her soft curves molded to my body; my cock pressed into her stomach, and I watched as her eyes widened. "Rules that you'll learn one by one. Rule number one: Your name means nothing to me." Carmine D'Agostino's days were numbered. To the rest of the Dons, he no longer wielded power.

I did.

"Your father is nothing more than an old fucking man who is about to find out what it means to lose everything."

Leda didn't tremble like I expected her to. Instead, she lifted her chin and stared me straight in my eyes. "What makes you think I care about my father?"

She might not have given a shit about her father, but she was going to fucking care what happened to her.

I took a small step back and hooked my finger around her already tilted chin. "Rule number two: You belong to me, Princess, no one else."

"What if I don't want to belong to you?"

I let a cruel smile across my face. "Then I'll march you back onto that fucking stage and let those leery bastards bid for your virginity. Hell, for a few million more, I'll let all of them take a turn after the winner takes it."

Everyone wanted a piece of the D'Agostino heiress, and she'd come to her senses that she'd have better chances here with me than with any of those other ones out there.

Hell, at the very least I was the best-looking one.

The defiance in her eye flickered like a wavering candle and she asked. "What are you going to do with me?"

*Ruin you, and make you wish you'd never been born a D'Agostino.* "That's not your business anymore." I told her.

Leda did not expect me to say that, but I was already at the door, ready to be done with this place. I got what I wanted.

"Time to choose." I said. "Me. Or them." My hand gripped the doorknob.

"You," she said. "I'll go with you."

I turned to look back at her, that last flicker of defiance was fading away. "Final choice?"

She straightened, and her chin lifted again. "Final choice."

"Fine. Come," I told her, as I stepped outside and held the door.

She looked down at her thin clothing. It was meant to entice me to sample my wares: give me a clear shot of her body and what twenty million had bought. It was cheap and meant to be ruined for the moment that I claimed her.

But for some reason, I felt that I wasn't ready for that.

Not with her. Not yet at least.

"Can I have some different clothes?" she asked. "At least some shoes?"

"No," I said, keeping my voice hard and flat. "You come like that."

She opened her mouth to respond, but I cut her off.

"Rule number three," I growled. "You will obey my every word. If I tell you to go naked, you go naked. Everything you thought you had is gone. From this day onward, your freedom is gone. I fucking own you, Leda. Never forget that."

"Like hell you do," she answered. "You don't own me. You will never own me, you piece of—"

My hand clamped around her mouth and I pushed her against the door. Her eyes widened in surprise as I pulled my face close to hers. She tried to push me back to no avail. I kicked her legs apart and kept her pinned to the door.

"Don't talk back like that again," I warned. "Do we have an understanding?"

The look she gave me was nothing but hatred. But her head dipped in the smallest of nods and I released her from my grip.

Leda sniffed and moved past me, drawing up short when she saw my capo Rocco standing at the door.

"Did you think I hadn't planned on you running away?"

She refused to look at me as I pushed my hand into the small of her back, urging her forward.

"Escort Miss D'Agostino to the chopper," I told Rocco.

He nodded and dragged her by her arm into the car that would ultimately take us to the helipad on the Hudson. I turned in the opposite direction and found the auctioneer waiting for me with a tablet in her hand.

"So I assume you're taking your merchandise?" she asked, her lips pursed.

I nodded. "I will."

She nodded. "And you found everything to your liking?"

I knew what she expected me to do in that room. Leda was labeled a virgin, and it was my duty—since it it was my fucking money—to ensure that she was correctly labeled. When dons paid for a virgin, it was important that they got exactly what they paid for.

I could look into her eyes and tell that she was innocent. I didn't need to slide my finger into her to find out.

A virgin. Exactly what I wanted her to be: Something I could break.

"Yes," I replied. "I can make the transaction now if you'd like."

A small smile crossed her face as she held out the tablet. "Will that be paid in cash or cryptocurrency?"

"Crypto." I replied and took out my phone for her to scan. Twenty million.

Not that I gave a shit. I could make it back in a month's time if I wanted.

The tablet pinged, and the auctioneer pulled it back. "Thank you for your purchase, Don Valentino. I trust that you will be pleased."

"I already am," I told her, turning and walking away before she could respond.

It was money well spent in my opinion. Once Carmine found out that I had his precious princess, he might do us all the favor of dying from a second stroke.

Let him. The old man held nothing over me anymore. Neither he nor the other assholes that had been in attendance tonight. They didn't see me as their equal, and I doubted they ever would.

One look at my face, and they knew who I was—who and what I'd been before I became a Don.

The ones that I could kill, I did. I slit their throats, relishing in their horrified expressions as I ended them. The others knew I could ruin them, never once thinking that I would be in the position I was now.

To show them that their time was over.

Walking up the stairs, I felt the weight of what I had accomplished tonight pressing on my shoulders.

Old wounds uncovered. New wars to be waged.

By the end of it all, I planned to be the final one standing. Leda was just the beginning, a timely transaction that would benefit me well in my plans.

I was going to strip away all defenses, all comforts that she was used to until she had nothing and no-one else but me.

Carmine had plans for his daughter, plans that I was ruining. Soon, he would know who had taken his daughter, and I only wished I could be there to see it.

The wind tore at my coat as I exited the underground building and into the car. The drive to the Hudson was short, barely five minutes and we were walking towards the helicopter. Rocco waited for me at the door, and I allowed myself a glimpse of my purchase on the seat.

Mine. Leda D'Agostino was mine.

Climbing in, I didn't acknowledge her huddled form next to me. My stomach lurched as the helicopter started to pull into the air. At this speed, we would be at my estate in a matter of minutes, and as much as I enjoyed showing off these days, I fucking hated flying.

Rocco caught my eye, and I gave him a single nod, letting him know that things were going exactly to plan. He would step up the protection now for all my capos and my estates, preparing for whatever war was inevitable.

It was coming; I could feel it in my bones, but it wasn't like I hadn't been through this shit before. I had been through far worse.

They tried to destroy me before, and now look at where and who the fuck I am.

I didn't expect Leda to have the same happy ending as I did. She might be strong now, but I was going to wear her down.

Night after night.

A grin slowly danced on my lips.

I was going to enjoy this.

## Chapter 8
## Leda

I huddled in the corner of the seat, the cold leather of the helicopter seat biting into my practically naked body. Flying in helicopters never bothered me like it did other people. But then again, I've never flown in such a state of undress.

Nor under such state of duress.

Blowing out a breath, I watched as the lights of New York City drop away behind us into the night sky as we ascended. I wondered where I was going.

Correction, where *we* were going.

Valentino hadn't even once glanced my way since he climbed in. The steady *thump-thump-thump* of the blades was the only noise between us. It was clear from his words that this wasn't going to be anything different than what I had already gathered.

He wanted to own me. He was going to own me. Valentino had some sort of vendetta against my father, and he already decided that I would be the one to pay the price of that vendetta.

A lump formed in my throat as I thought about my brother. Nico would be livid at what was happening, but he had too much to lose now. He had a family, a wife that loved him, and a son he had to protect. The last thing he needed was to be worried about me.

And besides, we both knew how strong my father's ties were to the other Mafias.

Well, that was until tonight. The auction proved that my father's support had practically evaporated overnight, which meant that no one was coming to save me. No one was going to stand up for the daughter of Carmine D'Agostino.

I was on my own.

It probably didn't matter either. Why Valentino even bothered to put me in this helicopter was beyond me. Maybe he was going to push me out once we were far enough. I didn't believe for one second that he was looking to do anything but destroy me.

But for twenty million dollars, I knew he was going to draw this out as long as he could.

Despite my resolve to not look at him, I couldn't help glance over at Valentino when the helicopter started to descend. His jaw clenched with the movement.

No way. Was my captor afraid of flying?

From the way he was clenching his jaw and flexing his hands on his knees, I would think so.

A smirk crossed my lips. So, there were cracks in his façade after all. The moment dissipated rapidly. Unless I was going to keep him in this helicopter forever, this small victory wasn't going to last.

As soon as the helicopter came to a halt, Valentino started breathing normally once more. His guard Rocco got out first, and he followed.

As he stepped out, he looked back at me. "Welcome home, Leda."

The rush of cool air forced me to move, my skin grew cold to the touch and my bare feet were freezing as they walked across the concrete slab. I couldn't believe just a short while ago, I had been complaining about my sandals. Now I wished I still had them.

"This way," he said, walking ahead of me without any concern.

I glanced back at the helicopter as it powered down, and saw nothing beyond the darkness. I didn't know if we were dangling off a cliff or if there was a forest awaiting me without the shine of light.

I had no idea where I was.

"Leda."

I closed my eyes against the harsh tone of his voice and forced my sore feet to move, not even looking at him as I swept past him and into the door he was holding.

The warm air replaced the cool one immediately, and I looked down at the hardwood flooring under my bare feet. Dim lighting illuminated the hallway. It was a modern home, one of those that were all angled wood and glass, with a floating glass staircase to my right.

"Up the stairs," Valentino stated, shutting the door behind him. "I will show you to your room."

I didn't want him to show me anything other than a way out, but I held my tongue. The more he believed I was meek and willing to behave, the more of a chance I had of him letting down his guard.

Then I would strike.

I walked up the stairs to the second landing, noting the open floor space over the railing as I passed. Everything about the house looked warm and inviting.

Everything but the owner.

A water feature spilled out of the wall to my right, and I faltered in my steps, letting Valentino brush past me.

"Move," he grumbled and the spicy scent of his cologne assaulted my nose.

I followed after him, and he paused in front of a door before pushing it open.

"This will be your room. There's no lock on the door, and you will stay in this room until I call for you. You do not have free rein of my home, Leda. You are not a guest."

*Yeah, tell me something I didn't already know.*

"Get cleaned up," he continued as I stepped inside. "I will be back."

I didn't ask what for when he shut the door.

## Chapter 9
## Leda

Finally with a moment to myself, I took in the sight.

The room was huge, with a king-sized bed dominating the center, all in muted earth tones. There was a balcony to my left, and I crossed the room immediately, sliding open the glass door and stepping out, shivering at the cold air the moment I did.

The soft lights on the balcony barely illuminated the space, but as I peered down, I noticed I wasn't as high as I thought I was. There was a patio underneath the balcony and it was surrounded by greenery. I glimpsed the faint glow of a pool in the distance against the backdrop of other lights in the distance.

So, we weren't far from a town or city, which was good. Maybe I could find some help if I could get out of here.

Turning back to the room, I located the en-suite bathroom and made use of it, stripping off the negligee and throwing it on the fluffy rug as I did so. I wanted to get under the warm stream of water and cry until I couldn't cry any longer, but Valentino told me he was coming back.

And the last thing I wanted him to do was catch me naked.

After I took a moment to gather myself, I didn't bother to look in the mirror as I walked back into the bedroom and threw open the wardrobe, frowning as I riffled through the hangers.

Nothing but lingerie. All in black.

There were long slips and short ones, sheer material and satin. I pulled out a bra and garter set, the satin glimmering in the light, and threw it back in disgust. Not even a set of pajamas in sight. I was nothing more than a plaything to Valentino, a set of holes not even fit to be considered a full human being.

I reached for a satin chemise and shrugged it on, surprised by how well it fit. Did Valentino *plan* for this?

There were matching slippers on the floor of the wardrobe, and I grabbed a pair, sliding them on my aching feet. I would have killed for a pair of sneakers, but these would do for now. At least these didn't have heels on them.

I closed the doors and walked over to the bed, frowning as I looked down at the creamy comforter. Was I the first woman to be in this room? Did this chemise belong to someone else? Perhaps another woman that he had broken and then destroyed?

A cry of frustration clogged my throat and I let a few teardrops fall, wrapping my arms around my waist as I did so. Valentino was a horrible asshole, someone who had literally purchased another human being. If he were just a Don, I could deal with him. After all, I had dealt with them all my life.

But he was something else, something that was dark and dangerous.

Something that my mind screamed at me to stay away from.

Something worse than my father.

I should have never gone back to my penthouse this morning. Nico had warned me to be careful, to at least get a bodyguard or two until our father could get completely cut off from prison life. He had warned me that our father would retaliate hard, and I hadn't listened, too caught up in the fact that he was truly locked up to worry that he still had his claws deep into my life.

Rory's best friend Emilia had also asked me to come with her to Paris, to forget about my life for a while, but I had been too stubborn. Emilia and I moved in the same circles, and I enjoyed her company just as much as I did my sister-in-law. She had been good to Rory, and she was good to me.

If only I had listened to either one of them and chosen to be cautious. I could've avoided this entire situation. I could be safe, looking forward to the rest of my life and not contemplating my death at the hands of someone who hated my father, who had bought me like a breeder buys a prized mare and was going to do who knows what to me.

I was alone, truly alone in this.

# Chapter 10
## Leda

Hastily I wiped the tears from my cheeks, and told myself to suck it up. No amount of crying was going to get me out of this situation. The only thing I could do was to keep my wits about me and remember that I was stronger than this.

I wasn't a shrinking violet and I was going to remind Valentino of this.

So, I started tearing apart the bedroom, looking for any weapon that I could use when he did return. Other than the lingerie and the towels in the bathroom, there was nothing. Everything was either bolted down or tamperproof, which meant he had expected a fight from someone in this room.

I could make a strangling device again, but he had disarmed me with just a stare and some words. No, I would be wasting my time going down that route. I still could feel the rapid beating of my heart when he pulled out that knife and slid it through the silk. I thought he was going to use it on me.

But more than that, the feeling of his strong body pressed into mine had nearly robbed me of my breath. His cock had pressed against my body, the hard bulge causing my stomach to quiver traitorously. No man had ever pressed himself into my body like that. Sure, men had ground against me, touched me when I didn't want to be touched and made me feel uncomfortable, but never anything like that.

Like he truly did own me.

There was a brief moment that I had thought about touching him, just to see if he was as hard as he claimed to be, but then my rational mind had kicked in.

He had stolen me, bought me, but he'd never make me want him.

Not in a million fucking years.

I walked over to the door and placed my hand on the knob, and found that it turned easily in my hand. At least Valentino hadn't lied about that.

I wasn't locked in, but I also couldn't keep him out.

If he wanted access to me, he could.

Whenever he wanted.

It would be easy for me to leave this room and try to make my way out of the house to the nearby city or town, where there might be some help. I could be quiet when necessary. And unless he was standing right outside, waiting for me to escape, I was pretty sure I could avoid guards looking for me.

After all, I had been doing it all my life. When I had finally understood what my life was, who I was, I had snuck out all the time.

*Or…*

Releasing the knob, I glanced over at the balcony, the door still standing open. He probably didn't think I would be brave enough to find a way to escape via the balcony. That was too bad. Valentino didn't know what I was capable of.

Quickly, I threw back the comforter on the bed and grabbed the top sheet. It wasn't a long way down, but I didn't want to jump if I didn't have to.

In no time at all, I tied the top sheet and fitted sheet together into a rudimentary rope, glad that they were cotton rather than silk. The knots were tight.

I kicked off the shoes, wishing I had something more durable for when I did reach the ground. I didn't know what sort of trouble might meet me once I did get to town, but anything had to be better than what I was likely going to suffer at his hands.

I would die before I let him touch me again.

Grabbing my lifeline, I made my way over to the railing of the balcony, not sure how much time I had. If I was still here when Valentino crossed that threshold, there was no way I was going to make it out alive.

There were going to be pieces of me that I would lose, and I wasn't talking about body parts.

Dignity, heart, and soul. He could tear me down until everything I did depended on him.

I wasn't one to depend on anyone. My father had never been there for me, only to tell me what to do that would suit his life. Everything I had, I had built for myself. I had grown a tough skin, put on the face that would hide my true self.

I wasn't going to give up that easily.

Looking over the railing, I made certain that I didn't see any guards on the patio first before tying off the sheet on the heavy chair on the balcony. It was going to slide, I knew that, but hopefully I could get down before it reached the railing and threatened to break the glass.

I threw the tied sheet over the railing, watching it snaked down the side of the balcony, and waited for a cry of alarm going up.

When there was none, I hiked the chemise high on my hip, glad I put underwear on, and slipped a leg over the side. My heart was hammering in my chest. This was it. I could turn around right now and forget this crazy plan of mine.

Or I could shimmy down this sheet to whatever waited for me.

The sound of the door opening in the distance caught my attention, and I barely saw Valentino's surprised expression before I went over the balcony.

## Chapter 11
## Lucas
*Moments Before*

I left Leda in the bedroom and walked down the stairs to my office, the automatic lights coming on as soon as I stepped over the threshold. It was sometime after midnight, but I felt like this night was going on forever, wanting nothing more than to crawl into my bed and catch a few hours of sleep.

Instead, I grabbed the decanter on the sideboard along the wall and poured a healthy swallow of whiskey into the glass, watching as the amber liquid filled the crystal. While I should have been upstairs, making good on my claim when I acquired Leda D'Agostino, I hesitated.

Mainly because I wanted her to wallow in the fear of what was going to take place for a little while longer. Call me a bastard, but I enjoyed watching her shrink from me.

I wasn't a sadist by any means. I didn't hit women or inflict any forms of abuse, but if a woman wanted to be spanked, well, I wasn't above doing that. The pain I inflicted on my partners was for pleasure, theirs and mine.

Picking up the glass, I took a long swallow, feeling the whiskey slide down my throat. I was certain that she was sitting in that room, wondering what was going to happen to her.

Fuck, I had so many options. I wanted her to beg for me, for my cock. I wanted her to have a flicker of distrust in those gorgeous fucking eyes of hers so that I could play on that distrust.

I wanted Leda to wish she had never been born a D'Agostino.

I drained the glass and set it aside, running my hands through my hair. I could already taste her skin on my tongue, drinking in her fear of me intermingled with passion that I would pull out of her. There was something lurking behind Leda's innocence, something that was begging to be brought to the surface, and I was the sort of man to do it.

Adjusting the front of my slacks, I forced myself to think of something else for now. If I didn't, I would be stroking myself in a few minutes.

My cell phone buzzed in my coat and I pulled it out, holding it up to my ear. "Yeah."

"Hello, Lucas."

My blood ran cold at the harsh voice. I clenched my free hand into a fist at my side. "What the fuck do you want, Adrian?" Adrian Gallo fancied himself to be something other than a member of the Cavazzo Mafia.

The fool fancied himself the Don.

Too bad I had already filled that position.

"I'm hearing rumors," he stated. "Rumors that you have the D'Agostino princess in your grasp."

I chuckled darkly, figuring that word was spreading like wildfire already. Now that the funds had been paid, I owned Leda. "Wouldn't you like to know?"

"I'm not going to war over the bitch," he growled.

My good humor left my face. "It's not your war to decide. You aren't the fucking Don, I am. Have you forgotten?"

Truly it had been a surprise to all, including me, that Cosimo Cavazzo would pick his enforcer to become Don in his will. I had watched the Mafia Don's back for five years after he had pulled me out of his shithole organization to serve him in a different capacity. Adrian had been his nephew, the heir who was destined to become Don.

The funny thing was, I knew the old man was having the last laugh. His entire family, including Adrian, had protested the will, but in the end, I had inherited the title and all the fucking money.

It didn't mean that any of them liked it. I knew I had a target on my back, not only from the rest of the actual Cavazzo family, but from other Mafias. To them, I was an outsider, someone who wasn't born into that inner circle.

And the truth was, I wasn't.

I was just a kid when my heroin-addicted mom sold me into the family—trading her son for her next hit.

I had suffered at their hands in ways that no one could even possibly imagine.

"So you keep reminding me," Adrian said with clear displeasure in his voice. "You are a disgrace on my uncle's name, Valentino, and I am going to ensure that his legacy, my fucking *family's* legacy, is put back together like it should be."

"Good luck with that," I told him. "You've been trying for five fucking years. Tell me what you are going to do differently this time."

"You have your day coming," Adrian replied.

I ended the call before he could go any further, and reached for the bottle once more.

He was an asshole, just like the rest of the family. There were some capos that had been willing to follow me without complaint, my second-in-command Rocco being one of them. For five fucking years I had fought Adrian and his family, and earned my place among the Dons.

I was ruthless, straying on the other side of the blurred line between what I wanted to do and what were unspoken rules. I was unapologetic in my kills and dealings, stealing from the other Dons when I could and laughing in their faces when they raised hell about it.

I took after the lessons of the Don from the good old days, building my empire as I saw fit and not what everyone expected I would do. There were even rumors that I bathed in the blood of my enemies—rumors that I encouraged.

I wanted my enemies to fear me.

Drawing in a breath, I poured another glass, and then set the decanter aside on the sideboard. Adrian was right about one thing. Everything was about to be out in the open about my purchase of Leda D'Agostino.

I did it for two reasons: one, to get back at Carmine, and two, to flex my muscles as Don. There had been a room full of Dons that had been running this world for generations. They could probably go back hundreds of years in their family trees, and it would have been impossible for one of them to take the D'Agostino princess into their Mafia like I had.

I overpowered them all with my money, and damn did it feel good.

After being the one they had used for years, I knew I held something enormously powerful in my hands. The fate of the D'Agostino Mafia. Their power might have been broken, but the foundation of their wealth—the string of properties and clubs and other investments—remained.

Everyone knew that Carmine's son Nico forfeited his rights as Don. He had no interest in the family business, and rumor was that he had a family of his own to take care of.

That, and the fact that Carmine just wouldn't die. I couldn't understand why someone who was poised to be in a position of power would give it all up for a family.

Families were shit. They didn't do anything but cause hurt and let down those that depended on them.

I threw back the whiskey, letting it burn my throat this time. I hated any sort of feelings. They reminded me of my weakest moments, moments where I didn't think I would survive past the morning.

If it hadn't been for Cosimo realizing I was better suited as an enforcer, I would still be living that life.

Or dead. Most likely dead.

Now I could defend myself with the best. I was a knife expert, able to hit a target from fifty yards away. I knew where to slice and dice for a slow death and how to find the quick kill without a sound.

I wasn't half bad with a gun in my hand either, but I preferred the intimacy of knives any day. That way I could see the fear in their eyes and feel their life drain out of their bodies.

My other skills, well, I could get close to just about anyone without them realizing that the fox was in the henhouse. And by the time they knew, it was already too late.

Placing the glass down, I drew in a breath. The other Dons must be passing word to their capos and soldiers. I would now be targeted for having her in my presence. There were many that wanted to make Carmine pay, many who wanted to watch him suffer at their hand. Leda was an easy way to make that happen. Some might kill her outright, send her head to Carmine's prison cell.

Others might marry her off to their sons, so their worthless heirs might plant a brat in her belly and extinguish the D'Agostino bloodline altogether.

Some would want her to hurt, to pay for his crimes.

Me?

I wanted to make her submit to me in every way a woman submits to a man.

I wanted Carmine to know that his little girl was worshipping someone else, someone who would take her fears and craft them in a way that would have her crawling to me for protection instead of defying me.

That was my plan for his little girl, and unless I wanted to have others attempting to kill me, I needed to start executing my plan.

"Boss."

I turned to find Rocco at the door, his bulky frame filling up the space. "What is it?"

"Guards are all in place," he stated, his eyes piercing in the dim lighting.

Where I was fucking great at my knives, Rocco could kill a man ten different ways with his bare hands. A former Navy SEAL, he had taken up with the Cavazzo Mafia when his fiancée had been killed in a turf war.

Cosimo had told me many times that he had never seen such a big man move with such stealth or elicit such screams from his victims. I had the good sense to keep Rocco on as my second when Cosimo died.

"Good, because word is out."

He chuckled. "Did you think it wouldn't be? You practically rub your balls in their faces and dared them to come after you."

I gave him a rare grin. Rocco was the only person that would ever see me like this, not as the powerful Don but as a man who was hell-bent on making a name for himself. I knew he wouldn't betray me and would take a bullet for me if there ever came a need to do so.

If I had been keen on having friends, he would have been the closest person to take that title.

"Did you expect me to do it any differently?"

He shook his head, his eyes flickering to the ceiling. "Want me to put a guard on her too?"

"No," I stated, the grin fading. "I'm about to handle her myself." My cock ached at the thought of her on her knees, big eyes looking up at me while her plump lips were wrapped around it.

Rocco shrugged. "I'll be around then."

I waited until he had left before I exited the office, and headed toward the stairs. Leda was mine. I didn't need anyone to help with watching out for her, which was one of the reasons that I had left her door unlocked.

I wanted to see how far that defiance was going to be pushed. I had expected a meek and mild Mafia princess, knowing she had grown up in a world where she had always expected to be a trophy wife one day.

I hadn't expected a hellcat with claws, but that only made me want her more.

I liked the challenge. Hell, I relished in it.

It would make breaking her in the end so much more rewarding, and she was guaranteed to give me a fight.

The thought of her trying to fight me made me fucking hard as a rock.

I reached the second landing, passing by my bedroom as I walked to hers. Likely by now she had found the lingerie in the wardrobe and knew what my plans were for her.

My cock throbbed as I thought about which outfit she was wearing or if she was wearing anything at all.

Would she give herself to me to get out of this situation? Would she be lying on the bed, those hazel green eyes flashing at me warily as I entered the room, her body primed for my touch?

Fuck, I hoped so. It had been some time since I had buried myself in a woman with some fight in her, and Leda was already driving me wild.

The door was still closed, and I turned the knob, pushing it open slowly in case she had decided not to give in and had found a weapon instead. Rocco had walked through the room himself, removing any chance of her arming herself. But she was crafty, and I left nothing to chance.

There was no attack, but my feet faltered on the plush carpeting when I saw the open balcony door and the flash of a leg as Leda heaved herself over the railing.

Fuck me. I raced over, my heart fucking stopping in my chest. She had jumped.

But then the gleaming white sheet caught my eye, and I came to the railing just in time to watch her shimmy down the rest of the sheet. She looked up, and I wanted to smirk at her.

"Run if you want," I called out. "You won't get far."

Leda's eyes narrowed, and she shot me the middle finger before taking off across the grass. When she was out of earshot, I chuckled to myself, watching as she disappeared into the night. A monster stirred in me and

I felt my balls ache for release at what was about to happen.

I liked when they ran.

I loved a good chase.

And when I caught up with Leda, she was going to wish she had never run.

## Chapter 12
## Leda

The ground was hard under my feet as I ran down the grass and onto a rough gravel road, realizing that it was surrounded by woods. The road sloped downward, but I didn't let up, hoping that I could get to the end before he came after me.

Valentino had seen me. More specifically, I had flipped him off for seeing me, for what he was doing to me and how he was treating me like he owned me.

I guessed for twenty million, it was easy for him to believe that he owned me.

Believed, not did in truth. No one owned me. I was my own person, and not even my father could lay claim to me completely.

A rock bit into my heel and I cried out, limping a bit as I continued to descend. Suddenly, I wished that I kept those slippers on.

I couldn't give up. I wouldn't give up. He was going to find me, but I was going to give him a hell of a time before he could.

I couldn't stay here. I couldn't let him catch me.

The gravel road ended at a paved one and I looked over my shoulder, not seeing lights behind me. Maybe he was going to let me go. Maybe he was going to wash his hands of me and leave me to my own fate.

A hysterical laugh left me. No, he wasn't. He was making some point that I didn't fully understand.

I was part of a bigger plan.

One that I wasn't going to like at all.

My feet slapped against the cool, paved road, and I nearly cried out in joy as I saw lights up ahead. I knew I looked a fright, wearing a skimpy chemise and nothing else, but maybe they would take sympathy on me and I could get a chance to call Nico.

No, I couldn't call Nico. I couldn't drag him into this mess and potentially put his family in danger.

I would call Vincent. Vincent DiMara was Nico's second-in-command, having chosen to stay on as his personal bodyguard even after Nico quit the Mafia life. Vincent could keep my secret from my brother and get me somewhere safe until I could figure out what to do next.

The building came into view, and I saw that it was a small diner instead of a house, with no cars in the parking lot. What the heck was a diner doing out here in the middle of nowhere?

Still, I could see someone moving inside. I forced myself to run faster and rapped on the glass door once I arrived.

"Please!" I cried out, startling the woman inside. "Please let me in!"

She hurried over to the door and unlocked it, her eyes wide. "What on earth?"

I rushed inside, nearly knocking her over in the process. "I need help. Do you have a phone?"

"What happened to you?" she asked as I hurried behind the counter. "Where did you come from?"

I found the phone cradle but not the phone. I looked at her in desperation. "Please," I croaked. "I need a phone. I need to call someone."

The door opened behind her, and I gasped as Valentino strolled in.

"Sir," the woman whispered, and bowed her head.

"Martha," Valentino replied evenly, his hands in his pockets, his eyes on me. "Thank you for finding her for me."

The woman didn't even bother meeting my gaze, and I fought the urge to scream as the strength sapped out of my body. Was there no one that could help me now?

"Forgive us for interrupting you," he continued, his eyes hard. "Come, Leda. You are bothering Martha."

"I'm not leaving," I growled, gripping the worn counter. "He's kidnapped me! Please don't make me leave."

The woman continued to look at the floor, and I heard a faint sigh escape the Don's lips. "Don't make this hard," he stated, holding out his hand. "I can either have you walk, or you can be dragged out of here. Either way, you are coming home."

Home. Tears smarted in my eyes. That was not my home, nor would it ever be. My home was with my brother, with Rory and my nephew.

His home was a prison.

Valentino arched a brow, and all the fight left me. I wasn't getting out of here, and unless I wanted to threaten his life, he was going to win.

"Don't even think about it," he said softly when he saw me eyeing the utensils on the counter. "You won't like the consequences, and Martha doesn't want to clean blood off that counter tonight, do you, Martha?"

Martha looked up at him, and I swore there were stars in her eyes. "No, sir, I don't. It's hard to get the stains out of the wood."

My mouth dropped open. What kind of blood did this kind woman clean up? Was it because of something Valentino did?

"That it is, Martha," he said smoothly, a ghost of a smile on his face before looking at me. "See, Leda? Martha already has enough to do. Now apologize for scaring her."

What choice did I have? I moved from behind the counter and ignored his hand. "I'm sorry, Martha," I said as I passed. "For scaring you."

She didn't respond, nor did I imagine she would. She was on Valentino's payroll.

Once outside, Valentino took my elbow and guided me back toward the house. Before I could move another inch, however, he yanked me around until I was facing him.

"You disobeyed me, Leda," he growled, reaching out for the neckline of the chemise. I yelped at the sound of the material tearing. A gaping hole appeared down the front.

Oh God, what was he going to do?

Valentino wasn't done. He yanked one side down until a long strip tore from the flimsy material. He grabbed my hands and bound my wrists with satin.

"Please," I begged, attempting to squirm away.

"It's too late for begging," he said harshly as he knotted the material tightly. "You should have thought about the consequences."

When his hand drifted lower on my body, I gasped, feeling his fingers brush my stomach before he ripped off the lace panties, and tore them in half. Something warm crept across my stomach, interlacing with my fear.

I swallowed against the flood of need coursing through my body.

No. No, I couldn't want this!

I *shouldn't* want this!

"You will remain silent," he said, his hand curling around the scrap of panties. "In fact, I'm going to ensure it."

Before I could say anything, he stuffed my panties in my mouth, tying the torn ends together behind my head. "There," Valentino replied, grabbing my wrists. "Let's go home, Leda."

## Chapter 13
## Leda

I had never felt so humiliated in my life as when he tugged on my wrists and walked me like a dog. Tears leaked out of my eyes as we yanked me down the road, my nipples puckering in the cool air each time the torn fabric rubbed over them.

This wasn't happening. This couldn't be happening.

Valentino was relentless in his walk, not caring that I stumbled a few times on the gravel road leading up to the house. In no time he had me inside, and I was at least grateful that no one was around to see my humiliation as he forced me up the stairs into a different bedroom than the one I had escaped from.

This one was darker in color, from the bedding to the walls, and I knew immediately it was his bedroom that we had come to.

*This is it. He's going to rape me.*

My stomach flipped at the thought. My mind imagined his powerful hands pressing me into the bed while his cock filled me up. The warmth of desire rose up and I felt my cheeks flush. Why was I reacting to this?

Valentino let go of my wrists, shut the door hard, and leaned against it.

"You have not obeyed my rules," he said calmly as he took off his coat. "You have defied me at every turn in the short time you have been here, Leda. Can I anticipate this to be the fight you will continue to put up?"

When I didn't answer, he started rolling his sleeves up. The sight of him exposing his strong forearms sent another course of desire through my veins. I caught sight of a tattoo on his left forearm, my eyes darting away quickly so that my heart wouldn't race any faster.

Despite the fact I had my panties shoved in my mouth, I could feel a moan tickling the back of my nose as a trace of wetness trickled towards my thighs.

*What the hell was going on with me?*

Was I looking *forward* to whatever sick punishment he was going to dole out? He could plan on killing me at the end for all I know! Yet here I was, turned on by the image of him rolling up his sleeves!

"Why?" Valentino asked softly, catching my attention once more. "Tell me, Leda. Why did you run?"

I glared at him. *Are you serious?* How about I don't want to be *owned!*

I wanted to go home, go back to my life without my father's influence. I was just learning how to live without him breathing down our necks, and Lucas Valentino stole it from me before I had a chance to even start enjoying it.

But then again, it really didn't matter to him why I ran. It wasn't like he was going to take pity on me and let me go because he liked my answer.

"You are far too hardheaded for your own good," he muttered as he advanced on me. I stumbled back, the backs of my knees colliding with the bed. The look on his face was positively murderous, and I couldn't help but wonder if this was it.

Was I looking at my death? Was I really going to die wearing a tattered chemise and with my own panties shoved in my mouth?

"You need to be taught a lesson," Valentino continued as his body pressed against mine. "For breaking my rules."

*Wait, is that a bulge? Holy shit, that feels huge.*

Up close, I could see the tic of his unshaven jaw, the slope of his nose that had clearly been broken once before. His hard eyes were framed by the longest lashes, and my heart did a funny swoop when I looked at them for too long.

What a shame someone this gorgeous was so dangerous.

When his hands gripped my hips, I gasped behind the gag, the electric shock against my bare skin sending my thoughts scattering. He must have felt it, too, for his eyes widened just a hair before I was flipped over, my face pressing into the soft mattress.

"You will learn to obey me," he said roughly right before my ass erupted from the sting of his hand. Pain bloomed through my body. But something else, something *dark* and unbidden coiled in my stomach.

The second slap was just as painful as the first, and I was barely able to contain my cry—half a squeal of pain, and the other half a moan against the gag. My traitorous body arched against his touch.

Oh God, I actually liked this! The wetness between my thighs intensified, and when his fingers stroked my ass cheek before he slapped it again, I couldn't hold back my moans.

He flipped me over so that he might look at me. My cheeks reddened as I saw the look on his face. His hand reached out and I flinched, wondering if he was a man who liked to hit.

But all he did was pull my balled up panties out of my mouth. "Tell me you liked that," he growled, his own chest heaving.

I didn't know what to say. *Did I like that he spanked me?* I had never been spanked before, but the way that my body was dialed up to one thousand right now, I felt like I had liked it far too much. Every nerve fiber was pulled taut, waiting for whatever was going to happen next. I wanted his hands all over me.

Clearly Valentino wanted me as well. I could see it in the stubborn clench of his jaw now, the way that his eyes were bright with heat.

The bulge in his pants was unmistakable. The size of it sent a shiver down my spine. Fear and anticipation and want mixed all at once.

Before I had a chance to say anything, he hauled me against him, his hand grasping the back of my neck roughly as his other hand trailed down to my very core. "Tell me you liked it, Leda. don't lie to me, or there will be consequences."

I wasn't even focusing on anything he said now, his fingers pushing between my legs. My dripping folds gave him the answer before I could.

"Hmm," he said as his other hand tightened on my neck. "I think I have my answer, but I want to hear it from your lips."

"Yes…" I breathed.

"Yes, what?" His fingers spread me, daring me to fight him.

"Yes, sir," I cried out as his thumb pressed against my throbbing clit. I wanted release, and I would do nearly anything to have it.

"Good girl," He whispered, rewarding me with another lazy circle around my clit. "I wonder what else you like."

I wanted to touch him, but my hands were still bound, my body at the mercy of what he was going to do next. "Please."

There was a chuckle, and I felt Valentino slip at the entrance of my sex. "I like it when they beg. Tell me, Leda, how many times have you begged?"

God, I couldn't think straight. His finger teased into me, pushing in and out to stoke a fire that was already simmering under the surface. Between that and his thumb, I wasn't going to last much longer.

"Come for me," he growled, his fingers flexing against the nape of my neck. "Come only for me."

And I did. Holy fuck did I come. I cried out as the orgasm hit me full force. My knees weakened, and when Valentino let go of my neck, I practically collapsed to the ground, the impact rattling my bones.

"Good girl," Valentino whispered as I gasped for breath.

The orgasm had shattered me, turned my bones into jelly. Daringly, I looked up to find him fumbling with his zipper, a hard look on his handsome face, and my breath caught.

He was going to fuck me. My body shivered at the thought, wondering what being dominated by someone like him would feel like. Clearly this was a role he had a lot of practice in.

"Give me your hands," he said roughly. I held them up, and he ripped away the material bounding them like it was nothing. He placed my hands on the top of his slacks and slowly, I gave them a tug until his cock fell out.

And boy, did it *fall out*.

His cock was huge, the purple head already adorned with a drop of pearl at its tip. His hand gripped my chin, and I felt him pulling my mouth towards it.

He wanted me to suck him. Involuntarily, I licked my lips, curious to know how he would taste in my mouth. I knew my thoughts were irrational, considering everything that had happened up until now.

But something about how he handled me, how he made me do whatever he wanted awoke a feeling that was now itching to break free from deep within my core.

So I didn't protest when he shoved his cock in my mouth, his thumb between my teeth to keep my jaw open in order to accommodate his size. Valentino grunted, his other hand shifted to the back of my head, and relaxed just enough for me to bring my own hand up to wrap around his shaft.

He jerked slightly at the contact and swatted my hand away. "Mouth only, Princess."

It was clear. This was for him. Not for me.

I clasped my hands behind me for balance as he shoved himself deep into my throat, gagging me. Tears blurred my eyes. Pleasure and pain, excitement and degradation, all mixed together at once.

I should be ashamed, but surprisingly, I wasn't.

I wanted *more*.

His thrusts became harder, and I knew he was getting close. Never in my life had I let anyone do this to me. Never had anyone had this sort of control over me, and I was scared at what I felt about it.

His scent—musk tinted with a hint of smoke—drowned out all other smells as he gripped his hand tighter behind my head. His cock was stiffening.

With a guttural groan, his taste flooded my mouth, and he pulled me close to him as he came. I had no choice but to swallow every ropey spurt. *Too much. It's too much.* I placed my hand against his thighs, desperate to breathe.

He held me—struggling—against his bucking hips as he continued emptying himself in my mouth and down my throat. My world grew blurry in a haze of tears. I coughed, and felt his seed running down my chin.

Finally, he pulled away with a grunt and I gasped for air, coughing. A thin gossamer stream clung to the corner of mouth and dropped to the floor, pooling between my legs. I refused to look at him.

My cheeks burned with shame, not because of what he made me do.

But because I *liked* it.

No, not just *liked*…

I *wanted* it.

# Chapter 14
## Lucas

I braced myself against the bed, heart hammering in my chest. *Fuck!* It had been a long time since I enjoyed myself like that. I looked down and saw Leda's head was bowed, her own heaving from what we had just done.

Her mouth. I could spend all day fucking her little mouth.

My cock started to rise again. I hastily backed away, shoving it into my slacks.

"Up," I said roughly, not wanting her to see how much she had affected me. Our eyes met, and I quickly reined in my surprise at the simmering heat in hers.

She liked that.

I fucking knew it.

When she rose, I was rewarded when she didn't attempt to cover herself up. The shreds of her chemise framed her willing body. I could take her now: throw her on the bed, bury my cock in her, and leave her a quivering mess.

*But it wasn't time.* The thought came out of nowhere, and I clenched my jaw. "Move."

Only when she gathered the sides of her ruined clothing did I see her chafed wrists, and the redness that encircled her tender skin.

The sight bothered me. But I wasn't about to let her see it.

I escorted her back to her room.

"Rest," I ordered.

Leda turned her eyes at me, and for a moment I wanted to say more. Never in my entire career of dominating women had I wanted to wrap my fucking arms around someone as much as I wanted around Leda.

I wasn't a touchy-feely man. My touches were reserved for pleasure and pain in equal measures. I didn't know how to comfort.

Especially not someone I wanted to break.

Disgusted with my own weakness, I closed the door behind me and walked back to my office, picking up the same whiskey decanter I had been drinking from earlier. I poured it straight into my mouth, letting the burn override what I was feeling.

My body was sated, but my soul felt restless.

Why the hell was it restless?

I pushed open the patio door and stepped out into the predawn morning, whiskey in hand.

This house was situated in the hills high above the nearest city, giving me the luxury of privacy whenever I needed it. I purchased it shortly after being named Don for the purpose of having a space of my own hidden from the world.

For years I had been surrounded by people who always wanted something from me, and to live in this sort of solitude was a welcome respite.

Now, the silence—once soothing—was damning.

I hesitated with a woman. I *never* hesitated before, especially not with someone as fiery as Leda. Cosimo taught me to never let women see the other side of me. I was to maintain an air of arrogance, to make it at least appear that I was someone not to fuck with.

But when Leda had attempted to grab my cock with her hand, I had nearly lost all control.

A part of me *wanted* her to touch me all over, to surrender myself to someone else taking the lead—to see where it could go.

Hell, I would probably enjoy it far too much.

The problem was: she would have power over me. She'd make me crave her touch when it should be the other way around.

That was something I could not tolerate.

Shoving a hand through my hair, I took another pull off the whiskey. I had started that interaction between us with one goal in mind: to dominate her—soul and body, willing or unwilling.

The defiance—damn, she'd played that up well. When she arched against my hand, all rational thought on my plans had been burnt away like morning fog. Suddenly I wanted to draw out our time together, to bring her to the brink of wanting me but not give her what she wanted just yet.

A cat-and-mouse game that I hadn't initially thought about playing. At least, not with her.

But right now, I couldn't figure out who was the cat and who was the mouse.

"Fuck," I breathed softly. Exhaustion started to pull at my bones. I needed some sleep if I was going to face her again, if I was going to maintain some resemblance of control. Because right fucking now, I felt like control was the one thing I didn't have.

It was those fucking eyes of hers that bothered me the most. There was something hidden in their depths, a secret that I wanted to uncover.

My cock jumped at the thought and I willed it down, taking another long swallow of whiskey before I placed it back on the table.

It had taken me years to get to this point, and I would not risk losing it all just so that I might pretend to play house with Leda.

Being Don was a twist that I hadn't seen coming. I had been perfectly happy with killing people for Cosimo. After all, he pulled me out of the slums of his organization and gave me something to look forward to—something that would bring me true pleasure.

I didn't have that. Not when I was the person I used to be.

I steeled myself against the memories that threatened to resurface, knowing full well it was a combination of being drunk, tired, and pleasured. But for a moment, I didn't care.

At age fifteen, I hadn't known much about the world I was getting into. I thought the day that my mom had handed me over for her next fix was the first day of freedom.

Instead, it had been the first day of being in chains. Gone was the ability to escape by attending school. Gone was the need to stay out as late as I could so that I wouldn't have to come home and find her passed out on the bed.

My owner later told me that my face was my downfall. I was too good-looking to be anything other than what he made me. I was put to work and made to serve—did things that I didn't want to remember but would never forget.

Cosimo dragged me out of that world. He told me that once he had seen the *anger* in me, he knew that my talents were being wasted doing anything else.

And that was that. He put me into enforcer training, kicking my ass for a few months before I learned to fight back. Soon, I was being put on assignments in the name of the Cavazzo Mafia.

I put more cold bodies in graves than warm bodies in beds.

When Cosimo asked me to be his personal enforcer, I jumped at the chance. Because now it meant some of those who had once treated me like shit was now afraid of me.

I craved that fear. Fear from others held me together. It forged me. Strengthened me. Became my shield and my sword.

It had also made others despise me.

Adrian was a perfect example. He was weak, as I had heard many times from his own uncle, not fit to lead an empire. I could keep myself in control, but Adrian couldn't. He was always causing one shitstorm after another that his uncle was forced to clean up.

Usually, it was me who had to clean up his mess—one life at a time, one name at a time. I didn't know that I was auditioning for the ultimate role at the time.

I shoved my thoughts away.

I wasn't that man any longer. I was a Don, one that was going to outlive them all and put them out of commission. There was a new era coming, one that was more ruthless and bloodier than they could have imagined. Not one of them thought that it would be me who'd come to haunt their future.

I was going to ruin them all.

## Chapter 15
## Lucas

*Leda rose from her knees, lips pursed in a saucy smile. "Tell me what you want, sir," she whispered as her hands trailed up my abdomen to my chest. "Tell me how to please you."*

*"Bend over the bed," I growled, my cock in my hand. "Let me see that ass of yours."*

*She did as I asked, raising her ass in the air. "Like this, sir?"*

*Fuck, yeah, just like that. I ran my free hand over her skin, tracing softness in her curves. I knew she would let me do anything to her, anything I wanted, and she'd fucking love it.*

*She was mine, my pet, my fucking everything.*

*My body stilled at the thought and I looked down, finding the black ring encircling my finger. What the hell?*

*"Lucas?" she asked, looking back. "What's wrong?"*

*I backed away quickly, my heart slamming in my chest. No, this couldn't be happening. I couldn't have done something like that.*

*I didn't want anyone else in my life, in my fucking existence.*

*I didn't want to care.*

*"What the fuck did you do?"*

*Leda rose from the bed, confusion marring her perfect face. "What are you talking about? Lucas, you are scaring me."*

*Scaring her? My eyes flew to her hand, and I swallowed hard at the ring there. "You aren't my wife."*

*"I am," she said slowly. "This is our honeymoon, remember?"*

*I shook my head, wanting to free myself of the thought. Honeymoon? No, no, no. I would never. This couldn't be happening. I would never let someone in. Not like this.*

*"You're lying," I growled.*

*Leda stopped in her tracks, and tears welled in her eyes. "Lucas, what's wrong?" she said, holding out her hand. "Please come here. I love you."*

*Panic clawed at my throat as I ran to the door, but it was locked. I had to get out. I couldn't deal with this. This wasn't what I wanted. I was supposed to chain her, not the other way around! Let me out!*

I gasped as my eyes flew open. I was drenched in sweat. Morning light streamed through the windows, and I was in bed, alone.

Taking a deep breath until the dream was nothing but uncertain memories, I pulled myself into a seated position and untangled the sheets. Somehow, I could still feel her body on my fingertips.

I pushed the thought away, climbed out of bed, and wrenched the balcony door open. Walking out bare-assed onto the balcony, I let the morning air cool my skin. *That would be the last fucking time I would finish off a bottle of whiskey before bed.*

I braced my hands on the balcony, and looked out over the wooded lot behind the house. Leda already wormed her way into my head. How the fuck did that happen? Was it because she surprised me with her escape, or was it something else?

The sheer panic I had felt watching her go over that railing had been a foreign feeling to me. Suddenly I cared for someone else, someone else's safety.

I didn't like it.

I didn't need anyone else. I didn't need to subject myself to feelings like that.

I was a Don, and not one that was going to be soft. I wasn't about to let my personal life collide with my professional one. I wasn't going to be the Don that had heirs, or a family, or concerned with his legacy.

I'd live fast, die young, and take all the bastards down with me when I go.

I wasn't going to make the same mistakes all of them did: grew weak because my wife or my kids were used as pawns.

Case in point: Carmine. Leda was his weakness, whether or not he wanted to admit it; and I just took his precious princess while he's watching from the sidelines. I was using her as a pawn. She would end up being sacrificed for his actions.

I didn't want that to happen to me. To have my attachments to someone else be the reason for my downfall.

My chest tightened and I, swearing, stalked back into my bedroom. Today was going to be a reset day for me, a way to exact my true notions on why I had Leda in my grasp to begin with and not because I liked her.

I didn't like her.

*Liar*, my mind told me as I started toward the bathroom.

She had impressed me when she showed that she wasn't going to wilt under pressure—that I wasn't going to scare her into submission. She'd fight me tooth and nail.

And last night.

I started the shower, and gripped my cock hard as I thought about her moans, the way she had felt under my fingers, her mouth on my fucking cock. That had surprised me like nothing else. What would she do when I took her?

What else would *I* do?

I could no longer be cautious with her. I went at sex like a starving man at the sight of Thanksgiving. And she was the full table spread.

Would that scare her? Or excite her?

"Fuck," I growled as I felt the pressure start to build. My hand moved faster on my throbbing cock.

Scaring her was the whole fucking point.

When I finally let go, however, it was her name that clung to my lips.

## Chapter 16
## Leda

*"Tell me what you want."*

*I stared into Valentino's eyes, feeling my heart flutter at his nearness. "I want you," I whispered, reaching out to cup his cheek.*

*He shuddered under my touch, and for a moment, I felt utter devotion for the man before me. He was powerful. He was dominant.*

*He was mine.*

*When he opened his eyes once more, I saw the fiery heat in them, the passion that he was going to bring to my body as he had many times before. Our love was, well, it couldn't be put into words what I felt for him.*

*"Leda." My name came out in a whispered plea as he dropped to his knees, his face inches from my throbbing core. "Let me love you."*

*"Yes," I breathed, my hands fisted in his hair. "Please."*

*His thumb brushed over my clit, and I whimpered. "You don't ever have to beg for me."*

*Oh, but I wanted to. I wanted him to make me cry out his name, make me beg him to stop as he brought my body repeatedly to the brink.*

*My favorite thing about him.*

*When his mouth touched me, I nearly lost it. His tongue glided over my swollen nub, worshipping me as he pushed apart my folds.*

I bolted awake, my eyes flying open as I struggled to catch my breath. It was just a dream.

It had to be a dream.

Groaning, I rubbed my hand over my face. Sunlight was streaming through the open balcony door. I tried to stay up after Valentino had left, waiting in restless anticipation for the moment he would.

But the pull of exhaustion finally won out and I fell asleep naked.

Refusing to get out of bed, I stretched my body and winced as my feet screamed in return. There were probably scrapes and bruises cuts all over the bottom from my failed escape last night.

A shower would do me some good.

*That, and maybe something more.*

The thought came unbidden, unwanted, and I realized my body was still flushed from my dream. My hand wandered over my aching breasts. I wasn't one to touch myself often, but *something* about that dream left me feeling…

Incomplete.

A grin flitted over my lips as the image of Lucas Valentino on *his* knees worshipping *me*.

Now wouldn't that be a sight?

My hand slid down my stomach and I closed my eyes, thinking of the way that he had commanded me with his touch. He dominated me from the very start, and molded my response to what he wanted.

What he craved.

My finger brushed my clit, and I gasped lightly. I was already soaking wet.

*This can't be happening.* I couldn't possibly walk around all the time wanting him…

Could I?

I shook my head. No. I shouldn't want him like this.

He took me from everything I knew. He swore he'd ruin me. That should be enough to remind me that he was a dangerous man, not to be trusted. But somewhere, deep in my core, a monster opened a curious eye.

And it wanted *more.*

It wanted him to pin me down into the bed, hold me down, and push me open. The thought made me close my eyes, and my brain flooded the darkness with flashes of clenched fingers, tangled limbs, and hot heavy breath hovering by my ear.

My fingers opened me of their own volition, and I gasped as I felt the heat start to build.

"Yes," I whispered to an empty bedroom, wondering if he had any hidden cameras so he could watch. On one hand, I positively die of embarrassment if he was. But on the other, I *wanted* him to watch.

My orgasm came quick and fast, and I cried out as my body bucked against it. But as quickly as it came, the pleasure started to fade, and all that remained was a burning need—a need that I knew only one person could fill.

"Great, just great," I muttered.

I was already starting to want him, and it was only day one. My getaway plan was a wash, and I hadn't done anything but crave his touch this morning.

This day was shaping up to be the worst day ever.

Throwing covers away, I got up, walked to the bathroom—naked—and turned on the shower as hot as it would go. I needed to erase him from my skin, to not want him any longer. Get my brain back.

I needed to forget he even existed.

When I stepped under the spray, I yelped at how hot it was and turned on the cold slightly so that I wouldn't scald my skin. There were small things of shampoo and body wash, along with a razor, which surprised me. Wasn't he afraid that I would use it against him? Or on myself?

I mean, I didn't want to go around looking like a hairy woman, but I would have thought…

Picking the razor up, I decided it didn't matter. This was probably just another one of his tests. Another one of his rules that he expected me to break.

Besides, I wasn't dumb enough to consider ending my own life right now. I still had options.

So far he hadn't hit me. He hadn't tortured me, unless you called the sexual encounter torture.

I could still get out of this.

I shaved my legs and under my arms before picking up the shampoo and working it into a lather.

The shower gave me time to reflect. *Has it even been a full day?* It was an entirely different life. One Leda walked into prison to see her father, and another Leda emerged.

But just who was this Leda? I sighed and scrubbed at my skin. That would be a question I'd answer later.

Rinsing out the shampoo, I quickly lathered up my body with the bodywash, and thought about what I was avoiding. For one, my father was definitely going to blow a gasket, and I won't be there to see it. Won't be there to bear the consequences.

That was the one positive. He had no hold on me. In a way, it was an odd type of freedom. If I had to take my father's wrath or Valentino's wrath, I'd take Valentino any day.

At the thought of his name, his piercing eyes popped into my mind, and I sighed. I really wished I knew what his deal was, how he became a Don, but I hadn't heard the story. I didn't even know anything about him. I've heard of the Cavazzo Mafia only in passing, but nothing else.

If I had to guess, I'd say he was somewhere in his early to mid-thirties. His hard nature made me think that he had some tragic backstory that left him the way he was. He liked to be in control, which meant he wasn't the type to soften over anything. To lose the upper hand would be like death for him; I was almost sure of it.

If I wanted to find a way to beat him, I'd need to take the upper hand. But how?

I washed the suds off me, shut off the shower, and picked up one of the fluffy towels to dry my body off.

Only then did I take a look in the mirror. And the image looking back startled me.

Eyes that I've known all my life stared back at me, but inside the mirror stood a woman I almost didn't recognize as me. She had a height of flush on her cheeks that I'd never had. Her wrists were chaffed an angry pink. And her eyes shocked me.

They stared, and they *wanted*.

I blinked, and I saw myself once again.

*Get a grip, Leda!* I reprimanded myself.

I wrapped the towel around my body, walked out of the bathroom to the wardrobe, and sighed as I beheld my skimpy choices.

What did it matter now? Valentino pretty much made his intentions clear. We were going to play his game. He laid out those ridiculous rules of his, and now he was going to take his time using me, either in bed or not.

*And after?*

Well, I didn't want to think about an *after*. Mostly because I wasn't sure if there would *be* and after. And if there was, I wasn't going to like it.

So I needed to make sure I delayed the *after* as long as I could.

A secret thrill ran through my veins as I selected a black teddy, one that left nothing to the imagination. If I was going to make him lose control, I'd need a little help.

I needed him to *feel* something.

## Chapter 17
## Leda

I dropped the towel and slid on the teddy, tying a black ribbon at my breasts. The material was sheer, just like most of the things in the wardrobe, with ribbons that held the bodice together. Would Valentino even bother untying those ribbons? Or was he going to rip this like he ripped all of my other clothing?

"Leda." I closed the wardrobe. "Get. A. Grip."

That bastard. He shouldn't make me feel like this. I was sex-starved now, and it wasn't like I had a whole lot of other experiences up until now.

Really, it was all just too overwhelming.

I held onto my virginity, waiting for the right moment and not wanting it to be some drunken encounter in the back of a bar or a club. I wasn't naive in the act or any foreplay that came before it, but letting a man touch me somewhere so intimately?

Well, that wasn't something I had experience in. The closest I had come was with my last boyfriend, Frederick. A French model that lasted four months. First a rebellion against my father, until a bag of money and a not so veiled offer of a choice in broad daylight sent him running back to Europe.

Yes, Carmine D'Agostino either paid off my boyfriends to keep them from ruining me for my future husband, or had them disappeared altogether.

It wasn't something I ever wanted to know. The first time I learned about this arrangement was when an unfortunate boy—too young and foolish—chose to turn down the money.

I locked myself away for days after finding out what my father did to him.

I shrugged on a short robe from the end of the bed, and walked out onto the balcony, letting the sun warm my face. Now that it was daylight, I could see the town below. It was a typical upstate New York town. Small enough to feel cozy, but somehow big enough to accommodate a couple of apple orchards, pumpkin patches, and two breweries.

*And all on Valentino's payroll.*

The house was surrounded by woods on three sides, and the grounds were carefully manicured and. I realized now that there was no way for me to escape in the dark. But after our interaction from a few hours ago, I didn't know if I truly wanted to.

My lips pursed at the thought. Of course I *wanted* to. This line of thinking had to be some sort of traumatic issue that any kidnapped person ran across. I didn't want to stay here.

I wanted to be free. I wanted to enjoy my life as I saw fit and not as others did. I wanted to take my life into my hands and figure out what made me happy—to find what I needed.

To make that happen, I had to get out of here.

Which meant I needed to take down Valentino—or at least give myself a big enough distraction so I could escape. I had to either play to his conscience, or find a way to bring him to his knees so that I could control him somehow.

A man like him would probably recognize the signs of somebody trying to control him. This wouldn't be easy.

I grasped the railing, and closed my eyes, letting the breeze fall over me.

I was a survivor. I wasn't weak. I wasn't going to give up so readily to Valentino or anyone else that came into the picture, especially not if I wanted this life to be mine.

Right now, all I had done was trade whoever was going to be my husband for the mysterious Don Valentino that I knew nothing about. Truth be told, either option would probably have taken on the same course of events as last night.

So where did I stand? What was I dealing with? What could I turn to my advantage?

One, as much he affected me, he was equally—if not more—affected *by* me. He *wanted* me last night. The way he filled my mouth and emptied himself down my throat told me everything I needed to know right there.

Two, he didn't want me to touch him. Now, that was curious. I wanted to say that it was because he wanted that sense of control, to show me how powerless I was.

But the way he practically jumped when my fingers brushed his cock.

*Almost as if he was about to lose control.*

My eyes flew open, and my lips curved in a smile.

Maybe that was the answer.

If I could touch him when he was exposed to me, then that could be the moment where I'd find my chance. The moment where I'd find his weakness.

*Would it work?* My heart raced with my shuddering breath. *Could I make him lose control? Did I really* want *him to lose control?*

My monster purred at the thought, and I felt a flush rise to my cheeks.

*What choices did I have?*

"You can do this," I whispered to myself.

Valentino was going to rue the day that he came up against Leda D'Agostino.

And when I was done, I'd put him on *his* knees.

## Chapter 18
## Lucas

Rocco opened the door for me, and I stepped out, my gaze going directly to Leda's room as I did so. There was business back in New York City that I couldn't put off any longer, so I had left Leda in the care of the guards.

She, of course, never knew I was gone, and that was how I wanted it. I wanted her to have that measure of uncertainty to keep her in her room until I was ready for her to cross the threshold.

The problem was, she hadn't strayed far from my mind today. It didn't help that the client I was meeting with had brought up the fact that I had D'Agostino's daughter in my grasp, the glee in his eyes now far too common. The rest of the Dons thought that I was going to kill her and make a spectacle out of owning her. And maybe I was.

But it would be on my terms, not anyone else's.

"She's been in her room," Rocco supplied as we walked to the side door of the house. "Hasn't caused a scene or tried to kill herself by climbing down the balcony again."

My grin was quick. "I didn't expect her to have the balls to do so."

"Yeah, me neither," Rocco admitted. "She's not what I would have thought."

I welcomed the cool air in the house. That was one of the many reasons I had thought about Leda today, and the object of my thoughts disturbed me greatly. I didn't think about anyone like that, especially not anyone where I could paint a vivid picture of what I wanted to do to her.

None of them included what everyone thought I was doing to her. Hell, I had a reputation of making people suffer before I killed them, using various methods that I had learned as an enforcer. My teachers had been more sadistic than I could ever be, but among those trainings, I had picked up some tools that had served me well over the last few years.

Now, as Don, I still liked to get my hands dirty. One of the lessons Cosimo had taught me was to feel my enemies' pain, that it was the only way I could understand how to torture them effectively.

What could I say? I was a fucking monster.

And I loved it.

"I'll go check the perimeter," Rocco said when he realized I wasn't going to carry on a conversation.

He left me at my office door. I stepped inside, ignoring the newly filled whiskey decanter as I did so. Hell, I no longer wanted to touch the stuff if it was going to have the same effect on my fucking dreams as it had last night.

I fell into my chair and leaned back, looking up at the ceiling. The meeting hadn't gone well. The fucking client wanted to hire my Mafia out to move his guns, and while I wasn't opposed to the idea for a few of my capos, he low-balled me on the price.

If he wanted me to do the dirty work, then he was going to pay the right price for it. He left with a threat to go to one of the other Mafias. So naturally I told him to fuck off, knowing he would be crawling back in a few days.

I could be accommodating when I wanted to be, but I wasn't going to do it for pennies.

That wasn't the sort of Don I would be. When I first took the title, the power had been tenuous. It wasn't easy adapting to giving orders. It wasn't easy managing everybody constantly asking for a share, or figuring out who was going to backstab me.

But I adapted to the task. I spent days trying to sort out information on the entire family, meeting with the capos—even the ones that didn't see me as their Don—and laying down my version of the law.

It hadn't been easy. Even now, there were still capos who whispered that I wasn't the true Don.

Adrian hadn't helped at all, of course. He kept giving me shit, did everything in his power to be a pain in my ass. He tried to sway the votes and get the other capos to call for me to step down.

An outright mutiny.

But then Carmine's empire collapsed. A single article, a couple of dead men, and all of a sudden, the boot of the NYPD came down on Carmine's neck. Seemingly overnight, there was no more D'Agostino Mafia.

His own son dismantled everything he built up. Now, I didn't doubt that there were loyalties left for the old man's name, but their days were numbered.

And suddenly, those capos' whispers got a lot quieter. They'd all seen what happened when a Don falls:

The jungle tore itself down, and guys like them were caught up in it. Chewed up by the sea of change that churned through them. They knew this could happen to Cosimo's empire. They knew, and so did I.

There were times I had considered letting the same thing happen to Cosimo's empire and absconding with what I could. But I had a change of heart when even the most mutinous capo knelt down and pledged his life to mine.

All except Adrian.

I used the Cavazzo Mafia to crush the other Mafias, and I spent the last five years doing just that. I leveraged what was left of Cosimo's influence to steal contracts. I took businesses that had been part of some other Mafia's for generations.

Money talked, and Cosimo's dead pockets were deep.

And the entire time, Adrian kept undermining me. Say what you wanted about that little shit, he had a way of swaying enough men to his cause.

Did it matter that I reminded him Cosimo's will made it plenty clear that I was Don?

No.

And even though the will had been upheld, Adrian had spread the poison of dissent among my ranks. Those capos wouldn't last long anyway. Either they would fall to me, or I'd send them onto their deaths.

That was the real point of Leda at my side. Once the war inevitably came, the unfaithful would be the first ones to die.

Adrian thought I was bringing Carmine's wrath down on the family's head by taking Leda. *Not mine, you little shit. Just yours.*

My cell rang, and I fished it out of my pocket. Number withheld. Probably that client who came crawling back.

I answered it. "Yeah?"

"You think you're some hot shit?"

Grinning, I braced my arms on the desk. "Hello Carmine, to what do I owe this pleasure?"

"You have my daughter," he growled.

"I do," I replied evenly. "I trust you've also heard the price she fetched?"

He huffed into the phone. "I made a deal. How the fuck did you get your hands on her?"

Well, I wasn't going to tell him that he had been sold out by his own men hired to take Leda to her husband. But he should've seen it all coming.

Men like him were old fashioned. Always bloodline this, and family ties that.

The moment I had heard that he had been arrested, I knew that he would be looking for a way to cover his ass. His son Nico wasn't looking to become Don, just to destroy his father.

Which meant Leda was Carmine's only card left to play. It hadn't taken much to figure out her whereabouts, track her, and see the moment when she was practically dragged to prison, I had seen my chance.

They had no idea she was already mine before she stepped foot on that stage. They never stood a chance at getting their hands on her.

"Wouldn't you like to know?" I replied casually. "It's too bad, Carmine. I imagined you had other plans for your family."

"I'm not dead, asshole," he seethed, his anger clear through the phone. "You think that I don't have back-up plans? You think you're untouchable? You think you got away with this scot-free? Do you have the slightest idea who you are messing with?"

"I know exactly who I'm messing with," I growled, dropping all pretense of a casual conversation. "A pathetic man who's nothing but a has-been. Whose own son dismantled his empire. A man whose supposed allies were tossing down stacks for the chance to fuck his daughter. You are done. You've been done."

Carmine chuckled, not fazed by my words. "If you think that this little setback is going to ruin me, *Don Valentino*, you have another think coming. I earned that fucking title the old fashioned way. The dignified way."

The sneer in his voice made me want to reach through the phone and wrap my hands around his neck. He thought, like the rest, that I got to where I was because of what I used to me. He thought that I didn't claw my way to the top.

"Think what you want." I kept my voice smooth. "But I'm on the outside, and you are inside that fucking prison cell, with nothing more than time on your hands."

"I will give you this offer only once," Carmine said after a moment. "Give my daughter back to me, and I will forget this ever happened."

*Never!*

I let out a snort. "Give her up? I've bought her for twenty million, and I intend on getting every penny's worth out of her. Would you like to know what I've been doing to your precious little princess, Carmine? Would you like to know in excruciating detail of how I made her beg?"

"Fuck you," Carmine growled. "If you even think—"

"I'll take good care of your little girl," I interrupted. "Don't you worry."

I ended the call and smirked as I thought about how the old man was likely raising hell that I hadn't given him the respect he thought he had earned.

Blowing out a breath, I slammed the cell phone down onto the desk, feeling some of the anger drain from my body from the exchange. There had been one thing that had bothered me all day, one thing that I hated above all else.

When Carmine demanded his daughter back, a feeling sliced through me.

I was worried about Leda.

I was worried about what would happen if she were to go back there. So much so, that I wanted to protect her from her shithead father and anyone else that came to lay claim to her. It wasn't in my nature to be a protector.

I was the savage that did the hurting.

I was supposed to be her worst nightmare, yet after our exchange hours earlier, I had an uncomfortable feeling when it came to my captive Mafia princess.

The same feeling that I had right now, after my parting words with Carmine.

I was going to take care of Leda, but not in the sense that he thought.

"Fuck," I breathed, my eyes straying to the liquor on the sideboard.

## Chapter 19
## Lucas

As much as I would have liked to drown out that feeling with some good whiskey, there was more of a pressing need in this house, one that I hadn't seen for hours.

I wanted to know what Leda was doing. I wanted to know how she had spent her day and if she was plotting my death yet or not.

Knowing her, she probably had it all laid out, and hell, I liked the viciousness. I didn't want to like anything about her. I wanted her to remain the enemy, to use her and throw her aside like the plan had been all along. I wanted to fuck her and move on, let her think that she was nothing more than trash to me, a means to get back at her father.

I no longer had any of those plans. Hell, I didn't even know what the plan was at this point.

Maybe I should cut ties with her, sell her off to the highest bidder and forget I ever crossed paths with her. In the few short hours she had been in my presence, she had caused more trouble than she was worth, frankly. She had escaped, made me do things that—well, I liked those things. I liked them a lot.

Yet I still hadn't taken her completely, and that was the reason she would stay. I wanted to taste all of what Leda could offer me, the passion that I had just gotten a glimpse of when I had spanked her and shoved my cock into her mouth.

I wanted to have her beg for me, beg for my cock and know that I had her under my complete control. If I sold her now, I wouldn't have that chance.

My cock throbbed painfully as I thought about my next steps. For some unknown reason I was looking at taking this slow, drawing it out so that when I finally did fuck Leda, it would be a culmination of pleasure and pain that she hadn't felt before. I liked the fear in her eyes, but I also liked the fight she was going to give me.

I wanted her to fight me. There had been a point in the beginning when I had planned this little snatch and grab when I had wanted someone who was scared of their own shadow, something that would be easily broken and easy to walk away from.

Now, though, I didn't want that. I wanted her to give me everything she had, for it would be far more satisfying breaking a wild woman than someone who laid down and let me do whatever I wanted.

My eyes drifted to the ceiling as the late afternoon rays started to darken the office. Perhaps I would try and bring her around again, see how far I could push her before she gave in. Her orgasm had been easily accomplished, but I wanted more.

I craved more from Leda.

One thing was for certain; I wasn't about to give her up to anyone, not even her father, not until I had my fill of the Mafia princess.

For there would be a time I would be ready to push her aside and move forward, but we weren't to that point now.

I was about to show Leda what it meant to come up against Don Valentino and how much I could show her before she was begging at my feet, wanting no one or nothing else but me.

A grin crossed my lips and I pushed out of the chair, my thoughts in motion. Last night she surprised me, but I was onto her game now.

And this would be a game that I'd thoroughly enjoy.

Leda wouldn't know what hit her until I have her pinned under me.

When it would be too fucking late.

## Chapter 20
## Leda

I picked at the comforter with my fingers, watching as the sun started to sink in the sky. Another day down. Was the word now out to Nico that I had been purchased by Don Valentino? Was he starting to scramble resources to find me?

Was my father aware of what had transpired? Did he even care?

I traded one prison for another. But this time, there was no ending that I could see.

Sighing, I moved off the bed and crossed the room for what seemed like the hundredth time today, wishing there was something—anything—else that I could do. There were no books, no TV, nothing to keep me entertained in this room. And I wasn't stupid enough to step outside of it on the off-chance that this would be another one of Valentino's tests.

The only interaction I had had today was the guard that had brought me my lunch, which had consisted of a salad and the best salmon I had tasted in quite a while.

I briefly thought about throwing it against the wall and demanding to see Valentino, but my hunger won out in the end and I devoured the food.

The guard made sure that everything was back on the plate when he returned to pick up the dishes. The only thing I was allowed to keep was the water bottle.

I was a crap prisoner if I wasn't constantly looking for a way out of here. Maybe it was because I was wearing lingerie and had no wish to traipse through the woods again barefoot.

Maybe I had given up.

I shook my head.

No, I hadn't given up, not even in the slightest.

I just had to be more strategic in the way that I got out of here. I had to play Valentino and beat him at his own game. I knew he wanted me to be panting after him, to rely on him for everything so that he could say he had won.

I wanted him to do the same with me. I wanted him to lose control again and again until he couldn't remember what he even wanted to control in the first place.

I wanted him to take his tastes of me and not be able to get enough. Could I delay the inevitable moment when he would demand that I spread my legs for him? No, probably not.

But there was a part of me that wondered if I could get him to be the one who begged me.

Picturing Valentino begging between my legs brought a smile to my face, but the image also brought that bothersome heat to my gut at the same time. I didn't know *how* he had such a quick hold on me, on my body, after one orgasm and him shoving his cock in my mouth. It was crazy, really.

It would have to be a fine line that I'd walk. Push him too far, and too hard, and he might just take what he wants from me by force.

But there was no other way to find out.

I had no choice but to press his buttons. I needed to take him to the brink of what he thought he controlled, and make him realize he wasn't as much in control as he would like to be. I *had to* mess up his carefully laid plans for me, and I was pretty sure there was only one way to do that.

I would have to become the spoiled brat he imagined me to be.

Up until this moment, I had done everything he had said. I had put on the clothes he had offered, stayed in this room even though I was bored to the point of tears, and eaten the food he offered.

In short, I obeyed.

I hadn't given him a reason to think I would defy him, aside from my one single desperate attempt at an escape.

Maybe that was the problem.

I could play the spoiled princess rather well. After all, it came out every once and a while when I hung out with the wrong crowd. I found it too easy to get caught up in the lives of the rich and famous, too easy to demand things that I wouldn't have normally demanded otherwise.

The few times I had participated in a runway walk, I had luxuries sent to my dressing room because I *could*. Granted, I felt horrible afterwards, especially at the thought of forcing the staff to run around and make it happen, no matter how unreasonable the demand had been.

But I could still do it.

And at any rate, I wasn't about to feel bad for what I was going to do to Valentino or his staff. As far as I was concerned, every person who saw me in this house was complicit in my captivity. Every single one of them could have chosen to help me. And in the end, none of them ever did.

So, yeah. He wanted to be in control? I'd show him just how out of control I could be.

I just hoped I could handle any fallout that might take place in response to my act of rebellion.

I wished I knew more about him so I could do more than just try and piss him off.

*Think, Leda, think. He took you for a reason. Why? Getting back at father didn't require YOU.*

I needed to find out more about him. I needed to uncover the unforeseen bad experience in his life and bring it to the forefront.

But that was the thought that I feared most of all: I was afraid that if I knew too much about him, it might be enough to make me unable to quit him.

What if his past is so dark that I ended up falling for him?

What if bringing up that past made him lose control in the worst of ways?

Would he spank me again? A secret thrill ran through my body at the thought of his hand on my ass, drawing out the spark of pain that had nearly sent me into an orgasm alone. I hadn't known that I could like something like that—equal parts humiliation and equal parts pain.

What else would he draw out from within me?

There had been a moment today that I had caught a glimpse of him climbing out of an SUV when it pulled up under the balcony. I had crept over to the curtains and watched him interact with what probably was his second-in-command.

I wondered where he had gone and what he had done during that time. Did he go to taunt my father about having me in his grasp? Was he gloating to the other Dons about the fact that I was back here at his mansion, waiting for his touch?

I felt like that would be the worst of it all: the idea that I was here, waiting for him. The power he held over me with that simple action of *neglect* was more than I could've ever expected. He knew he could move on with his day—even with the D'Agostino princess in his home—but he knew *I* would agonize every little decision.

Well, two can play that game, and he was about to see what sort of princess he had acquired.

# Chapter 21
## Leda

The door suddenly opened, and I turned to find the object of my thoughts coming through the doorway, a tray in his hand.

He was wearing a dress shirt and slacks, the collar open at the neck and his shirtsleeves rolled to his elbows, exposing that tattoo I had seen on him earlier. Did he have other tattoos?

It was only a matter of time before I would find out.

"Good evening," he stated, setting the tray on the small table near the balcony. "I trust your day went well?"

I crossed my arms over my chest, rewarded with the way that his eyes drifted to my raised breasts that were barely contained in the sheer material.

I did my best to put on my annoying spoiled brat voice. "I am bored." I pouted.

He arched a brow, and my insides quivered. How could a man possibly look so unbelievably sexy by just arching his brow?

"Bored? Princess, you are a prisoner. It's not my job to fucking entertain you."

"Still," I replied. "There should at least be *something* to do in this room. I mean, do you really expect me to just sit around and stare at my nails all day? I want entertainment, Valentino."

His gaze narrowed, and I gave myself a mental high five. This was going to be easier than I thought. He wasn't someone who got a lot of challenges, apparently, and this was a challenge that he definitely didn't see coming. "I expect you to stay in this fucking room and not cause trouble."

"Oh?" I asked innocently as I dropped my arms and let my robe fall open. "What kind of trouble could I *possibly* cause?"

His eyes drifted over my exposed skin. Just the thought of his eyes raking over my skin sent my nipples puckering to a painful point, but I kept my chin high. This was all about getting *him* off his game, not about *me* being seduced by him.

Valentino wasn't a seducer by any means. He was a conqueror.

It was time I gave him a little push. "You know that D'Agostinos love to stir up trouble." At the word *trouble*, I teased the robe apart—just enough to give him a better look, but not enough for the full thing.

"Is that so?" He crossed his arms over his chest. He looked, well, maybe amused, which meant I wasn't there just yet. I needed to step up my game, piss him off where he least expected it.

I knew exactly how to do it.

I nodded and tipped the end of the tray with my hand suddenly, the dishes sliding to the floor. Mentally I mourned what looked like a delicious pasta dish splatter against the carpet. Oh well, small prices to pay. The sauce spilled out of the bowl and splashed onto Valentino's slacks. He looked down at the ruined fine material of his pants.

This was certainly working out better than I could have even imagined!

"Why did you do that?" Valentino growled, meeting my gaze. Oh my. He was visibly pissed, his jaw clenched tightly, so tightly I thought I could hear his teeth cracking.

"Because," I said flippantly, even tossing my hair back to further irate him. If I was going to do this and likely starve tonight, I was going to go all out. "I don't want to eat if you can't give me what I want."

"And what exactly do you want?" he echoed, his eyes narrowing.

I let out a little huff, as if he were irritating me. "Quit repeating my words. I know you can hear just fine. I have certain requirements that I need if you want me to stay in this room any longer. I mean, just look at these sheets. They're nowhere up to par with what I want."

Well, that was a lie. Those sheets were actually great, but I wasn't about to admit that to him.

His expression grew harder still, and I sucked in a breath, keeping the half smile on my face. Was he close to his breaking point?

If he wasn't, then the man was a saint. I had all but insulted his room, his accommodations, and his hearing.

"Pick up those dishes."

I eyed him, seeing how tight his body had grown. It was a shame that he was so gorgeous, honestly. "Or what?"

Valentino grew very still, and I felt like the air had been sucked out of the room as his eyes glittered. "Excuse me?"

"What are you going to do about it if I don't pick up those dishes?" I challenged.

My insides twisted in turmoil. Truth be told, he could do a number of things. He might pick up the dishes himself and bash me in the head with it if he really wanted to. He might push my face into the pasta on the carpet like an unruly dog. Different scenarios flashed through my mind. Each one ending with the same scene: me, dead, dead, dead.

Fuck, had I gone too far?

But it was too late, I couldn't back out now. To do so would be to admit that I was afraid of him. I had to keep going.

"Well? I'm waiting." I said sweetly, doing my best to keep the tremor out of my voice. "And besides, are you really a Don to begin with? I've never heard of you."

The moment the corner of his mouth lifted, I knew I had gone too far. There was no inch of softness in him, and the last of my bravado fled.

*This wasn't* his *breaking point, Leda. This was* yours.

He stepped over the food and I backed up against the bed, torn between telling him that I was sorry and wanting to find out what he was going to do next.

He looked at me like a wolf looked at a wounded sheep. I was suddenly very aware of the fact that before me stood a dangerous man, a man who didn't like being told what to do and who didn't care for the woman I was portraying at all.

*Oh no.*

His body pushed into mine, and a whimper escaped through my lips when I felt the evidence of what my little taunting had done to him. He was hard as a rock, his erection pressed against my belly, and I fought the urge to lick my lips.

"Do you know?" He leaned closer until his face was the only thing I could see. His arms flanked me on both sides. I was trapped. "What I do to girls that don't listen?"

Heaven help me. "N-No?"

His grin became feral, and I felt every nerve ending stand at attention. My own body was flushed with heat, the wetness starting to leak through the thin material that was between my legs. The monster inside of me was dancing in happiness.

He flipped my plan onto its head with a single simple gesture.

I wanted him; I wanted him far too badly. This wasn't the sort of response I had wanted for myself. I wanted him to suffer, to figure out what in the heck he was going to do with me acting up like this.

Instead, I had turned on the floodgates to my own arousal, desperate to know what he was going to do to me next. What I wanted him to do to me next. Would he fuck me now? Would he throw me on this bed and have his way with me like he had planned on all along?

If he walked away, I might be partial to begging this time around. Valentino had left me wanting more last time, and my body hadn't forgotten the fact.

His hand came up, and I gasped as a finger trailed down my cheek lightly, his blue eyes never changing color.

"So, you're a bad girl now," he whispered, the barest hint of mint tickling my nose. "And bad girls get punished, Leda."

My knees weakened as his finger slid down the column of my throat, over the frantic beat of my pulse under my skin before he grasped ahold of the neckline to the teddy. I squeaked as he tore it down the middle—much like he had done with the chemise hours before—and as the sheer material fell to the floor, he pushed me onto the bed.

I overstepped.

And now he was going to make me pay.

## Chapter 22
## Lucas

My nostrils flared as I looked at her naked form, my cock pressing against my pants. Fuck, she looked excited by what I had just done, which made me want to fuck her harder than before.

Normally I didn't act like this. Normally I didn't lose control like this, but Leda was making me want to do things to her that went far beyond just physical domination.

She made me want to truly own her, body and soul.

The moment that thought crossed my mind, I knew I should have walked away. This wasn't part of the fucking plan. I was supposed to have taken my time with her. I was supposed to have broken every fucking wall she had up until she was nothing but putty in my hands.

I was supposed to make her worship me, and beg for my cock in humiliation before I took her.

I hadn't done any of those things.

Instead, she became like a drug to me—an addiction that I couldn't quit.

Leda looked up at me, and there was defiance reflected in her beautiful eyes. I thought she might be weak, nothing more than a spoiled princess who spent her daddy's money and got her way. Hell, I had seen a lot of those types in my day.

More importantly, I knew when they were acting.

And as hard as Leda tried, the act today was just that: an act.

It was an act that I was sucked into. Everything she did—all of the little provocations—was done specifically to get me to react like this. From the way she pushed the dish onto the carpet, to the way she challenged me.

It made me want to ruin her. It made me want to take that defiance on her face and transform into submission.

I needed to put her in her place, before I lost my own fucking mind.

I reached for Leda, watching as her lips parted before I flipped her onto her stomach. Her pert ass rose into view. I braced my forearm on her lower back, and rubbed my hand over her ass before I gave it a rough, sharp smack.

"Bad girl," I growled, watching as the skin reddened under my touch. "You are a bad fucking girl that needs to be punished."

A moan escaped her, and I frowned. This wasn't the reaction I had expected. I thought she would at least have cried out in pain. But this moan of pleasure?

It was almost like she *liked* this.

As if she *craved* this.

My cock was begging to be inside of her glistening entrance, and I had to grit my teeth to keep myself in check, to keep myself from doing exactly that.

Leda was brought here as a tool. She was the key to my personal war of consolidating control over the rest of the Cavazzo Mafia. I was supposed to dangle her before the other Dons as the bait while Adrian's loyalists died by the droves.

Not wasting time in here, playing with her body.

The thought that she kept me from doing what I was supposed to do spurred on the rage building in my heart. She needed to be taught a lesson—a lesson in knowing her place—but I didn't feel like I was doing that correctly. It felt like she was the one who was teaching me a lesson: that I was hopelessly addicted to touching her.

This addiction was something that I did my best to stay the hell away from my entire lifetime. I spanked her again, and Leda's moans grew louder. She turned her head, her eyes hidden by the tangle of hair draped across them. Another moan escaped from her lips, low and needy, and her ass practically wriggled.

She was going to make me blow my load in my pants by moaning like that. I wanted tears, maybe even a scream, but she wasn't doing *anything* that I wanted her to do.

Another smack, and another moan.

My head was filled with the memory of her eager mouth caressing my cock, her throat opening as I slid my cock deep into it, and tears leaking from the edges of her eyes as I emptied myself. I knew she hadn't had much experience in the bedroom from that moment, but it didn't matter.

Given who she was and what I had seen before her purchase, I had expected more out of her.

Leda was a worldly woman, having traveled to places I hadn't even fucking gone to. I had seen pictures of her hanging out with models, arms draped around each other, and a woman like that didn't stay a virgin for long.

Not to mention the world that I knew far too well from my past. Mafia Dons and their wives didn't stay faithful to each other, and their children bore the brunt of that infidelity. Those kids learned from either their fathers' mistakes or their mothers' liaisons.

I'd even seen depraved moments when a daughter was to be introduced to the world of sex: to be taught in ways of not only pleasuring her soon-to-be husband, but also to be used as a siren for her father's bidding.

I fucking hated those moments. Those girls were to be pure for their husbands, and their fathers made certain of that purity.

Maybe that was what D'Agostino had done with his daughter.

The very thought made me rage, and I pushed it away. My own feuds were relegated to the back of my mind. Now, a singular purpose drove me forward.

After tonight, Leda would be intact no longer.

I was going to ruin her.

## Chapter 23
## Lucas

My curiosity piqued at Leda's reaction. I spanked her a few more times so that both cheeks matched before I flipped her around. Her eyes were wide with heat, her entire body flushed in a delicious shade of pink, and my hands twitched to roam down her body.

*No. Fuck. No.* My touches had to dominate, not explore. They were meant to be harsh, to show her who was in control.

There would be a time for pleasure, but not from my touches. That honor was reserved for my cock. Everything else was off-limits.

When my hand went to my waistband, Leda unknowingly licked her lips, and I fought back a groan. It was almost like she *wanted* my cock in her mouth, almost as much as I did.

"On your knees," I ordered as I opened my zipper and pulled out my cock.

Leda did as I asked. I stepped forward until my knees hit the side of the bed, my cock in my hands.

I gripped at my cock hard to keep my hand still. Maybe it was her eagerness that was affecting me, but I had never felt like this before with anyone. "Put it in your mouth."

She didn't even give me a protest as her tongue darted out and touched the bulging head, tasting me tentatively.

"All of it," I demanded, not wanting to play fucking games. I needed to gain control again, and this was the best way to do it.

Leda needed to know she had no control over me. I was the one in fucking control, not her.

Stretching her mouth, she slid my cock between her lips, and I felt a tremor slide through me, torn between wanting her to stop and wanting to continue. This was fucking torture at its best. The Mafia princess before me had no fucking idea just how much power she wielded over me in this exact moment.

For a brief second, *she* owned *me*, and I didn't hate it as much as I thought I would.

I couldn't let her discover that power.

Angrily, I pushed deeper until she started to gag against my cock.

I was pissed at myself for allowing any thoughts other than ruining her to cross my mind. *Fuck her beautiful body. Fuck the fact that she wasn't scared of me.*

She was going to be.

Leda reached up to adjust herself, and I slapped her hand away, pulling out slowly before ramming back in. Tears welled up at the corners of her eyes as I thrust, and a twinge gripped my chest. I was supposed to teach her a lesson, wasn't I?

This was Leda D'Agostino, the daughter of the most hated Mafia don at this moment.

She deserved far worse than what I was doing to her. She deserved to pay for her father's crimes, to have real fear in her eyes as I did unspeakable things to her. I should chain her to this fucking bed and use her repeatedly until I was the only person she answered to.

I wanted to mark her body with my seed, to cum all over her until there wasn't an inch of her skin that hadn't been violated by me. I thought I would use her up and then drop her off right on her father's doorsteps as a sign of my own power.

To show the other Dons: look at the D'Agostino princess. Her father thought she was untouchable. You thought you were untouchable? You thought wrong.

Yet here I was, about to ruin all the plans I had drummed up in my head. Now, all I could think about was burying my cock deep between her legs until she forgot who she was.

Until I forgot who I was. The terrible things I had done and endured.

I watched her suck my cock with an enthusiasm I hadn't planned on, and it took every fiber of my being to utter the next word.

"Stop," I gritted out, feeling the pressure build in my balls. If she kept doing it like that, I wouldn't be doing anything but embarrassing myself all over her fucking face or in her mouth.

Leda did as I asked, her gaze meeting mine, but her hand still held onto my now wet, aching cock like she owned the damn thing. Her fingers trace the bulging head, idly finding the vein that stood out against the stretched skin. She was exploring me at her leisure, her lips parted as if she wanted to take me in her mouth again.

Every touch and every stroke was fucking ruining me.

Without a word, I grabbed her hand, stilling her touch as I tried to find harsh words to say. What I *really* wanted to tell her was to continue torturing me like she was—to bring me to the edge only to pull away until nothing could hold me back anymore.

"Valentino?" she asked hesitantly. Did she even know my full name? Why should I even care? I shouldn't care, but there was a small piece of my dark soul that wanted to hear my name pass through her lips the same way that my cock did.

No. This was getting out of hand. I was going to end these warm feelings right here and now. I hadn't bought her to explore my desires. I bought her because I needed her as just another part of my plans.

That was why she was here, no other reason but that.

I squeezed her hand tightly until she winced under the pain. That was more like it. She was supposed to be scared of me.

That had been the plan. "You don't get to ask any fucking questions," I snarled before pushing her away. Her chest heaved as she fell onto the bed, but I was no longer paying attention to anything but the glistening pussy before me. Did this turn her on?

It sure as hell turned me on.

I was acutely aware that I was hard as a rock. It was almost painful.

One look at Leda's face, however, only pissed me off more. She looked hurt, and her eyes begged me for an explanation. As if she did something wrong.

*No. You did nothing wrong.*

"Turn over," I told her in a near growl. I didn't want to watch her expression as I fucked her. In fact, I preferred to keep my partners facing away from me because to meet their eyes was too much. Eyes were a fucking glimpses to a person's soul, and right now, I wanted nothing else but to keep mine hidden.

When Leda flipped over, I grabbed her hips and pulled her to the edge of the bed, ignoring the softness of her skin under my fingers. She felt like heaven to me as my rough and callused hands ran over her skin, the same silky skin that begged to be kissed.

I rested my cock at her entrance. "Wait," she breathed. "Wait."

*No.*

I had waited long enough. All my plans had gone to hell at this point. All I had now was Leda D'Agostino.

No more fucking waiting. I was taking what I wanted.

I pushed the head of my cock into her warm moist entrance. She gasped. I reached out and covered her mouth as I started to push myself deeper.

"You don't get to fucking talk."

# Chapter 24
## Leda

I didn't know what to think.

My heart hammered against my chest as I felt him start to nudge my entrance with his cock, the tingling causing me to bite back a moan so it wouldn't make him angry again. Never before had I been in this situation, a situation that I couldn't handle. Normally if a guy was getting too handsy, I could handle it, but right now, it seemed that Valentino was in complete control.

I was scared. I was nervous. I was—heck, I was excited about the prospect. My mind felt drunk, even though I was fully aware of what was going on. A million questions raced through my mind, but only two stood out.

Why did this Mafia Don feel so... right? Why didn't this scare me more?

That was what truly scared me: the fact that I wasn't fazed by the way he was treating me, that I wasn't trying to fight back and deny him the rights to my body, to my mouth.

I *wanted* this. I *wanted* to watch him lose control in my mouth again. I *wanted* to feel like I was taking a piece of him away.

I *wanted* to watch Valentino take my virginity, but he clearly didn't want me to meet his eyes when he did so.

That was completely odd. This position was meant to be humiliating, but I found it far too exciting.

"Wait." I breathed. *Let me savor it.* But the only thing I could do was muster another "Wait."

One hand reached up and covered my mouth, and I felt him move deeper inside of me. His voice hung hot and heavy by my ear.

"You don't get to fucking talk."

And without another word, Valentino pushed himself deep inside of me. I cried out against his hand as my body accommodated his thickness, contracting as he reached places no-one has ever reached before. There was a burst of pain—fiery and hot—as he stretched me.

A sharp sting, almost like a needle, took my breath away. I gasped as the smoky smell of his fingers filled my nostrils. His other hand clenched my hips tightly, pulling me closer to him and driving his cock even deeper..

The sensations were almost indescribable. I felt—well, I wasn't in pain. My lower half felt heavy, like it was waiting in anticipation for more, and I knew there would be more.

Surely he wasn't going to just take my virginity and not do anything else. That would be the worst torture!

My mind was only dimly aware that he was barebacked. Oh God. At least I'd had my IUD recently replaced, but the thought of us touching like this, without anything between us, left me shivering.

I moved just slightly, and his grip tightened before he started to move, sliding out without warning. Gasping, I felt the barest brush of an orgasm starting to build. It was mere seconds before he was plunging into me again.

His hand released my mouth just in time for a sound to escape my throat. I was unable to hold back my own lust. My hands clenched the comforter. This was slow torture.

Deliciously slow torture that I was willing to die from. Every girl pictured the loss of her virginity when she was old enough to know what it was, but this wasn't how I expected to lose mine at all.

Valentino's pace started to build, and I whimpered as my orgasm started to build. My body tightened to an unbearable point. It was hard to tell where he ended and where I began. The pain was nothing more than a distant memory, having been slowly replaced with a delicious pleasure that I was dangerously close to losing control over.

My body seemed to know what to do as well, arching to meet his thrusts and hearing him grunt in appreciation when I did. Oh, how I wanted to see his face! Was he enjoying this?

Why did I care?

The orgasm crashed through me and I cried out, unable to hold back any longer. My body quivered against his cock, and I felt his hand bunch around my hair, pulling my head back like a man would rein in a horse.

"Who do you fucking belong to?" he snarled, his body never losing rhythm. "Tell me, Leda, who do you belong to?"

God, I was wet again. "Y-you," I breathed, meeting him thrust for thrust now. "I belong to you."

"Don Valentino," he said. There was just a little bit of pain at the roots of my hair as he pulled, but it only heightened the way my body was responding to his intrusion.

"Don Valentino," I panted, my eyes squeezing shut as I cried out against the orgasm.

He let go of my hair, and I felt his cock grow even harder inside of me. Was he was about to lose himself.

"Please," I blurted out "Don't cum inside me." I didn't know what made me say it aloud, but just the thought that he *might* do so caused my nipples to tighten.

Valentino let out a harsh laugh and forced my face into the comforter as he fucked me deeper into the bed. The sound of our bodies clapping together filled the room. The scent of musk was overpowering. His hands gripped my ass and squeezed roughly. My pussy clenched automatically, gripping his cock even tighter.

Somewhere inside of me, I wanted to reach out and feel him. I took the chance and reached my hand between my legs. I felt something wet drip onto my wrist—whether from him or from me, I'd never know.

I reached further and found his balls. My hand cradled them. I felt them tense up at the touch. I barely had time to register his shout as he stiffened inside me.

The warmth came a moment later. Waves of pleasure washed over me. Flowers of sweat blossomed as they fell from his brow to my body. His cock twitched and emptied, and I felt his balls trembling in my own fingers.

He had done exactly what I had wanted him not to do. Why was I not angry about it?

Valentino grunted as he pulled out of me, my sore muscles flexing around him as he left. There was a temporary moment of emptiness, and I fought the urge to beg him to return inside.

The moment his weight disappeared from my back, I scrambled upwards to a seated position, watching as he took several steps back. His cock glistened with my wetness, and I had to fight the shock that was now settling in.

I was a virgin no longer.

He raked a hand through his hair before tucking his cock back into his pants.

"You're mine now," he said softly, buttoning his pants. "Make no mistake of the fact, Leda. No one can save you. No one is coming for you. You are mine. I can do this to you anytime I want. Never forget that."

I swallowed at his statement, my traitorous heart deciding that I might not care if anyone came for me. Who would anyway? Nico? Probably, but if he hadn't come by now, he probably wouldn't be coming any time soon. I was a big girl, and so far Valentino hadn't done anything but grow my sexual experience unabashedly.

I should be ashamed, but I wasn't, and that was what scared me.

Without saying a word to me, Valentino walked out of the room, shutting the door behind him. I watched the door for a few moments, torn on whether or not to move if he came back

When the door didn't reopen, I let out a shaky breath. There was a smear of pink on the comforter, the proof that I no longer had my innocence. A drop of pearl leaked out, tinged with spirals of pink. *This really happened*.

He bought me.

He fucked me.

He made me bleed.

I didn't even put up a fight.

And I liked it.

## Chapter 25
## Leda

I didn't understand what was going on, but I couldn't stop thinking about the fact that I *liked* what had just happened. I *liked* that he had dominated me, that he had taken me and came inside of me even though I begged him not to.

The right person would have fought back. The right person *should* have fought back. The right person wouldn't have reached out to cradle his balls right before he emptied himself inside of her—like she wasn't just as wanton as her kidnapper was.

I hadn't done any of those things. I didn't even think about fighting back. Instead, I allowed Valentino to order me around like I was some sort of slave craving her master's touch. I let him inside of me. I held him there while he filled me.

Swallowing the harsh truth, I climbed off the bed and walked to the bathroom, wincing as I did so. My ass was sore from his slaps, but I knew that I would be sore for other reasons come the morning. Most of the women I had been around in my adult life had lost their virginity long ago.

None of them told me what to expect. They all assumed that I was like them and knew my way around a guy.

Judging by how my body instinctively reacted to Valentino, maybe that was the right assumption.

A bubble of laughter escaped me before it turned into an all-out sob, and I quickly turned on the shower to drown it out.

I wasn't upset about what I had done. What I was upset about was that I didn't know what the hell was going on and what would come next.

What would Valentino do now? Had he accomplished what he had set out to do, and was he now going to kill me?

Or was this part of his plan to take my virginity and now flaunt it in front of my father so that he would know he couldn't sell me again? I would be tainted goods, though I somehow doubted that would stop Carmine D'Agostino from getting what he wanted in the end. He had been extremely specific in what his plans were for me.

The water felt hot on my skin as I stepped inside, sliding down the wall of the shower before drawing my knees to my chest. Whatever Valentino did decide to do with me, it was a far better thought than what my father had in store.

I'd rather be Valentino's slave, to have him fuck me repeatedly night in and night out, than to be married off to some Don that my father had picked out.

A laugh escaped me as I thought about how my father was likely spewing venom at this moment, having lost his opportunity to take the reins of his own Mafia once more. It was disbanded, disgraced, and probably never likely to pull back together again, at least not under my father's thumb.

That was enough for me to face whatever was next. Knowing that my father was ruined beyond his comprehension would keep me warm at night.

*My father had summoned me from my summer vacation in France. It was supposed to be a present that he gave me for my high school graduation.*

*When I walked into my father's study, I saw him sitting behind his desk like he always did. My stomach twisted. There would only be bad news "Leda," he stated, not looking up from his papers on the desk. "Did you have fun in France?"*

*I straightened my shoulders. "Why would you care?"*

*He chuckled, but the laughter never reached his eyes. "You have no problems spending my money to do so. Don't you think that entitles me to know whether or not you enjoyed it?"*

*"What do you want?" I asked instead.*

*He was right. I had spent his money without a care in the world. I was finally free of him, or would be the moment I packed up my things and headed off to college.*

*My father leaned back in the chair, placing his hands behind his head. "I've summoned you here to tell you of your future."*

*"My future?" I asked. "I've already gotten into Columbia. That's where I'll be heading in a few weeks."*

*"No, you aren't," he replied. "You don't need college for what I have planned for you."*

*Sweat broke out over my skin. "I'm eighteen now. You can't tell me what to do." More so, I wanted the freedom, the independence of not being under his thumb any longer. I had done everything he had wanted me to for eighteen years.*

*The look he gave me said that I could not have been more wrong.*

*"You will be wed," he stated after a minute. "To a husband of my choosing when the time is right."*

*My mouth dropped open. Married? "I—"*

*"This is not a negotiation, Leda," he continued. "You will not run, or I will hunt you down and deal with you myself. Your brother will also suffer, so keep that in mind if you decide to fuck me over."*

*My lips parted, and I wanted to tell him how I truly felt about him, that I wasn't going to go along with his precious plans. But the moment he threw in Nico's name, I knew I had no choice. My brother had already suffered so much under my father's watchful eye, hating him just as much as I hated him. I couldn't let him take any more hurt, any more pain.*

*I couldn't let Nico take the fall for anything related to me.*

*"So, my dutiful daughter," he stated, leaning forward. "Do we have an understanding?"*

*I lifted my chin, ignoring the devastation swirling in my gut. "We do, father."*

*He smirked. "That's what I like to hear. Go get dressed. We are having a soiree tonight, and I expect you to be all smiles and your usual gracious self."*

*It took all I had to walk out of the study and not do something stupid like shoot him on the spot. If I did, many would cheer, that was for certain.*

*My legs trembled as I walked up the stairs to my room, waiting until my door was shut before I slid against it, letting myself fall to the floor. My father was still ruling my life, and all hopes of me getting away from him were now a moot point.*

*I was never going to get away from Carmine D'Agostino.*

*Never.*

Shaking out of the horrible memory that had spawned all this, I rose from the floor and washed Valentino's scent from my skin.

I had learned to be stronger than I ever had been, to not let anyone get their claws into me and await the day that I would be handed over to my husband, a husband that my father had chosen for me. And now those plans went to shit, and it was all because of the man who had just left his seeds inside of me.

The thought that he did such a thing sent a tremor through me. I was already craving Valentino's touch again. I could only hope that it wasn't the last time he did that to me, or anything else for that matter.

I had enjoyed it, and my mind was whirling with possibilities of what he could do next time.

Or at how I could push him.

A little smile flirted on my lips as I thought about my original plan to get him to lose control so that I could find his weakness. He had certainly broken down my walls.

And though I had no idea what to expect next, I knew that I reached something inside of *him*.

That was a start.

Snorting, I shut off the water and stepped out of the shower. I pulled the towel down off the rack and covered myself. I was used to covering up my internal pain with a smile, a sneer, a flick of the wrist.

I could do the same with him.

The wardrobe still had nothing but lingerie hanging there. As much as I wished I had some comfortable pajamas, I slipped on a black floor-length gown with an exposed back, and climbed into bed. Exhaustion washed over me and I was suddenly aware of just how tired I was. The sheets smelled like him, and heaven help me, I might have pressed my face into them.

I already wanted him again.

That couldn't be good.

It didn't take me long to fall asleep, however.

My body was sated.

And my dreams were filled with Valentino.

## Chapter 26
## Lucas

I sat on the terrace outside the study, a drink in my hand as the still night moved around me. I hadn't touched the drink since I poured it, too busy thinking about what had happened earlier and what the hell I was going to do about it.

I had fucked Leda D'Agostino. It hadn't been the plan, not this soon. But now that it was over and done, all I wanted was to take my happy ass upstairs and do it all over again.

Leda wasn't just some object I had bought, a pretty vase that I could keep in the room, touch once, and ignore for the rest of my lifetime.

I had a taste of her.

And I wanted more.

"Stop it," I leaned my head against the chair and breathed.

What had possessed me to lose control like that? I had tried to do it the way I wanted to, to keep her face away from me so that she would be nothing more than a plaything.

Yet every time I closed my eyes, I heard her breathy moans, the way she had started to meet me thrust for thrust, and how I wished I had turned her around to see her reaction.

It wasn't what I needed to be thinking about. Leda wasn't what I expected from a Mafia princess. Actually, I had no idea what I was expecting. Certainly not the hellcat that she actually was—one who was just as turned on by being humiliated like she was.

And to add to that, she was a virgin. A surge of primal pride ran through me. I was the only man who ever had her, the only one to have given her pleasure like that. And no matter how hard I tried to keep it cold, she wanted it as much as I did.

But one thing continued to bug me.

Why the hell hadn't she broken down in tears? Other than a token resistance at the end, she never once begged me *not* to take her. *That* was what I expected from her.

I blew out a breath and looked up at the stars. What would she be like the next time I opened her legs? Would she hurl the insults I was supposed to hear for a man who stole her innocence? Would I find a completely different person in the bed by morning?

Whichever it was, I wanted to go back and find out.

It wasn't just lust. It was curiosity.

Oh, don't get me wrong. I wanted to fuck her. Hell, I would keep fucking her until neither of us could walk. But there was a part of me that—and I fucking hated to admit this—wanted to find out more about her.

She was a fighter—strong, resilient, and made of sterner stuff than I had given her any credit before.

I wanted to know why.

And how.

It was bad for me to care like this, to have this craving inside that couldn't be sated even after I had her. She did something to me just now.

I didn't fucking like it.

I didn't go back to her for the rest of the night. Instead, I resolved to lock myself in my own room to keep myself from going to hers. Sleep was nonexistent. By the time morning rolled around, I was pissed off and exhausted, craving the woman who haunted my dreams.

When the sun flooded my room with light, I went to the kitchen and fixed her a tray for breakfast, having some myself before I got ready to see her. Maybe it was just the anticipation. Maybe once I see her, I wouldn't feel the same way.

But every step on the stairs sent my pulse racing, anxious to see what she was going to be doing or what she'd be wearing when I opened the door.

## Chapter 27
## Lucas

I found her sitting on the bed. The remains of the spilled dinner from last night had been cleaned up and the broken china sat on the tray on the table.

"I couldn't take the smell," she explained as I walked in.

My cock swelled at the sight of the pink blush of the morning light playing on her cheeks. Definitely not a one-time thing. I was getting obsessed with her, and that would be a problem.

A huge one.

"Balcony." I said and motioned to the chairs that faced the morning sun.

She shrugged and threw back the covers, the long gown moving around her legs as I let her open the door. I could see the entire expanse of her exposed back. My eyes traced the spine to the cleft of her ass cheeks. I suppressed my groan as my balls tightened.

I needed to put her in some decent clothing.

I set the tray on the table. She sat down in the seat beside it and tucked her legs under her.

"Why are you like this?" I asked immediately as she reached for the coffee carafe I had brought.

Leda's eyes found mine, and there was genuine confusion there. "Like what?"

"Like this," I grumbled, thrusting a hand through my hair. "You aren't even fucking afraid of me."

To my surprise, Leda laughed.

She poured a cup of coffee and handed it to me. I took it silently, berating myself that I had asked something so straightforward. "Thanks." I told her.

"You're welcome," she answered as she fixed her own coffee. Steam rolled off the black liquid and she breathed in the curls.

"To answer your question: because I'm my father's daughter. I can't afford to look weak to his rivals. That means you, Valentino."

"Lucas," I corrected her. "Today, you call me Lucas."

Leda's lips parted in surprise, and I had the urge to press mine against them.

"All right, then. Lucas," she finally said. "My father is a monster. He's done horrible things, things that no one should know about. Things to his own children. Fear wasn't an option since I was a teenager."

I knew the stories of Carmine. His feuds with the other Dons, his feud with Wall Street moguls, and his feud with pretty much anyone who didn't acknowledge that he was top dog. He made a name for himself, and every

Don speculated in hushed whispers about what Carmine made his own son do.

Hell, if half of the rumors and speculations were true, then I couldn't blame Nico D'Agostino for wanting to tear down everything his father built.

I hadn't been able to confirm the story. And now here was my chance.

"What *has* he done?" I asked.

Leda shook her head and stared at her coffee cup. "That's not for me to say. I don't want to talk about it."

Motherfucker. So she was still keeping her own father's dirty secrets. What did he do to his own daughter? Leda refused to meet my eye, as if the patterns in her coffee were the most interesting thing in the world.

Carmine must've broken something inside her long ago. But it hadn't broken her. She was strong.

Stronger than I cared to admit.

Leda wasn't going to be the type of person that would take my hits lying down. She was going to meet me stride for stride, at least in my presence. What she did afterward, I wouldn't know. But something about the way she held herself together told me she wasn't about to cry on anyone's shoulder.

A few silent moments passed before she drew in a breath and turned her intense gaze on me. "You aren't what I expected either, Val—I mean, Lucas."

"In what capacity?" I asked. My heart lurched at the sound of my name on her lips. How the hell was she doing this to me?

She smiled, and the corner of her eyes lifted ever so slightly. "I really don't know. There's something about you that I can't put my finger on. But I know that you're just... different. You don't seem like the other Dons."

"What do you mean?" My breath caught in my throat.

"The other Dons," she explained. "Well, they have this way they act—like they own the world. But you? You act the entire opposite of that. Like the world owes you. Kind of makes me wonder. How did you get here?"

I froze. This wasn't why I had come out here this morning. I didn't come here to check on her because I wanted her to play therapist.

Leda's smile dimmed when she caught the look on my face.

"I'm sorry," she said quickly, tucking a strand of hair behind her ear. "I didn't mean to pry, I just meant that..."

I let her voice trail away as I fought the demons clawing their way inside of me.

Hell, she made me all kinds of uncomfortable, and my past would make her run for the hills. Would I really tell her that my drugged-out mother held it against me that I had ruined her fucking life? That she sold me to the worst people in the world?

That I was a bastard in more ways than one?

No. Hell, no.

Leda would never even begin to understand the darkness that molded me. And I had to remind her of that.

"Be careful," I told her harshly. What little light she just shown me died out like fireflies in the morning.

"Lucas, I—" she started, but I already rose out of the chair and moved back into her bedroom, getting as far away from her as I possibly could.

\*\*\*

It wasn't until I was on my own balcony that I allowed myself to breathe.

What the fuck just happened back there? Had I really taken her breakfast, told her my name, and almost told her something completely personal about myself?

Leda was here for one reason and one reason only, for me to use. In every way someone could be used.

I had fucked her, and my damn traitorous cock wanted me to do it again. *That was what drove me to have that stupid cozy moment with her.* I thought. *Had to be.*

I took a fistful of my hair, tugging on the roots to bring on the mind-clearing pain that I had so relied upon over the years in order to think straight again. I didn't give a shit about small talk or feelings or anything of that nature. I was a stone-cold killer before I became a stone-cold Don. the one that lurked in the shadows and had an air of mystery around me.

I didn't need this shit. And I certainly didn't need someone prying into my past. Especially now.

Almost everyone who knew my story was fucking dead, either by my hand, someone else's, or circumstances of their own making. The past was dead, dead, dead. And once I put Adrian in the fucking ground, nobody could ever threaten me with it anymore.

*You don't care for Leda. You can't.* I told myself.

She was becoming a weakness I could not tolerate.

I released my hair and stared out over the fields of trees that kept my privacy. Something had to give. I had to put some distance between us because she had only been with me, what? A couple of days? I didn't bring her here to play house.

A tortured laugh escaped me. Leda was dangerous, far more dangerous than I could have ever foreseen. Now, instead of her being the one with fear in her eyes, it was I who had to watch what I say and do around *her*. I was, but not because she could physically hurt me.

Not because she might physically hurt me.

But because she could do something far worse.

My walls were there for a fucking reason.

And no way in hell would I allow Leda D'Agostino to bring them down.

## Chapter 28
## Lucas

The next morning, I woke with a shitty headache and a throbbing cock, forcing me to take care of business in the shower before I could even get my day started. After putting on my custom black power suit, I jogged down the stairs, and found Rocco waiting for me.

"I want her watched," I told him, ignoring the buzz of need that threaded through me at the mere thought of her. "No one goes in; no one even fucking looks at her."

"Is that really what you want?" Rocco raised an eyebrow. "You want her watched, but nobody actually keeps track of her? That's going to be fucking hard."

I gave him a murderous stare as I walked past him toward the door.

"You know what I mean. Remind her that she's my prisoner."

"Yes, Don," he answered and he opened the door. I walked out into the dreary day, feeling the smattering of rain against my face. It would do nothing to improve my mood today. Which suited me just fine.

I spent the majority of the night dreaming about Leda, about her under me, about her riding me, about her whispering words in my ear that I never wanted to hear.

Words that I eagerly echoed in the dream.

She did something to me and didn't even realize it. This had to stop now.

I slid into the SUV, pulled out my phone, and tapped it against my leg. I had business today, and where business normally gave me my pleasure, instead there was a need. A need to climb back into bed with Leda. The need to see her and to touch her.

It was nearly unbearable, and I needed to turn off that part of my brain today.

"There was a list waiting with her breakfast tray this morning."

The SUV started down the drive and I glanced at Rocco, who still had that shit-eating grin on his face. "What?"

Rocco crossed his arms over his chest. "She made a list of things she wants."

I smiled inwardly. Only Leda would feel like she could make demands. "What sort of list?"

"You can read it if you'd like," Rocco responded, pulling out the small piece of paper and handing it over to me. "Figured you wanted to."

I took it and read the elegant handwriting. Leda had requested a few beauty products, some real clothing, and books.

She wanted books, nonfiction preferably, maybe with some suspense. There were even a few authors listed, and an unexpected chuckle escaped me. "She knows she's a prisoner, right?"

"Was that what you've been telling yourself, boss?" Rocco asked, arching a brow.

I glowered at him before looking at the list again. Normally I would have laughed and crumpled the paper, not giving it another thought. After all, Leda wasn't here on some leisure trip. She was supposed to be suffering.

Yet something deep inside gave me pause, and I swallowed hard. "Get her this shit," I told Rocco, handing the list back over. The surprise on his face was priceless.

"Yes, Don." He tucked the list in his shirt pocket. "I will make sure it's done today."

I ignored him, flipping through my phone idly to bring up my emails. It was out of character for me to give in so quickly and readily. Rocco knew it, which was why he was looking at me with that shit-eating grin on his face.

The trip didn't take long, and when the SUV pulled up to the warehouse, Rocco was the first one out. It took me a while to get used to the habit of someone else opening my own door. I was too used to stepping out first and surveying the scene before opening it for Cosimo. Old habits died hard.

Rocco opened the door and I stepped out, buttoning my suit coat as I did so.

One of my other capos, Emil Corvo, waited at the entrance to the warehouse. He dipped his head in acknowledgment as I approached.

"Don."

"Emil," I said smoothly. "Got something to show me?"

He nodded and I followed him inside. The smell of wood shavings hung heavy in the air. Crates upon crates were stacked high against the walls, and Emil cracked one open to let me see the guns tucked in there.

"These were ready for shipment, but Adrian has held them up. I asked him about it and he kept coming back with excuses."

Fucking Adrian. If he wanted to stage a fucking coup, at least have the brains of doing it with some fucking grace and common sense.

"What was Adrian's excuse?"

"He said that he was acting on your word," Emil replied.

"Of course he fucking did," I snorted. I trusted Emil, and there had never been a need for him to prove his word to me. "What else did he say?"

"Nothing else." Emil cleared his throat. "But word among the capos is that Adrian wants to change up who runs which shops. Some are saying that the boys in the

Lower East ought to be put closer to the Battery, and vice versa."

That bastard. He wanted to play my own games against me. I had threatened him, stolen what he thought was his, and the only way for him to get rid of me was either to kill me or get the capos to turn their backs, to leave me vulnerable to attack.

"And how are they taking this news?" I asked.

"Well, depends on who you ask. The ones in the Lower East don't want the shit detail. But the ones in the Battery are chomping at the bits." Emil replied.

"Getting restive?" I asked.

Emil nodded.

I had seen this coming. With some guns in the mix, Adrian had gotten himself a nice little army. The exact kind he could use to violently take over the Cavazzo Mafia. Unless I did something about it.

"Ship them today," I said. "I want confirmation by the end of the day that they have all been sent."

"Yes, Don."

The boy showed some real promise and initiative on that front. Too bad he couldn't have put that same initiative on behalf of working *for* me. But he was too goddamn dumb to realize that once Dons started taking control of Mafias by force, it would be a long time before the cycle of violence stopped.

It was always more preferable for someone else to do the dirty business.

"Anything else?"

"There's also rumors," Emil continued. "About the D'Agostino girl. Rumors that you're willing to go to war over her. And the thing is: I don't think the rest of the capos like the idea of dying for some bitch."

My heart bristled at the word.

"They may not like it," I growled. "But need I remind them that Cosimo demanded they give their loyalties to me?"

"No offense, Don," Emil said after a moment as I struggled to keep my anger under control, my outward appearance still impassive. "But the prospect of a war really isn't popular with the boys. Might be best to put her back on the auction block. Adrian is turning more heads than I like right now, telling the boys that you are using the Cavazzo money to bring the D'Agostino Mafia to our doorstep."

No other capo was brave enough to talk to me like Emil was, mainly because Emil had been an enforcer with me. We shared plenty of great times—kills and girls—together. The day that I had elevated his status to capo was probably the best day of his fucking life.

Still, I wanted to deck him for telling me that I should give up Leda. He didn't know the internal war that was raging inside me, how she tore me up with just a single night together—making me question who was really ever in control to begin with.

"Keep an eye on the rest of them." I ordered Emil as I straightened the cuffs of my sleeves. "If you get so much as a hint of treason from any of them—"

"Car crashes, gas leaks, and other unforeseeable accidents." Emil finished my sentence. "I'll keep them quiet. But I gotta say. It'd be nice to know why we're doing all this shit."

"All in good time, Emil." I said. "You'll just have to trust me."

Emil cocked an eyebrow but ultimately, he held his tongue.

"As you say, Don." He gave me a curt nod and walked away.

I couldn't reveal my play to Emil. The more people who knew a plan, the more likely somebody ended up talking. Right now, only Rocco and I were privy to this. When the time was right, Emil and the appropriate capos would be clued in.

Adrian blabbing about this shit was forcing my hand. Killing him would just prove to the capos on the fence that he was right. Leaving him alive meant that he continued to spread these rumors.

No, I needed this war to come now.

I had to escalate.

Which meant that giving up Leda was not a fucking option.

# Chapter 29
## Leda

I pushed off the bed with a sigh, taking a familiar route to the balcony and back again. When you were stuck in a prison that had nothing to do in the form of entertainment, you started memorizing every nook and cranny real quick.

Not that I was locked in or anything. I tried the door handle every day since Lucas stormed out. It was unlocked every time.

But I didn't want to push my luck.

"Ugh." I pushed my hair off my forehead. Lucas had been all that I could think about.

And dammit, every time the door opened, my heart would beat just a little faster, only to be disappointed when it wasn't him.

He hadn't come back since that morning. For two days my only companions were the guards who dropped off my food and left as quickly as they came in.

What had been a complete surprise was the bag full of everything that I had asked for. Yesterday, a gruff guard delivered it to me, not bothering to answer any of my questions. I spent all day pouring through the contents of the bag. There were a few trashy paperbacks, not the sort of thing I wanted to read, but better than nothing.

And then there were the beauty supplies I had asked for.

He actually bought them. This was my test to him, and it was a test that he failed. I had gotten to him. Somehow.

A small smile played on my lips as I thought about how quickly Lucas Valentino hightailed it out of my room when I had started asking a few questions about his past. When I took notice of what kind of person he acted like.

I wasn't completely surprised at his reaction. In many ways, he *was* like most Mafia Dons—all business and next to no personal feelings.

But when I told him that he thought the world owed him rather than him owning the world? *That* had been the button. All I wanted at that moment was to exploit my advantage against him. But he walked away.

And I didn't realize just how much I missed his presence.

The problem was, I was pretty sure that I started developing feelings for him. Oh, how I hated the fact that I had slept with him! But the feelings weren't because of my no-longer-involved virginity. Actually, I was kind of glad to be done with it.

No, I didn't like the fact that I hadn't stopped dreaming about him, or that I continued to crave his touch.

More, the desire for wanting to know about his life spanned far beyond any plans for escaping. There was what I felt was a genuine interest.

And with that interest, came a terrible realization: if I wanted to know about him, then I'd be opening myself up to caring for him.

For a man who paid an obscene amount of money for my body.

Something had to be seriously wrong with me. I wasn't even putting up a fight at this point, for God's sake!

I was a D'Agostino, and yet I had caved at the first crazed touch from him.

I walked back to the bed, wishing that I had something else to wear other than the short robe that had come with the other presents. I had asked for *real* clothing, not the gossamer threads that barely covered my ass.

Apparently his generosity didn't expand to my clothing.

The door opened, and I paused at the bedside.

My heart raced as Lucas stepped through the door.

He was clad in a dress shirt with the sleeves rolled to his elbows and a pair of sinful dark jeans that molded to his body like a second skin. His hair was slicked back, but I could tell that it was still wet.

And his scent. Oh God, he smelled *delicious*.

Lucas's blue eyes raked over my face, no hint of emotion in their depths. My knees weakened. After days of not seeing him, his arrival plunged into my core like a spear of fire.

"Leda," he said, his deep voice rumbling through the silent room.

I swallowed. "Lucas."

What was he going to do? My body hummed with the anticipation of him throwing me on the bed, and having his way with me. Desire climbed up in my throat. My nipples hardened underneath the silk material of the robe, and I had to draw in a breath to keep my breathes steady.

"Are you hungry?"

"H-hungry?" I asked, as if I didn't know what the word meant.

"You know," he stated, pushing away from the doorway he was leaning against. "Food."

I looked around the bedroom, mainly because I couldn't bear to stare at him any longer or else I might do something really, really stupid. "I don't see my tray."

"You won't," he answered matter-of-factly. "I want you to have dinner in my room with me."

His room. My heart tumbled over in my chest.

"The food is getting cold," Lucas prodded as I tried to process what was going on. "Will you be coming, Leda?"

*Only if you made me.*

"Yes," I answered quickly.

It wasn't like I had any other choice.

## Chapter 30
## Leda

Lucas moved aside, and I crossed the room, wrapping my arms around my waist to keep my flimsy robe closed. I thought I heard a sharp intake of breath as I passed by him, and walked up to the bedroom down the hall.

The room was dark, but there was a flicker of light on the balcony, and I crossed the room to find an intimate table setting behind the door. Candles danced in the cool night air.

"Here," Lucas said as something settled on my shoulders. I looked down and saw that he'd draped a thick coat—heavy with his scent—over my body. I slid my arms into the large sleeves. It was warm, far warmer than anything I'd been allowed to wear, and a small shudder of satisfaction rolled through me.

He was being nice to me.

Why was he being nice to me?

Was he about to throw me off the balcony?

I whirled around to face him, and found him right behind me.

God, I never realized before now how tall Lucas was.

I narrowed my eyes at him. "Something's up."

"Something is always up," Lucas said slowly. "The sun, the stars, maybe even the moon."

"Is this like my last supper or something?" Not that I really wanted to know that it was. I would have preferred for him to strangle me in my sleep or shoot me when I least expected it.

To my complete and total surprise, he smiled, and two dimples appeared on his cheeks. Dear God, he was gorgeous when he smiled! Still, the smile never reached his eyes. A shadow clung to the depth of his beautiful blue gaze.

"If you want it to be your last supper," he said. "I can have that arranged. But you will be quite hungry for the next few days."

I stepped back, only because he was so close, and grasped the edges of the coat. "Who are you, and what did you do with Don Valentino?"

"I think we got off on the wrong foot," Lucas answered. "I'm not going to kill you. I'm here to dine with you, Leda."

My conscience told me to run as far away as I could. But where? I was on a balcony. This couldn't be right. I just got used to his gruff demeanor, but now he was being something completely opposite, and I didn't know how to handle that very well.

Yet I was insanely curious where this night was going to end up.

I crossed the threshold and took one of the chairs at the table. Lucas took the other, stretching out his legs before him as he sat.

He held his piercing gaze on me, and goosebumps ran down my body—even underneath the thick coat.

"So," he said after a few moments, reaching for his glass. "Did you enjoy my gifts?"

I took the wineglass, inhaling the heady scent as I swirled the liquid in the glass. "You conveniently left off the clothing I requested."

As I lifted the glass to my lips, Lucas smirked. "You are dressed how *I* want you to be, Leda."

The sensual timbre of his voice sent shivers down my spine, and I busied myself by taking a sip of the wine.

"Eat," he continued, his finger tracing the rim of his glass. "I insist."

I pulled the dome off the plate and inhaled the tangy scent of Bolognese. "God, you must have an Italian master in the kitchen." I picked up a fork.

"I have a weakness for pasta dishes," he responded as I shoved a small forkful of pasta in my mouth.

It tasted like heaven, and I moaned as the flavors exploded on my tongue. Lucas sat up straighter in his chair, and that predatory gaze turned heated. I swallowed the lump in my throat and looked down at my pasta, feeling the same wanton need deep in my stomach.

"This is really good," I said quickly, wanting to keep my mind focused on anything other than the fact that Lucas Valentino looked like he wanted to devour me whole.

"I want to know about you," he finally said.

I placed the fork down. So that was what he wanted: more information.

"I have a brother," I started hesitantly. "But you knew that already. And he has the cutest little boy."

"You must miss them."

It wasn't a question but a statement, and my heart squeezed in my chest. I did miss them terribly. After a lifetime of being under my father's thumb, Nico finally escaped. I thought that I would also find happiness like Nico did with his wife Rory.

Instead I was sitting on a balcony with a man who had paid to have me here.

Yet, it didn't feel as bad as I imagined.

"I do," I finally said. "I miss them more than anything in the world."

I'm sure that his son Anthony had already hit some crazy milestones. Rory and Nico both would have been over the moon. We had never had any other babies in our family until Rory came. I had been excited to hear about Anthony's first word, his first tooth, finding something other than the depravity that was my father's influence.

Something that could be cherished.

Something that I should not have mentioned to Lucas Valentino.

"What are you going to do?" I asked.

"Nothing," he replied. "I merely wanted to know more about you."

I allowed myself to meet his gaze. His expression was contemplative at best. Did he have a life as fucked up as mine and my brother did?

I felt like he did. The way he had shut down when I asked about his past told me more than what I needed to know.

He probably wasn't the type of guy that craved something other than the Mafia life. A life that I desperately wanted to escape from. A life that I was still hopelessly stuck in.

Tears threatened and I tried to blink them away.

I wouldn't cry in front of him. I wouldn't let him see a shred of weakness.

"Tell me what's going on in that pretty head of yours," Lucas said suddenly, breaking through my thoughts.

I looked up, clearing my throat. "What?"

"That look," he responded, his fingers drumming on the table. "I can practically hear you think."

I let out a mirthless laugh. "I doubt that very much."

He didn't smile as he leaned forward. "What were you thinking about, Leda?"

*No, you don't get to fucking ask.* "Do you sleep well at night?" I asked suddenly. "With everything you have done in your lifetime?"

Lucas widened his eyes, caught off balance by my sudden pivot. "What?"

"You see," I began. "My brother was caught up in the middle of being a Mafia Don, like you. He did some horrible things, but the entire time he had a righteous goal in his mind. So I want to know

"Do you sleep well at night, Lucas? Because from where I'm sitting, you have no righteous goal. You're a black-hearted bastard who likes hurting people."

A hint of a smile crossed his lips, and there was an unreadable hardness behind it. I was rapidly starting to recognize what he would hide behind. Despite what I *should* have felt for him because of what he did to me, a piece of my heart was also softening.

Lucas leaned forward, eyes hard in the candlelight. "I sleep very well, Leda. Even better now that you're here."

I rolled my eyes and his smile vanished. "Liar."

"Choose your words carefully, Leda." He said slowly, his expression darkening. "Or else I may punish you."

"Go ahead," I challenged him. There was a boldness growing inside of me. I mean, what did I have to lose? "You won't gain anything by it."

His mouth worked, and I saw a vein throbbing at his temple. Here was my chance.

"So, you want to know what's going on in this pretty head of mine? I'll tell you: I think that you're hiding something from me. Something that you're afraid of admitting.

"Because like it or not." I continued. "You forget who my father is in your weird desire to punish him through me. I've seen what he's capable of. And one of the first things he ever taught me was to *know* when someone was hiding something."

"In other words: you, Lucas Valentino." Leaning forward, I pursed my lips. This was going to be either my salvation or my demise. Either way, I couldn't go wrong. "*You* are what's going on in this pretty head of mine."

## Chapter 31
## Lucas

"*You* are what's going on in this pretty head of mine."

I stared at Leda, every nerve ending in my body pulled tight. She had surprised me tonight, not being the scared rabbit I had expected once I released her from her cage.

No, she had taken me stride for stride, not even flinching under my stare. It had been two fucking days since I had allowed myself a glimpse of her, hoping that whatever feelings I had would dissipate over the separation.

I threw myself into my work, refusing to even lift my head as I tried to straighten out the shit that my capos and Adrian were getting me into. Shipments were delayed all over the city. Seditious whispers had taken wing.

No one trusted me enough. Not even in my own organization. All they saw was the slave they had all abused, the enforcer that had stolen the title of a Don.

But I would never be good enough in their eyes. I would never be the Don they wanted because I wasn't born with the name. I could kill; I could make a shitload of money. But I could never erase the sin of my name. No matter what I did, my name wasn't good enough. My blood wasn't good enough.

And Leda D'Agostino kept reminding me of that.

With every mention of Carmine, she challenged me. And she dared me to reveal my past to her. Those questions about whether I could sleep at night? I've heard more than my fair share of them in all sorts of variations.

The real question she asked—the one that they all asked—was simple: who was Lucas Valentino?

I didn't want to tell her, yet there was a pull to do so deep down inside me. No one ever challenged me the way she did and lived to tell the tale.

She should be begging for her life. Hell, I should be putting fear in her. But watching her as she sat across from me, eyes flashing with defiance, I felt something far different.

I wanted to bare myself to her. I wanted her to look at my black soul and darker past, and make her own judgment. But I knew better. She'd run if she knew. Hell, anyone would.

No one gave a shit about me, and I preferred it that way.

"What do you think I'm hiding?" I asked softly.

"How could I know?" Leda retorted. "I ask, and you stonewall me. You tell me that I'm not allowed to fucking talk. You tell me that I don't get to ask questions. You tell me that you'll punish me if I pry. So why should I guess?"

"I wasn't supposed to be a Don," I interrupted her as she got ready to launch another tirade. "The will was changed at the last minute. I never even knew I was in the running."

"What?" Leda's eyes widened.

I picked up my glass, and drained it before I continued. "Cosimo Cavazzo changed his will and told me on his deathbed that I was to take over. I was his enforcer, and before that—" The words refused to move past my lips.

I didn't need Leda to look at me with disdain in her eyes, the way that I had been looked at for years before Cosimo elevated my status.

"Something else." I muttered.

Clearing my throat, I stood and walked to the railing, gripping it under my hands. "He was an asshole," I said softly, thinking of all the times he had beaten me within an inch of my life in the beginning.

Cosimo knew the kind of violence I was capable of. He'd seen it before, when I was pushed to the edge of survival. He wanted to bring that part of me to the surface.

And the only way to do that was to beat me until I started fighting back. Every scar on my body was a testament to his torture. But in return I had learned valuable lessons that had served me well to this day.

"Why would Cosimo make you his heir?" Leda asked softly. "You weren't even a capo."

"He said it was a debt," I told her, my teeth grinding together. "A debt owed to my mother." I snorted. "The bitch who sold me to him for her next hit."

I didn't even know he knew her until after he died. The will was straightforward. He was absolving himself of everything he owed her, and making me the Don of the Mafia that he built was the ultimate payment.

To this day, I never knew why. I stood up and walked over to the railing, clutching it as memories of the day I was made Don washed over me.

## Chapter 32
## Lucas
*Five years ago*

I walked into Cosimo's office and shut the door behind me. The smell of the cigars he preferred hung heavy in the air. It was exactly as it had always been: the massive oak desk that Cosimo liked to joke about. "Size is everything!" He'd always say.

The same books lined the walls. The man was an avid reader—everything from economics to military theory to pulpy detective books.

The only things conspicuously absent were personal mementos. No pictures. No little gifts. Nothing to suggest he had anyone that he gave two shits about.

Not that I expected there to be. Cosimo Cavazzo had married young, as expected. After all, an heir was necessary as early as possible to ensure the bloodline continued, he had told me once. That lesson had come after a few too many whiskeys, the only time that Cosimo had given me a glimpse into his personal life.

His bride had been picked out by his father, and he had done his duty, gotten her pregnant almost immediately. Lust turned into love, and Cosimo admitted that he grew fond of his new wife, happy with the son she was carrying that would be part of his future.

But like most Mafias, the rest of his story was full of pain and blood. His wife, weeks before she was due to give birth, was kidnapped and murdered by his enemies.

As a final insult, they even carved Cosimo's unborn child from her belly and cut him up into seven pieces.

Cosimo personally hunted each and every person that had been involved and made them pay for taking away his slice of happiness.

He never married again. A wife was a weakness that he couldn't afford anymore. He welcomed death like an old friend: a chance to reunite with his beloved and his unborn son.

And he left me here with no fucking clue on what to do.

I rounded the desk, sat in the familiar leather chair, and stared at the door. The fool made me Don. He placed me in a position of power that I knew not how to wield. Now, the entire Mafia was in an uproar at what the old fucker had done.

He had claimed in his last words that I was ready for this, that I was the only one worthy of inheriting his empire. If it hadn't been for the will he had also drafted, no one would have believed his dying words.

And now it was a reality.

Cosimo was really gone, and his capos waited to pay respects to their new Don.

"Why did you do this to me?" I whispered into the empty room. I swore I could hear him chuckling in response. I had muttered those words to myself more than once over the past few days. What on earth had the old man been thinking?

A debt owed, he claimed.

This was the worst thing that could've happened to me.

As an enforcer, I could see my enemy coming. Things were easy. But now, I had to read men who hid daggers in their smiles.

I pushed myself out of the chair and straightened my suit coat. I was the new Don of the Cavazzo Mafia. I would address the capos and make my plans for the future.

But I would never live up to their standards. I already knew that. Whatever shit Cosimo thought I could overcome wasn't going to happen. I wasn't him, and they would be reminding me of that until my very last breath.

A cool mask of indifference slid over me, and I clenched my jaw as I walked to the door. It didn't matter. I was going to show them that they meant nothing to me.

No one did.

## Chapter 33
## Lucas
## Present Day

I released the railing and clenched my hands into fists instead. I hated and cared for the man at the same time. My greatest tormentor and my only benefactor. He gave me his world, and provided me with the opportunity to rain holy terror on everyone if I so chose.

I had an influx of cash, properties, and connections all over the world.

But I was alone.

The thought hit me more than I cared to admit it. I had a core group of capos that *did* follow me, those that wanted to continue the work regardless of who was the Don. They believed that I was going to make this Mafia the top dog now that D'Agostino's reign had ended.

And then there were the doubters, dissenters like Adrian who refused to believe that Cosimo would ever hand his entire empire over to me.

Even after I grew his millions.

Even after I stole lucrative contracts away from other Dons and left my men richer than before.

Eve after I eliminated any potential competition along the way, and built an even larger empire than had been Cosimo's vision.

They could never stop looking down at me. They were too used to doing just that.

Turning toward Leda, I saw she had been watching me with bated breath. "And that's it."

This would be all I was going to tell her tonight.

"I'll admit," she finally said. "I don't know much about the Cavazzo Mafia. I mean, I didn't even know who you were. And I thought I knew *all* the Dons out there."

Thank fuck for that. "How involved were you in your father's business?"

"Look." She shook her head, and gave me a small smile. "As far as I was ever concerned, I was always going to be married off to one Don or another. My father did his best to keep me out of his business. I had an idea for how it would end. And after Nico put him in prison, I just thought…" Her voice trailed.

"I mean, I hoped that my life would be different," she finally said.

Her words affected me far more than they should. I had taken that hope from her. I was the real villain in her story, not her father.

I wasn't a hero by any means. I wasn't the good guy, nor would I ever be. There was too much blood on my hands—enough that I could spend the rest of my life in penance and the guilt would never wash out.

The devil would greet me when my time on earth was over. I was sure about.

But if I hadn't bought her that night, her fate could have been far worse.

I doubted that was any consolation to her.

But it was to me.

When Leda rose from the chair, I became still. I didn't like to admit it, but I enjoyed my time with her, mainly because she had been on my mind since the night I had her.

Every night, she appeared in my dreams. She wouldn't let me rest, wouldn't get out of my blood.

Something deep down told me that it was because I didn't want her to be gone. I wanted her to be with me. Emil's words came to me. *Might be best to put her back on the auction block.*

I would never put Leda back up for auction. I wasn't about to give her up.

Call me a selfish bastard, but I wanted more from her.

Leda didn't turn to the balcony door. Instead she joined me at the railing, leaning against it with a slight smile on her face.

"Look, I'm not going to tell you that you are a good guy," she said softly. "Because you aren't."

"No, I'm not." I agreed.

"But for what it's worth." She placed her hand on my arm. "I'm thankful that you shared that with me."

I turned and caged her between my body and the railing. My cock hard as a rock as it sensed her proximity. A familiar thought returned—to bury myself in her warmth and forget who I was. Forget what I had done to her and anyone else in my fucking life.

My nose was inches from hers, and her citrusy scent was like a drug. I inhaled her, hoping that it would calm the raging storm inside.

"I'm a monster, Leda. I always will be."

It was my mantra when I was an enforcer, and I had stuck with it as a Don.

Shadows and darkness were what I lived in. Not her.

"So don't think you can save me."

## Chapter 34
## Leda

He was breaking my heart.

Somewhere between the dinner and his short but halting admission about the fact that he wasn't supposed to be the Don, I had let go of any residual anger that I had for Lucas. It was crazy to think that I didn't hate him.

I couldn't. He was trapped in a life that hadn't been his choice, just like I was. He did evil things—I mean, my being here was a product of that—but I could see the hurt in him in the brief moment it swam to the surface of his eyes.

He knew nothing but violence in his life. There were dark secrets he didn't tell me about, secrets that he held close to his heart.

And his mother… Was she like Angelica Griffin? A woman who had been abused by a Don for his own diabolical reasons and Lucas her constant reminder?

Was Cosimo his real father? It would make sense for a Don to hand off his empire to a random person that was not of his blood.

Unless he was.

Pulling myself back to the present, I reached up and cupped his cheek with my hand, feeling it jump in response. "Everyone is worth saving." *Even you.*

To my surprise, he closed his eyes as he took a shuddering breath. "You're fucking killing me, Leda."

"Well, I hope not," I nearly choked on my words. "Because I'm not very good with dead bodies."

A choked laugh escaped him, and his intense blue gaze found me again. "I can give you pointers."

My breath caught. Was he teasing me? Was Lucas Valentino *joking* with me? This had to be a dream.

I slowly moved my hand from his cheek to his forehead, smoothing my thumb across his skin.

"That's a bit morbid," I whispered, tracing his eyebrow next.

"I'm a bit morbid," he growled when my finger slid down the arrogant slope of his nose.

I believed it, but he was also attractive in a dark, mysterious way. My stomach tightened as I brushed over his lips next, wishing that they returned to press against my skin. I expected Lucas to pull away at any moment, to hold me down as roughly as he did before. Instead, he stood there—still as a statue—and allowed me to trace his features.

I didn't even think he was breathing at this point. I dropped my hand, my cheeks burning at what liberties I was taking.

"Can I make a request, Lucas?"

His pupils dilated. "You can."

Somehow I didn't believe him, but that would be something I would work out later when I was alone. "Will you kiss me?"

Lucas's jaw clenched. "Why?" he asked, his breath stirring my hair.

Why did I want him to kiss me? I really didn't know, but it felt right.

Lucas felt right.

"I don't know," I told him, my hands sliding up to touch his chest. I felt the rapid beat of his heart under my palm, and my lips parted. Was he really into this as much as I was? Was he affected like I was?

"But I want you to kiss me." I told him again.

His hand released the railing. When it slid behind my neck, I shivered at his touch. My body reacted in familiar ways from the brief encounters we had between us.

My breath quickened as he moved closer until our bodies touched. His leg was wedged in between mine. Oh God, I hoped that the railing was bolted tight, or we might end up tumbling into the darkness from the way he pressed me against the iron.

"Why?"

"I don't know."

"You're right," he said softly as he angled my face toward him. "You don't."

His lips covered mine, and I whimpered against the feather-light touch. I half expected him to kiss me with ravenous hunger. The gentleness took me off guard.

He nipped at the corners of my mouth until my lips parted and he swept in, his tongue tasting of whiskey and mint. The flame that had been simmering in my stomach now ignited to a full-blown wildfire, and my hands slid up to his shoulders and around his neck in an effort to pull him closer.

I wanted this.

Oh, I wanted this like there was no tomorrow!

Lucas molded his lips over mine, his free hand finding my hip and pulling me into him as his other caressed the nape of my neck lightly. He held me almost like a cherished possession, and I didn't want the feeling to ever end.

When he finally pulled away, I nearly tumbled against him.

"I want you, Leda," he said, his nose nuzzling my ear. "I want to have you. Will you allow me?"

Was he... asking? It didn't feel like he was asking. It felt like he was *begging* me to allow him to do something. I pushed the thrill deep down inside, even as warning lights went off inside my head.

I didn't care.

I wanted him just as much. "I want to see you naked."

Lucas pulled away so suddenly that I thought I had run him off with my request. I hadn't seen him naked before. I'd only been intimate with his cock and truly little else. Of course, in my dreams, I had conjured up what his body looked like many times. But I wanted to see it now.

When he reached for the buttons on his shirt, I realized I was about to get my wish.

"Are you sure, Leda?" he asked huskily.

I nodded and he obliged. When he shed his shirt and tossed it on the chair, I gasped.

Even in the soft candlelight I could see the scars, and my throat closed unexpectedly. There was a tattoo on the left side of his torso, too dark for me to see, but the silver scars dotting his torso told the story he hadn't been willing to.

Unconsciously I stepped forward, and Lucas's hands stilled on his jeans. "What are you doing?" he asked roughly, watching my hand touch the large scar on his shoulder, like someone had tried to hack his arm off.

"What happened to you?" I asked instead, my finger tracing the deep groove. What did Lucas suffer through?

Were these scars the reason he kept those walls so tight around him?

If so, I couldn't blame him. Not even Nico had these kinds of wounds.

Lucas caught my hand and pulled it to his chest. "Another time."

*Another time.* Always another time. Fine. I would wait, but he was going to tell me everything one day.

Wait. Was I really thinking about this being more long term?

Gazing up at Lucas, I realized that I was.

## Chapter 35
## Leda

This was crazy. He had bought me, but he had also saved me from whatever my father had planned for me.

Lucas clearly needed someone in his life, someone that could chase away the darkness that was his life. No matter how hard he insisted that I was not the one to save him.

"You're changing your mind," Lucas said flatly, catching my attention.

I shook my head immediately. There was no way I was backing out of this tonight. Something was shifting in him, something I desperately wanted to explore. "I'm just wondering how much longer you are going to stand here and hold my hand."

His smile was slow and genuine, not the grins or smirks he had given me up to now.

It was breathtaking.

"Demanding, aren't you?"

I forced myself to step back, severing the connection between us. "I can be when I want something."

"Don't let me be the one to make you wait then," he murmured, undoing his jeans as he stepped out of his shoes.

When he pushed them down off his hips, it felt like I'd forgotten how to breathe.

Perfection.

Even with the scars, Lucas was pure perfection. From his broad shoulders to his perfectly formed abs that ended in a plunging V towards his cock, he was every woman's dirty fantasy.

And that cock. It jutted out from his body, hard and heavy in the dim evening air. The part of his body I was intimately familiar with.

Lucas stalked toward me, and I held my ground as his hand brushed my hair off my face.

"Your turn, Princess."

Though he had seen my body numerous times, I still felt the blush rising as I placed my hands on the coat he'd draped over me. This was new territory for me. His niceness had thrown me for a loop, so I wondered where this was going to go from here.

I had started this, and I wasn't about to leave any time soon. The coat puddled at my feet. Cool night breeze caressed my skin. It didn't take long for me to be as naked as he was, and I shivered when Lucas's eyes slowly slipped over my body.

"You're fucking gorgeous," he growled, finding my gaze. "Leda, I—"

I didn't want to talk any longer. Something inside me broke, and I was closing the distance between us before the next word could pass his lips. Lucas murmured before he kissed me passionately, his hands entangled in my hair. I could feel the insistent way his cock was pressing into my stomach, my body flooding with wetness at the thought of having him inside me again.

That was the only thing that mattered right now.

Lucas tore his lips from mine and his hands found my breasts, his thumbs teasing my nipples. "I've dreamed of having you a hundred different ways," he admitted, tweaking one of them and eliciting a whimper from me.

Before I could respond, Lucas picked me up and took me into his bedroom. Gingerly, he placed me on the cool silk sheets. His hands found my hips and he pulled me to the edge of the bed, one hand sliding down my leg. "Put your legs on my shoulder," he rasped.

My entire body trembled as I did as he asked, and I gasped when he lowered himself to his knees, eye level with my thighs. "You will scream my name, Leda," he murmured, his lips trailing from my knee to my inner thigh. "Now tell me, who do you belong to?"

"You..."

I barely had time to say that single word before his mouth covered my mound. His tongue drew wicked circles around my throbbing clit. I tried to push him away, but Lucas grasped my thighs and pulled them apart for better access.

Never before had I let anyone do something like this. And with Lucas, it felt right.

Oh God, it felt like this was what I was made for.

His name bubbled on my lips as his tongue teased apart my folds, giving him better access to my core as he lapped at my wetness. My fingers bunched in his hair, urging him closer. But torturously, he held back, layering pleasure upon pleasure in delicious agony.

When he pressed a finger into me, I cried out his name, my body rising off the silken sheets as pleasure pooled, surged, and then crashed through my entire being.

When Lucas lifted his head, I met him through half-lidded eyes.

"Told you," he said, standing.

I couldn't even get my mouth to work, but I didn't have to.

Lucas positioned himself between my thighs, his eyes on mine. "Tell me this is what you want," he rasped as his strong hands found my waist. My sex ached with hungry need, missing the warmth of his presence against it.

"Yes," I answered, wrapping my legs around his waist. "Please, Lucas, don't stop."

If he did so now, I might not ever recover.

Some unknown emotion crossed Lucas's face as he pushed himself into me, filling me to my core. I arched my back at the familiar intrusion, but this time there was no pain, only the heightened burn of pleasure that I never wanted to stop.

Lucas's hands gripped my waist possessively and pulled me closer to him. Instead of feeling dirty, I reveled in the touch.

"Gorgeous," he whispered, beads of sweat popping out on his forehead. "So fucking gorgeous."

I moaned and arched my hips, wanting him to move. I wanted to feel him pound into me, to give me what I had been dreaming of.

But he didn't. Instead, he took it slow—pulling himself back in long, measured strokes as he brought me back towards the brink of orgasm, but always denying me the sweet relief of release. He leaned down and covered his mouth against mine.

The kiss was heartbreakingly gentle. I tilted my hips to him, and he bit my lower lip softly.

"That's it," he whispered against my neck as he quickened his pace. "Show me how much you want this, Leda."

I started to buck under him, pushing my hips into him. My hands found his shoulder and held on for dear life as he started to move my hips to the rhythm he wanted. Stroke by stroke, he picked up his pace. Each time he pushed back deep inside, I felt the slow dizzying spread of pleasure across my skin.

When his lips found my nipple and lapped at it, I felt my control slipping. A small tremor began, first at my core. It crescendoed until I was gasping, then crying—my voice rising up in a rasping note as he brought me higher and higher in pleasure.

Stars were dotting behind my eyes as my body shook, but I opened them once I felt Lucas start to pull back.

*No. No. Stay. Not yet.*

He was straining to keep control, I could tell.

I reached for him. "Lucas?"

"I'm close, Leda. I have to."

"Come inside me," I finished for him. "Please don't stop."

I must have gone crazy. That was the only way to describe it. But I didn't want him to leave me. I didn't want him to leave me unfulfilled.

Lucas's jaw clenched as he lifted my legs onto his shoulders and drilled into me. The bed was shaking under the force of each thrust.

"Yes! Yes! Yes!" I screamed.

The orgasm came sharp and fast as my pussy pulsed around his cock. I clenched around him and felt his cock doing the same.

With a low groan, Lucas came. His seed filled me as I held him there, refusing to let go.

For a moment, I couldn't believe what had happened. This wasn't the dominant sex that I thought he would give me. This was—this was something I couldn't explain.

If I didn't know any better. I would've called it lovemaking.

Lucas pulled out of me, and I lay there as he stumbled backwards, a small smile flitting over my face. What now? Why did I feel like I had just gotten the medal for first place with the very man I should be running from?

Should I leave? There was no way he was going to want me to stay in his bed now that he was done. I forced myself to climb from the bed, my knees watery and weak, but before I could round the bed, Lucas's hands were on my waist. "Where are you going?" he whispered into my ear.

I spun in his arms, a blush stealing across my cheeks as I saw his intense gaze. "I was, um, going to my room."

"Is that what you want to do?" he asked.

"Is that what you want me to do?" I countered, wanting to hear it from his lips.

I saw the internal war raging in Lucas's eyes as his nostrils flared.

"No," he finally said. "I don't want you to leave, Leda."

Oh God. This was uncharted territory. "But," he continued. "I might pass out if I don't get in that bed soon. It's been a long fucking week."

"Then by all means," I said nervously. "Let's get in bed."

When I climbed in next to Lucas, he hauled me against his chest, his warmth spreading through my own limbs. "That's better," he said drowsily, his fingers tangling in my hair.

I pressed my hand to his chest and felt the steady heartbeat there, the way that his arm cradled my head as if he cared.

He didn't, of course.

But it was nice to think he did tonight.

It didn't take long for Lucas's breathing to start slowing, and only then did I steal a glance at his face. It was slack and without the lines of deep worry that seemed to follow him.

He had done something far worse to me tonight than anything else he had done.

Something even worse than stealing my virginity.

He was starting to steal pieces of my heart.

## Chapter 36
## Lucas

I woke up to the feeling of a body pressed against mine. My hand felt soft skin underneath. For a moment, I felt a quick burst of panic race through my body before the events of last night came flooding back. I remained still, barely breathing as I felt Leda's body—soft and warm—against mine.

I've never slept with a woman through the night before. It always felt too intimate and too personal to share a bed with someone like that.

Yet I did it with Leda.

I didn't know what had possessed me to want her to stay. But in the moment, it felt right.

It still did.

She murmured in her sleep, and I instinctively pulled her closer, feeling lightness around my tortured soul for the first time in my entire life. Last night was different. We didn't just fuck. We did something else, something that I was afraid of putting a name to.

That bothered me the most.

Drawing in a slow breath, I allowed myself to bury my face in her hair, breathing in Leda's scent. She was ruining me.

Somehow, Leda D'Agostino sank her claws deep inside me. By all means, I should be pushing her away, putting some distance between us so that I could get my shit together. I should be finding each and every excuse on earth to get out of bed.

Instead, a smile was breaking over my face. And no matter how hard I tried to erase it, it kept coming back.

What if I didn't want to have my shit together? What if I was tired of being alone? What if Leda had touched something deep inside of me last night, something that I thought I'd locked away for good?

It disturbed me how much I wanted this.

Not just having her cry out my name as I filled her pussy. Not just having her beg me for more. But *this* – this moment right here: her body against mine as dawn opened the sky with rosy tips.

Companionship.

If I were a man who was looking at a future with a woman, Leda would be the woman I would picture.

Fuck, I sounded like a teenager with his first girlfriend. I had known Leda all of what? Four, five days? She shouldn't be affecting me like this. How the hell did she get past my walls that quickly?

But now that she was here, I didn't want to let her go.

Emil's words returned again, echoing in my head.
*Might be best to put her back on the auction block.*

But I didn't want to.

I wanted it all. I wanted Leda, and I wanted control over what should be *my* Mafia.

Nothing else would make me happy. I nearly let out a snort, holding it back at the last minute so as to not disturb Leda.

Happy? There was no happiness in my dark world. I wasn't born for happiness. That feeling didn't sit right with me. Hell, I didn't even know *how* to be happy.

But maybe with Leda, I could figure it out.

I toyed with the idea. Was that even a possibility? Could I even trust her with my secrets? To be happy with her meant that I would have to tell her everything.

I would have to tell her about my past, and all the sordid details that came with it.

She would find out soon enough anyway. I had her holed up in this house for now, away from others. But at the first opportunity, I was sure that she would start prying, start peeping into things that she had no right to.

I couldn't change my past any more than I could change the sun rising in the east every morning. I couldn't hide from it either. All my life since becoming Cosimo's enforcer, I pushed through it, using my anger to make myself stronger.

I thought I made myself damn near invincible.

And then Leda was about to shatter all of that with just her touch, her presence. I bought her. I was supposed to break her. But now, I wasn't sure who was on the verge of being broken.

I hated it.

And I hated the fact that she made me think that there might be the hope of a life beyond being a Don. A life beyond the Mafia.

Leda shifted again, and I let my hand roam higher until my thumb brushed the underside of her breast. My cock stirred to life, and I steadied my breath, thinking about how fucking well I had slept last night. It was because I felt like—hell, like I could trust her.

She didn't just pleasure my body. She shed light onto my pitch-black soul.

My choice was clear: I wasn't going to give her up. Not for Adrian. Not for Carmine. Not for anyone, and it was time I proved that to her.

I wanted her to trust me, to know that there was more I wanted from her than what was between her legs.

A thought came to me, and I grinned as a plan formed in my mind. A perfect way for me and Leda to get out, but not where our enemies could touch her. I would flaunt her eventually, but I wanted my trusted guards to ensure that I wasn't walking into a trap first.

Carmine wasn't about to let go of the fact that I stole his princess and ruined his plans. But first, I wanted—

no, needed—to bury myself in her warmth to start my day.

I kissed Leda's shoulder as my hand squeezed her naked breast lightly. Her nipple hardened in response to the touch and a slight whimper of sleepy pleasure escaped from her lips. I slid my hand down body, slipping between her legs, and found her already wet.

Had she been dreaming about me?

"Lucas," she moaned as I slipped my finger between her folds, massaging against her swollen clit.

"I'm right here," I whispered in her ear as I dipped a finger inside.

She whimpered and arched into my touch, urging me on. My cock pressed insistently against her ass, and I continued to roll her clit until she was flooding my hand with her orgasm. Only after her cheeks were flushed with lust did I place my cock at her slick entrance.

She turned slightly and I caught sight of her half-lidded gaze. Want glimmered in her eyes.

"This is how I like to wake," I told her as I slid into her. She arched her perfect ass to meet me, and I groaned as I pushed deep into her wetness.

I pressed my face into her shoulder. "You feel like fucking heaven."

"Lucas," Leda gasped, her hand reaching back to pull me closer, and I drank in her scent.

I started to move, and soon we were rocking the bed, my thrusts rapid as I brought her back to the peak of her pleasure. My free hand found her mouth, and she sucked on my fingers greedily as a shudder tore through her body.

Fuck, I couldn't hold on any longer. With a groan, I poured into her, my other hand tight on her hips as I took a shuddering gasp from my own release.

Leda turned around, propped herself up with one elbow, and kissed me gently. "Good morning to you too."

I wiped a hand over my face, my body relaxed to a point that I could just go back to sleep. "Sleep well?"

"Surprisingly, yes," she answered. "And you?"

"Well enough," I replied, turning on my side to stare at her. Leda in the morning was fucking gorgeous. Her long dark hair fell over her bare shoulder. Her cheeks were pink and red from our morning bout.

She gave me a little smile, and I found it difficult to not return it.

"I've got somewhere I want to take you," I said.

Her smile dropped, and then dimmed.

"Oh," she stated, looking away. "All right."

Fuck. She looked worried, and I knew immediately where her mind had gone. She thought I was going to take her to her next destination now that I had gotten what I wanted.

What Leda didn't know was that I was nowhere near done with her.

Reaching out, I brushed the hair off her shoulder. "You will like it, I promise you."

"I, um, okay," Leda said after a minute. "But unless it's a lingerie party, I'm going to need some clothes."

"As much as I would like to keep you fucking naked in my bed," I replied, watching as a blush stole across her cheeks, "I believe you are right. I will have some sent over immediately."

Leda pulled the covers over her naked body. "Thank you, Lucas. That's nice of you."

Nice? I wasn't nice. Throwing back the covers, I climbed out of bed, conflicted on my feelings of why I wanted to do this for her and what I genuinely wanted from her.

Hell, I didn't know what I wanted from Leda, but I sure as hell wasn't going to give her up.

## Chapter 37
## Lucas

I drummed my fingers along the door as the SUV sped toward the docks, glad that it wasn't raining at least. Leda sat next to me, dressed in a blue T-shirt and a pair of skinny jeans that clung to her ass in a way that had me wanting to take her in the back of the SUV.

How Rocco managed to find clothing so quickly was beyond me. But I was glad that Leda looked happy at least.

Not to mention fucking gorgeous. Even in a T-shirt and jeans, she looked positively radiant.

I already called ahead to ensure that the destination was prepared and ready for our arrival. I wanted no delays. I didn't want to have Leda out in the open any longer than I needed to.

But I also wanted her to enjoy this day. This was my gift to her, something that I hadn't felt the need to provide until now.

The SUV slowed, and I looked over at Leda. "We are here."

She peered out of the window. "The docks?"

I opened the door before reaching for her hand. "There's something I want to show you."

Confusion and questions swirled in her eyes, but she allowed me to lead her out of the SUV and down the floating ramp.

The captain greeted me. "Mr. Valentino," he said, his hands clasped behind his back. "Everything is ready for you and your guest."

"Thank you," I said, bringing Leda to my side. "Chris, this is Leda."

"Ma'am," Chris smiled. "Welcome aboard *Vengeance*."

"The *Vengeance*?" she asked, looking around.

I smirked. "Welcome to my yacht."

Her lips parted in surprise. Chris gave me a wink before he climbed aboard the yacht, and helped Leda over the threshold. I followed behind. Rocco and a few others would join us later. I couldn't risk floating down the Hudson by myself without some security.

But the yacht was big enough that they would stay well out of the way.

The *Vengeance* was one of those impulsive purchases, much like the helicopter. But what better way to flaunt your wealth than to buy big-ass toys? Like somebody told me a long time ago: money was like the wind, you only felt it when it was moving.

"So, this is the surprise you planned for me?" Leda asked as one of the attendants approached us with drinks on a tray.

"It is." I snagged one of the whiskeys. "I thought you would want to get out for a little while."

Though her lips were pursed into a line, I could see the sparkle of excitement in her eyes and knew that I did the right thing. This was the first step of proving to Leda that she wasn't just an object of pleasure, that she was more than a prisoner.

That she was something I couldn't possibly put a name to because I had no idea what that even was.

"Well," Leda finally said, wrapping her arms around her waist. "I can't wait then. Will you give me a tour?"

Of each and every bed on this fucking boat? Absolutely. I knocked back the whiskey and placed it back on the tray before holding out my hand. "Let's get started."

Leda placed her hand in mine, and I laced our fingers together, enjoying the way her hand felt in mine. Hell, I liked everything about her. She wasn't frightened of me or what I had done in the bedroom, she pierced the walls I put up with just a couple of words.

I wanted to see what else she could do.

What else she was capable of.

The boat set off away from the dock as I took Leda on her tour, watching as she took it all in. She was a fucking Mafia princess, yet it was like she hadn't seen something like this before. I held her hand as we walked from room to room, Leda laughing as she took in the massive bed in the master bedroom, surrounded by mirrors.

"My God," she giggled. "Is this your fuck room? So you can see yourself from all angles?"

"Not just me," I replied and pressed her against the bed. "You also get an unobstructed view."

Leda looked up at me, her eyes sparkling, and I couldn't help it. I kissed her.

This kiss wasn't like any of the kisses we shared in the past. It wasn't just hungry lust or want. This kiss was full of emotion, pent-up emotion that I was only willing to show her. She gasped against my lips as our tongues met and danced. Her hand snaked under my shirt, tracing lines as I explored the depth of her mouth.

We fell closer until we were half on the bed, still kissing as if the thought of breaking apart would leave us dying. When I finally pulled away, her lips still parted and she was panting.

"I'm sorry," I said, surprised that those were the first words out of my mouth.

"For what?" Her voice was breathless and husky.

Hell, I didn't know. I was sorry for a lot of things, some that I could control and a hell of a lot that I couldn't.

"For not showing you this room sooner."

She rolled her eyes and coyly pushed me away. I let her, only because she was making me feel like a different man, a new man.

"You are too much, Lucas Valentino. I can't figure you out."

I chuckled and pulled her back into my arms, surprising us both. I liked the way she made me feel whenever she was around.

"Come on. If we don't leave soon, I'm going to fuck you on this bed. And there are so many others you haven't seen yet."

Leda brushed her hand over my cheek. "I will hold you to that, Lucas."

## Chapter 38
## Lucas

We returned topside as the New York skyline came into view. Leda broke away from me and walked over to the railing to watch. I shoved my hands into my pockets and watched her, wondering what she was thinking.

If there was a moment for her to escape, now would be the time. My mind flashed back to the moment I saw her go over the top of the balcony on our first night. She could do it now and there'd be no way for me to reach her in time.

There were plenty of other boats nearby that she could easily be picked up before I or my men could get to her.

Of course, I wouldn't let her go so easily. I'd board any boat that picked her up to demand her return.

Nonetheless, I made no move to join her. She needed to trust me, and the only way she was going to do so was for me to back the fuck off. I wanted to show her that I could let her taste freedom. That she'd be given the choice to leave and she would choose to stay.

Could I be what she needed? Hell, no. I was a bastard with more secrets than she could possibly drum up. But I would still be a bastard who gave her a choice.

When Leda turned, I waited with bated breath to see what she was going to do. Whatever she decided, I could handle. I would *have* to handle it. If she left, I wouldn't blame her. After all, she was in this shit because of me.

So when she started to walk toward me, a knot in my chest loosened.

She was coming to me.

"What's that look for, Lucas?" Leda asked as she reached my side, her long hair blowing in the wind.

"I thought you would jump," I said.

"Jump?" she looked back at the railing. "Into the Hudson?"

I shrugged, carefully schooling my emotions so that I wouldn't let her see how much she affected me. "The easiest way out."

Leda opened her mouth and then promptly shut it. "Lucas," she said after a few moments. "I didn't want to jump."

Her words destroyed me. She didn't want to jump. She didn't want to leave me even though I had bought her like an object.

The man who stole everything from her: from her freedom to her innocence.

And yet… she chose me.

## Chapter 39
## Leda

The wild panic in Lucas's eyes faded with my words and left me breathless at the same time. He thought I was going to jump, to swim away from him and toward my freedom.

The truth was, I could have. Any sane person would have taken that opportunity to escape, even if it meant jumping into the Hudson. He was being far too nice to me, a completely different person at every turn. He was confusing the hell out of me today. But I never forgot the reality of what we were:

I was still his prisoner, and this could be just another test.

I hadn't chosen him. He took me, ripped me from my future without my consent, took my virginity, and used me in almost every way that a man could use a woman.

Yet here I was, staring at him and wondering why he looked at me like I was some lifeline for him.

"Why?" he rasped. "Why didn't you jump?"

I closed the distance between us and wrapped my arms around his waist, burying my face in his shirt. As much as I hated admitting it, I loved the way he smelled. Something dark and spicy that was equal parts off-limits and equal parts utterly intoxicating.

"I don't know," I said honestly. "I really don't."

Lucas let out a shuddering breath and his arms came around me, locking me against his chest. "The sun is setting."

"Oh?" I asked, turning around so I could watch it on the horizon.

The gorgeous sunset streaked the sky with perfect mixtures of gold, orange, and blue. In any other scenario, it would have been a perfect sunset, the sort that Edmond Dantes sailed off into at the end of *The Count of Monte Cristo*.

"You can see the best sunset from my brother's penthouse," I said. "Mine has an obstructed view, but Nico's was perfect."

I was rambling, but Lucas was making me nervous. This new Lucas acted like he cared. And truth be told, that was scarier than the Lucas who only demanded my submission and wanted me for my body.

"You should see it in Belize," he said after a moment. "My beach house has an unobstructed view of the ocean and the most spectacular of sunsets."

"That sounds nice," I admitted softly, my thoughts going straight to Lucas in a pair of board shorts and nothing else. "How often do you get to go there?"

"Not often enough," he responded as the sun dipped lower, setting the sky ablaze. "When I was younger, I never thought I would see a place like that or be standing on a yacht with a beautiful woman like you in my arms. Yet here I am."

"Here you are," I echoed.

His compliment warmed my cheeks against the cool wind coming off the water. I ached for him when he said things like that. He was holding something close to him, something he didn't want to share. Not even with me.

Not even after everything that had happened.

Bitterness crept into the edge of my thoughts. My own brother had years' worth of bitterness directed toward my father because of the horrible things that he was made to do. I hadn't even known about it, and if I had, I might have offered some degree of comfort?

Who did Lucas have? Did he have siblings? Did he have anyone close to him? All I had ever seen around him were his guards. Did he even know how to care for others?

The bitterness grew inside of my heart.

Ugh, I didn't *want* to feel this way about him. This all snuck up on me, and suddenly I started *wanting* to be someone close in his life! What was I thinking? He was my captor, yet, standing on this deck in his arms, I felt more.

So much more.

The first pop startled me, and Lucas shielded me immediately with his body, his hand going for a gun I didn't realize he had tucked at his back.

The sight of the gun was like a splash of ice water. But then, another thought entered my head. *He wanted to protect me.*

I let out a burst of laughter when the sky lit up in red. "It's just fireworks."

Lucas swore and straightened us both, the gun disappearing in his clothing.

"Sorry," he said as he pulled me close to him again. "Hazard of being a Don. Always think someone is shooting at you."

My laughter grew, and I felt a chuckle escape his chest against my back. "At least you are prepared. But I don't think your bullets would go that far."

He spun me around as a blue firework exploded in the sky, and I saw the smirk on his handsome face. "You think it's funny, don't you?" he asked softly.

I fought to rein in my laughter, wiping my eyes. "A little."

To my surprise, Lucas rolled his eyes, something very unlike what a don would do. "The thought of me taking a bullet for you amuses you?"

Truthfully? Yes. My traitorous heart soared at the thought. There was no one else here for me but him. I laid my hand on his chest and he stiffened, the mirth sliding from his expression.

"What are you doing, Leda?"

"Thanking you," I simply said, my heart doing a nervous dance inside my chest. "For being ready to protect me."

The monster that awoke inside of me since the first moment he put his hand on me stirred. I knew better than to fight her. It was time for me to lose myself in my own desires. Lucas was all that I thought about now, and the thought of him pressed against me like he was now left my mind feverish with want.

I wanted to see what he would let *me* do.

## Chapter 40
## Leda

My hand slid down the front of his body and cupped him through his pants. Lucas swore under his breath. How did he walk around already hard as a rock all the time?

One day maybe I would ask him.

"Careful," he said softly, his voice gruff. "You're playing with fire."

"That's the idea," I interrupted, standing on my tiptoes to brush my lips over his as I caressed him through the material of his pants. "Lucky for you, I like playing with fire."

My hand gripped him. "And I'm not afraid of getting burned."

I had never been one to seduce anyone before, but Lucas made me want to try. "Take off your shirt, Lucas."

"Let's go to the bedroom," he murmured, his lips tracing my jawline. God, I couldn't think clearly when he sucked the skin there! "Let me show you what it's like to be burned."

"No," I told him, gasping. "This is my turn." I pushed back from him; my eyes set on his. "Are you afraid someone might see you naked?"

His grin was slow and deadly, those horribly sexy dimples re-emerging in the dying light. The fireworks exploding over our heads chased away some of the darkness, but not enough for anyone to see what we were doing.

My body was trembling and I couldn't tell whether it was because of lust or excitement. I didn't think I would ever know. I had no idea why Lucas asked me to come on the yacht. Tomorrow I might be handed off to someone else for all I knew.

But tonight? This was my night with him.

"You want to see me naked, Princess?" he asked softly, his voice a deep timbre.

All I could do was nod, rooted on the spot and hoping that he wasn't going to deny me this.

Lucas grasped the edge of his coat and pulled it off, removing the gun from the waistband of his pants and placing them both on the cushioned seat nearby. He slowly unbuttoned his shirt, and my breath grew quicker with each button that popped loose, with every moment he revealed more of the tanned, muscular skin underneath.

I could hardly hear the exploding fireworks as his shirt joined his coat a moment later. The wind ruffled his hair, and the red glare of each new explosion in the sky cast accentuated the hard lines of his body.

My feet moved of their own volition, and soon I was touching his broad shoulders, my fingers drifting over the scars on his shoulder. I wanted to know everything about him, where his scars came from and who had done this to him.

I wanted to ease that pain, to show him that there was softness in his world, and that softness, that light could be me.

Was I really thinking about him in that manner? I should be running away, but all I wanted to do was to run toward him.

To embrace his darkness.

When I slid down the front of his chest, kissing his chiseled abs, he hissed. He knew exactly where I was going. Looking up at him, I saw his jaw clenched. He slowly losing control.

"Please?" I asked softly, wanting his approval first. I didn't know why that was so important to me, but it was. I didn't want him to be uncomfortable with my touch.

The nod of his head was barely noticeable in the darkness, but it was all that I needed. I made my way down, planting kisses and trailing my fingers downward as I knelt in front of him.

"You know," I started as I worked at the buckle of his pants and slid open the zipper. "I saw you that night."

"What night?"

"The night we first met," I said. The scent of his manhood was filling my nostrils. "I thought you were gorgeous."

His hand found my chin and he nudged it up, so I had to look at him.

"And you," he said, his voice barely heard over the *boom-boom-boom* of the fireworks. "You took my breath away."

Thank God I was already on my knees, or else I would have wobbled a bit.

My eyes bore into his. "Stop distracting me."

His lips teased into a rare grin and his fingers released my chin, letting me go back to my business. His cock sprang forth, warm and heavy in the darkening air. A drop of pearl hung at the tip and I licked my lips before I licked away the salty drop. His groan of approval spurred me on. But I held myself back, content to tease in small swirling circles with my tongue, savoring his taste as I greedily lapped at the throbbing head.

I didn't know why I liked tasting him. Maybe it was because it made him vulnerable and put him in a position where I held most of the power.

Or maybe I just liked it.

I grasped him lightly and he breathed out audibly, his cock twitching slightly at my touch. I believed that I made him this way, that he liked me doing this, and that he would never admit to it.

I took my time around the bulging head before I slowly took his length into my mouth. I looked up at him, daring him to set the pace. His hand went into my hair and excitement ran down my spine, but he didn't take over.

I was in control.

He let me guide myself the way I saw fit over his cock. It was a measure of trust, one that weakened my resolve and left my panties soaked at the same time. I wanted him so badly, but I wasn't going to stop until Lucas lost all control with me.

My tongue continued to swirl around his cock, even as I bobbed my head along its length. Salt and musk mixed in my mouth and I felt his hand ball into a fist in my hair.

"Leda," he growled as I worked him. "You're going to make me explode."

"That's the idea." I breathed along his length and returned to my work. His cock grew harder in my mouth, and my pace quickened with anticipation. He was close, I could feel it. I slapped his hand away, pinning them at his side as I swallowed his length. He was trembling. My throat and tongue and lips continued to tease him, to push him further and further until the point of no return.

"Leda," he gasped. "I—"

His voice cut out as his essence filled my mouth, overwhelming me with his taste. I swallowed him—one thick ropey spurt after another—until he clung to my shoulder for support. And only then, did I slowly pull back, gave his head another swirl of the tongue, and met his gaze.

There was a look on his face that I couldn't decipher, but when he helped me to my feet, it was clear that he wasn't done.

"My turn." He said as he lifted me into his arms.

I squealed in sudden laughter before his lips covered mine, and soon he was pressing me into the cushions.

Would he rip this shirt? A part of me wanted him to, but another part wanted him to ignore it and put his face between my legs.

Hard hands snaked their way under the shirt and suddenly I felt the cool evening breeze against my nipples. In a split second, the coolness was replaced with his mouth, hot and hungry, as it closed around the right nipple. His other hand found my left breast and squeezed. My body arched instinctively at the touch.

He suckled with equal parts intensity and equal parts softness. His tongue rasped over the delicate flesh. Warmth and desire pooled between my legs, radiated from the nipple between his lips, and collected deep inside my core.

When he pulled away, I almost begged him to come back. But before I could've uttered a word of protest, his mouth closed around the other nipple. The air around us grew heavy and sticky, and a drop of sweat ran down my body as Lucas kissed his way down. His tongue swirled around my bellybutton and finally, he knelt down between my legs.

"Look at me Leda." He breathed against my quivering sex. "I want you to look at me as I taste you."

I hadn't realized my eyes were closed until then. When I opened them, I was greeted with the most beautiful sight. Lucas Valentino, his face between my legs. Rough fingers made their way down my body until they hooked my thighs. Then, with an expert pull, my pussy was pressed against his hot and ready mouth.

My legs squeezed together instinctively and I felt the stubble of his chin against the soft skin of my thighs.

*Oh.*

He pushed my legs apart to give himself better access, his tongue lapping at the juices leaking from my slit, refusing to let even a single drop go to waste. A finger slipped inside and I felt myself squeeze out of instinct. My body shuddered and my breath quickened, torn between pulling away from the delicious torture and hanging on for dear life.

*Oh.*

I felt like I was flying, soaring above the water to the stars, and Lucas was the one who was taking me there. His touch and his tongue were setting me alight, bringing me higher and higher. My body felt like a string pulled to its very limits.

And when he pressed his tongue against my swollen clit, the string snapped.

The orgasm came slowly at first, just small eddies of pleasure as it swept through my entire body. My mind spun as my body rose off the cushion. I would scream, but I struggled to breathe. It was as if I lost control of all aspects of my body as I came against his mouth. For a brief moment, I blacked out from the pleasure, and when I opened my eyes again, Lucas stood before me, his cock swollen with need.

There's no way he could be ready that quickly again.

"Lucas," I whispered.

He silenced me with a kiss that stole the air from my lungs and swallowed my moans. I tasted myself on his lips as his tongue pushed into my mouth the same time his cock pushed into my pussy.

I hadn't realized just how much I wanted him inside, how much I *needed* him inside until he was already there. My hands clawed at his bare back when he grabbed my legs and pulled himself even deeper.

"Oh Lucas!" I shouted in wanton lust. "Yes!"

His hands moved up and for a moment, my mind begged him to squeeze my breasts. But instead, he found my shoulders and pinned me deeper into the cushions. His cock touched me in a spot that I didn't think it could touch as he drilled deep inside of me.

I squeezed around him again, my entire body shuddering as I sobbed his name.

*Please.* I begged him through tears of pleasure. *Please. Take me. Use me. Make me yours.*

"Leda," Lucas groaned. I knew what was coming. I pulled him down into a kiss, wrapping my legs around him so he could not back away, and squeezed as he filled me with his seed.

\*\*\*

What the heck did we just do? It felt different, just like last night did. Lucas was no longer trying to teach me a lesson, and I was afraid of what he was actually doing to me.

This wasn't the beginning of a relationship for us. This couldn't be the beginning of a relationship. I had to remember that. Lucas wasn't some dark avenging savior that was going to take me away so that my father never found me. He was the one who stole me. The one who I was supposed to be saved from.

"Fuck," Lucas muttered, catching my attention.

He was staring down at me, his jaw clenched, but there was something in his eyes that sent my pulse racing.

"That was," I panted. "Something."

His grin was quick, and he started to pull out of me carefully. "Yeah, it was."

My chest tightened at his soft words, almost like he was happy. I had done that to him. I made him lose control. And dammit, I enjoyed it far too much.

Lucas closed his pants and then reached for me, helping me to my feet. "I think I could go for a shower," he replied, tucking my hair behind my ear. "And some food."

I looked down at my clothes on the deck, and laughed. "I think I might need some new clothes."

His eyes followed mine and he leaned down, snatching the scrap of lacey underwear off the deck and shoving it into his pocket. "I want to take you into the city," he said as I tried to pull my jeans at least to my waist.

I fastened my jeans before looking at him, not sure what to say. At least on the yacht I could pretend that he wasn't who he was, and I wasn't the woman he had all but kidnapped.

But in New York?

In New York, we could run into a number of people who would think otherwise. Surely he knew that? He was a Don and I, well, I was Carmine's daughter. Was he doing this to flaunt it in my father's face or for another reason?

"I know what you are thinking," he said. "But I just want to take you to dinner."

Lucas sounded so sincere that my soul caved just a bit. He was going to be the death of me; I knew it. This wasn't how this was supposed to be panning out, yet Lucas was making me think of things we would never have, like a relationship or anything more meaningful between us.

I was going to lose my heart to him if I wasn't careful.

"All right," I replied, watching as his eyes lit up. "First, we'll shower."

Lucas held out his strong hand, and I took it, feeling the gentle squeeze that told me he was pleased with my decision.

## Chapter 41
## Lucas

I waited at the Battery docks for Leda, watching as people came and went from their own small boats. The night was early, and while I would have preferred to stay on the yacht with Leda, repeating what we just did again and again, I wanted to take her into the city.

Hell, I wanted to show her off, but not for the reasons she thought.

I didn't give a shit whether or not her father heard about our little trip or if anyone else saw us together. I wanted to keep that smile on Leda's face, to not make her constantly worried that I was going to turn on her and send her back to her father or someone worse.

Blowing out a breath, I realized that I was falling for her. That was it, wasn't it? It fucking terrified me to think of it that way, but to think anything else would be lying.

I didn't want to need her, yet I needed her badly.

"Will you be spending a few days in the city?"

I looked over at Rocco, who was looking out over the dark water.

"Yeah, I think so," I replied.

There was other business that I needed to attend to, and what better way than to have Leda here with me? I had a penthouse in the city, one that I hoped lived up to the sunset potential that rivaled what she wanted. Actually, I was looking forward to showing Leda my penthouse, giving her a glimpse of my life that she hadn't seen yet.

I wanted her to believe that I was looking out for her well-being now, not just as her captor but as something... more.

"You're starting to like her, aren't you?"

"Fuck you," I told Rocco, gripping the railing. "I don't want to hear a fucking lecture from you."

"Wouldn't dream of lecturing you," he chuckled. "What you will *hear* is a hale and hearty 'I told you so' when you realize that you can't let her go."

"I have no intention of letting her go," I replied, the thought making me sick. Leda was mine, if nothing more than the fact that I paid for her.

"Oh, trust me, I know." Rocco let a low whistle. "You've got it bad. I hope you know what you are doing."

I pushed away from the railing. Sometimes I wanted to deck him, and sometimes, well, he had been there when many hadn't. "I do. Trust me"

"While you're here," Rocco said. "Might not be a bad idea to shore up your support with the boys in the Battery. Y'know, considering we *are* here."

It wasn't a bad idea, but the sound of approaching footsteps took my attention away. I turned to find Leda heading towards us.

Fuck, she took my breath away, dressed in one of those wrap dresses that I was going to have a fun time removing later on. Her hair was down, and there was a tentative smile on her lips that made me want to kiss her.

"Hey," she said, giving me a once-over. "Is this okay?"

"It's amazing," I said and then turned to Rocco. "Get the fucking car."

He rolled his eyes and walked away.

As Leda joined me, the smell of citrus that she gave off drove me wild on the inside. I allowed her to shower alone, even taking one of the guest bathrooms so that I could keep myself from running my hands all over her body.

Every time she was in my presence, I wanted her. Every moment beside her was another moment I wanted to spend buried within her.

I took her hand and felt her trembling, causing me to pause. "What's wrong?" I asked immediately.

She looked everywhere but at me, focusing on the water over my shoulder. "What are we really doing, Lucas? I mean, what am *I* doing here?"

Hell, I didn't have an answer for her. "I'm taking you to dinner," I said.

Her eyes found mine, and I swore I saw another person in them, one that I didn't recognize at all. "You don't have to lie to me," she said softly.

Unable to help myself, I released her hand and framed her face, forcing her to see past the hard shell of a man that I was. "That's it. I swear it, Leda. Is it so hard to believe?"

"It is," she whispered, fear shining in her eyes.

I didn't know how to turn her fear into a means of trusting me, but I was going to fucking do it one step at a time. "Trust me. I know it's a hell of a lot to take in, but I'm not going to hurt you. Not anymore. I promise."

And I meant it. I didn't want to see Leda hurt.

Instead of responding, she leaned in and brushed her lips over mine. "All right," she mumbled against my lips. "I'll trust you."

Some of the tension eased out of my shoulders, and I gently kissed her before stepping back. "Let's go."

Leda nodded, and I tucked her hand in mine, leading her to the car. I made the promise, and now I had to live up to it.

We climbed in the car, and it started toward the destination, followed by the SUV that the rest of my guards would ride in. Idly I wondered if Leda was used to being so protected whenever she was in her father's presence. As a Don, it had been hard for me to get used to the guards' sudden and sometimes unwanted presence.

I was a loner as an enforcer, and I took solace in that fact. But all of that changed after I became Don. No matter where I went, there was always somebody in my shadows. The capos didn't believe in letting their leader alone. Whether they wanted to keep an eye on me to keep me from doing something stupid, or just wanted to keep an eye on me for other reasons, it didn't matter.

Rocco was right, if I were here, I should check up on the situation with the boys in the Battery. Sometimes, it was worth reminding them just who was the boss and who were his followers.

Not tonight. Not yet.

Likely, word had already gotten out that I was in the city. We just stepped off a yacht, one that even a blind man couldn't miss.

It both pissed me off and made me weary in the same breath. Being a Don was draining, to say the least, especially when you couldn't hide.

The car pulled up to the familiar place on Mott Street, and I waited for Rocco to open my door. "Make a perimeter," I told him as I buttoned my coat. "We won't be here long." I had every intention of taking Leda somewhere else after this stop. But whenever I was in the city, I liked to make an appearance, to show that this, too, was under my protection.

Walking around to the other door, I opened it and helped Leda out of the car. "Chinatown?" she asked, looking around. "I haven't been here in ages."

"There's something I need to check up on, and then we'll head out." I told her, not wanting to leave her in the car. The closer I kept her to my side, the better I felt that I could keep her safe.

"Oh, we aren't eating here?"

I glanced at her. I had already booked a table at Per Se at Columbus Circle, but the wistfulness in Leda's eyes made me wonder if maybe I had gone overboard. She wasn't what I would have thought a Mafia princess would be like, and continually surprised me with her down-to-earth nature.

It made me want more. "You want to eat here?"

"Can we?" she asked before biting her lip. "I mean, it's been a while since I had some good authentic Chinese food."

Well, hell. Leaning close, I brushed my lips over the shell of her ear. "Of course."

When I pulled away, there was a genuine smile on her face and I shook my head, leading her inside the small restaurant. The smells were instantly familiar; the décor had not changed since I first set foot in the place all those years ago.

It almost felt like coming home.

# Chapter 42
## Lucas

"*Xiao Lu!*"

I turned around and saw the familiar shape of a small Asian woman in her seventies hurrying toward me. She was dressed in an absurdly traditional red *qipao* that looked faded with age. She told me years ago that she felt powerful any time she put the garment on, and I imagined she must've had a closetful of the dresses in every color because I had never seen her in anything else.

"Ruhua," I answered in Cantonese, watching as Leda's eyebrows shot up. "It's good to see you."

"Baoshan!" she shouted, even though the old man in question was literally standing only a few steps away. "Look who it is!"

"I see him," he replied in Cantonese as he approached us, his weathered face wearing the same haughty look from my past. "And I can hear you just fine."

"He's going deaf," Ruhua said, shaking her head. The tiny gold coins hanging from the comb in her gray hair tinkled as she did so, and I bit back a grin. The Wongs had been married for over fifty years, running the restaurant for forty of those years. While their food might not be the best the city had to offer, it was the people that brought me here.

"Leda, this is Wong Baoshan and his wife Li Ruhua," I explained to Leda, who was watching the exchange with some surprise. "They own this restaurant."

"I, um, nice to meet you." Leda extended her head.

"Who is this?" Ruhua asked in Cantonese, giving me the appraising glance of a questioning mother. "She's pretty. Too pretty for you. You never brought a woman here before."

She was right. I had never brought anyone here save Rocco. "This is Leda," I said instead, ignoring her question. "She wants to eat."

"Well!" Baoshan exclaimed, his smile wide. "I'll fix you a plate."

Leda looked at me and suppressed a laugh as the small old man shuffled off, leaving Ruhua to entertain us.

"How is business?" I tore my gaze from Leda and asked Ruhua.

Ruhua's smile dimmed. "Not good. Times have been tough, but what else could we do? De Blasio shut down the city last year and we were left to fend for ourselves."

I couldn't even begin to think how much their business had been hurt by the pandemic.

The worst kept secret of New York was that Chinatown was the poorest neighborhood in the entire city. More than a third of its inhabitants lived below the poverty line. In normal times, its close proximity to the courthouses and the Financial District meant a constant flow of people getting lunch and dinner.

Then the pandemic hit, and what little money flowed into the community evaporated overnight. Restaurants and shops that had been around for generations shut down, and owners who had been the pillars of the community fell into even deeper poverty and ruin.

I had invested in the Wongs' restaurant a long time ago, buying the building so they didn't have to bother with rent. It hadn't been easy. Most of Chinatown's real estate was split between a number of different benevolent associations and other collective financial schemes. As the years went by, families split their share of ownership among more and more children.

Hell, just finding the sixty-odd owners for this single building took me more time than I'd liked. But it was something I was determined to do for the Wongs. They were the only ones who really ever looked out for me and asked for nothing in return.

And though I hadn't told them, I suspected they knew why they were no longer being hounded for rent each month.

Reaching into my pocket, I pulled out a roll of bills I had. "Here," I told her, pushing them Ruhua's way. "Take it."

Ruhua's eyes hardened. "We don't take handouts," she argued, shaking her head. "Not from you, not from anyone."

"Then take it to get Baoshan some better hearing aid," I urged, knowing that Leda was watching the exchange. "You know I have plenty. Don't be stubborn."

"Take the money!" Baoshan called from the kitchen. He knew what I was doing, and while he liked to pretend he would put up the same fight, Ruhua was where their pride came in.

She frowned before grabbing the wad of cash. "All right, fine, but you get to eat here for free all year."

I grinned, unable to help it. The amount of money I had given her would keep this place running for a few months without problem. It was worth more than a few free meals, but I didn't want anything from them.

Hell, they had a soft spot in my heart. Likely the only fucking soft spot that had existed before Leda.

"Come!" Baoshan stated, wiping his hands on his apron. "Sit. Eat!"

Leda looked over at me and smiled before she made her way to one of the small tables in the place.

"Girlfriend?" Ruhua asked, never switching from Cantonese.

I watched Leda interact with Baoshan, my jaw clenching. "No, not my girlfriend."

Ruhua would likely beat me over the head with her frying pan if she knew how Leda and I met. The Wongs knew enough about who I was, but they didn't know the full extent of it. And if they did, they sure as hell wouldn't condone the things I did.

"She seems like a nice girl," Ruhua replied softly, patting me on the arm. "Good for you, *Xiao Lu*. Good for your future and even better to forget about your past."

That part they *did* know, and not once had she or Baoshan ever judged me for it. *We all did what we needed to do to survive.* Ruhua had told me all those years ago. They had left their home, their families, and everything they knew in China when the Communists took over. They knew what suffering was.

"I don't know," I said softly as Baoshan tried to get Leda to try one dish after another. She was laughing with him, and nothing she did felt forced.

That was Leda. She wore her fucking heart on her sleeve, and I didn't think she had an enemy to save her life.

"I do," Ruhua replied. "Your future is all that you have to live for, *Xiao Lu*. Don't you ever let it or let her get away." She moved away from me, and I contemplated her words. Leda was supposed to be a wife before I snatched her away to become my property.

Could she be my future?

I hadn't given much thought to my future like this. As a Don, I was required to make certain there would be another generation to pick up where I left off. It meant I would have to eventually marry and have kids someday.

I just hadn't realized that having a future could be this soon.

Or that I would find someone that I could picture having that future with.

Realizing I was just staring, I forced myself to move over to the table and sat down as the Wongs fussed over Leda. Once they had put enough food on the table for half of New York City, they left us in peace.

"Well," Leda remarked, chopsticks in hand. "This is a complete surprise, Lucas. Thank you."

"I was going to take you somewhere else," I told her.

"No need," she answered, her eyes sparkling in the low light of the restaurant. "This is better."

I didn't want to go into that with her right now. I wanted to—hell, I didn't know what I wanted to do, but it would be with Leda. That I was sure of. "Eat," I said, picking up my own chopsticks. "We can talk later."

To my surprise, Leda reached across the table and laid her hand on my thigh. "I saw what you did. That was really nice of you. You're a better person than you think, Lucas."

I didn't respond, and shoved a piece of broccoli in my mouth instead. She still thought I was worth saving.

I was a bastard and a monster, one that Leda should stay far away from.

The problem was, every time I was around her, I just wanted to keep pulling her in even closer.

## Chapter 43
## Leda

I pushed the plate away and groaned, rubbing my completely full stomach. "I'm going to be sick if I keep eating."

Lucas chuckled lightly as he leaned back in his chair, his eyes on me. "You liked it?"

I winced. "Far too much, I'm afraid. You might have to roll me out of here."

"I don't know, I think they might ask you to stay," he replied, standing. "I'm going to go and settle the bill."

I watched Lucas walk away, my heart sighing in contentment. Never would I have thought he would be like this. He seemed to genuinely care for this old couple, and the way they had interacted with him—with their own pet name for him—told me that they reciprocated the way he felt.

Which meant he couldn't be this heartless Don with a chip on his shoulder all the time.

Tonight, I saw a side of Lucas that probably wasn't brought out much, if ever. It was a side that I wanted desperately to hang onto. If he could be open and sincere with the Wongs, then he could be with me as well.

Whatever this was between us could be more than just awesome hot sex.

I was alone in this restaurant, with Lucas in the kitchen talking with the Wongs, I had a clear path out. Any other person in my shoes would have already run for the door by now. But he didn't seem worried about me leaving, and honestly, I wasn't either.

I no longer *wanted* to escape. I hadn't been lying to him on the yacht. I was—well, I felt happy, and it terrified me to be happy with someone like him.

He was going to break my heart. I already knew that. Whatever he was playing up to with his sudden and drastic change wasn't going to last forever.

*Won't it?* I asked myself.

Was he testing the waters to see if he could let down his guard around me? Maybe he thought I was some sort of spy for my father, and once he realized how much I hated my father, he started to relax.

Or maybe I had punched through some sort of walls to him and earned his trust. He certainly wanted mine. He had said as much on the boat, and while I had told him I trusted him, I didn't.

Not completely.

Not until I could figure out what drove him.

Lucas returned, but this time the couple was trailing behind him, carrying a few boxes. "Food for later," Ruhua said, as she shoved them at me.

"Take them." She said in English for my convenience. "Stubborn man won't."

I took them, mainly because she frightened me a bit, and stood up. "Thank you so much for the lovely dinner," I told them both. "It was delicious."

The little woman smiled and, in the same breath, socked Lucas in the arm. "Bring her back, or else you no longer eat here."

I muffled a laugh as he peered down at her. "What happened to my free food for a year?"

She huffed. "Only if she's with you."

Lucas just shook his head as he took the boxes from me. "Fine. I will bring her back."

My heart warmed at the thought. Was he thinking something more, well, permanent between us? This was a much better setup than I could have dreamed of on the day that my father had me dragged away for marriage.

Was I misreading this all? Was he not interested in anything long term?

What if it was just the here and now? The thought didn't sit well with me. I didn't want to be just the instrument of his revenge. I wanted him to care about me as *Leda*, not as Carmine's daughter or any other motive he had in his mind.

I wanted Lucas to let me into his world, to move the darkness that surrounded him and bring something special into his life.

I wanted to be his personal heaven.

We said our goodbyes and climbed into the car, but instead of pointing it back to the yacht, we ventured further into the city. "Where are we going?" I asked as familiar buildings passed by. We were only a few blocks from Nico's penthouse, and I longed to see my brother, to let him know that I was okay.

"My penthouse," he said, tapping his long fingers on his thigh as he stared out of the window. I bit my lip and did the same, wondering what sort of fresh hell would await me there. Was that where he was going to turn me loose? Was that why he was bringing me into the city? Had he figured out who my father was going to give me to, and now that he had had his fill of me, he was going to turn me over to another sort of future?

My heart hammered against my rib cage as the car pulled up to a building not far from the Flatiron District, his guard helping me out and onto the nearly empty sidewalk.

"This way," Lucas said near my ear, his hand on my lower back as he led me into the lobby. The building itself was old, and I watched as he swiped a card from his pocket against the elevator button, having it open nearly immediately.

"Wait," I stated, turning to face him. "Just tell me what's up there." I needed to steel myself against what might be waiting and start to purge all of these feelings for Lucas at the same time.

He arched a brow. "Leda, I told you to trust me."

Oh, I wanted to! I wanted to trust him, but I was also a D'Agostino, raised to trust no one in case they stabbed you in the back the moment they needed something else.

"Please," I begged, my voice faint. "I can handle it."

Really, I didn't know if I could handle walking away from him, but I would have to. Lucas didn't want anything long term from me.

Why would he? He had gotten what he wanted, and now it was time to move on.

Tears pricked my eyes, and his gaze narrowed. "I'm not going to let you go."

I drew in a breath as the first tear spilled over, and he caught it with his thumb, brushing over my cheek lightly. "Trust me," he said softly.

There was a lot of weight in his words, but what else could I do? I was his prisoner, and if he were lying to me, I would have to deal with it.

Even if it meant risking that he might break my heart.

# Chapter 44
## Leda

I walked into the elevator and watched as he swiped the card again, leaving his guards watching us. I could see the tension radiating off his body as we ascended, and every fiber in my being wanted to comfort him.

Still, I refrained. Trust him. I couldn't trust him, could I? Lucas should be my enemy for what he had done to me, not my lover, and certainly not my friend.

Yet I wanted him to be so much more.

The doors opened, and Lucas stepped out, waiting for me to follow. A blast of cool night air greeted me as I realized the elevator opened directly into the penthouse shrouded in darkness. My feet were rooted to the floor as Lucas walked over to a table and switched on a lamp.

Light flooded the space. There was no one waiting for us, just the faint hum of the fridge in the nearby kitchen. "There's nothing to be afraid of," he said softly, crossing his arms over his chest. "Unless you're scared of stainless steel. And if you are, well that's something you'll just have to learn to deal with."

I burst into laughter at his attempt to lighten the mood, some of my worry sliding away.

"And gray, apparently."

Gray was everywhere, on the walls, the furniture, clearly a man's domain. A wall of nothing but glass peered out over the cityscape. Beyond it I could see the dim glow of the lights that illuminated the private hot tub built into the granite terrace.

To my right was a dazzling open staircase that led up to the second level, and I longed to go for a tour. This was far more than what Nico and I had in our own places, and clearly Lucas had spent a pretty penny on it.

"It's gorgeous," I said softly.

He held out his hand. "Would you like to see the terrace?"

I nodded and took it, surprised when he wrapped his fingers around mine. For a moment we gazed at each other, my pulse slowing to a dull thud, and I had the sudden urge to kiss him.

Instead he pulled his gaze away and led me to a door off the kitchen, opening it to the cool night. The balcony stretched the entire length of the penthouse.

"This is ridiculous," I said as I dipped my fingers into the hot tub.

Lucas leaned against the glass railing, watching me. "It's home. Safest place in the city."

I smirked, standing. "Are you sure about that? I mean, a good rock climber could get in here in a heartbeat."

He looked at me for a moment before he threw his head back and laughed, catching me completely off guard.

For the first time I saw the true Lucas, how the hardness of his face softened, and he looked younger, happier.

"Well, I will have to let my security team know about that," he said, wiping his face. "Because I'm sure that never crossed their minds."

I joined him at the railing and gazed out over the city. "I sometimes forget how it looks at night." The city was always my favorite, and many a night I had sat out on my own balcony, just watching the lights dance in the night.

"I miss it sometimes," Lucas admitted.

"So," I said after a moment. "The Wongs." I was dying to know how he knew them and why they meant so much to him. Would he tell me?

Lucas let out a breath, not meeting my eyes. "The Wongs' restaurant was a place for me to get cheap food and not be bothered. I started hanging out there to get away, and Ruhua started to teach me Cantonese in her spare time."

A brief smile flickered over his face before he let it drop. "One night, this asshole walked in and tried to rob the place. Scared Ruhua with a gun, but he never saw me sitting in the corner. I beat him within an inch of his life."

His words stole my breath. Sometimes I forgot how vicious Lucas could be, not having seen his violent side.

Yet.

"I was young and angry then," he continued. "And didn't realize at the time that the lowlife I beat belonged to a rival Mafia. I nearly started a turf war that night, but Cosimo saw something in me and pulled me out of my old role and put me onto enforcer training."

"What *was* your old role?" I pressed, curious. If there was any night he'd tell me, it would be tonight.

Lucas stiffened. From the dark look that crossed his eyes, I knew I had gone too far too quickly.

"Sorry, I didn't mean to pry," I said quickly, a twinge of hurt crossing my chest as I saw the dark look on his face. He wanted me to trust him, yet he wasn't willing to share those details with me.

Why should he? Maybe that was my answer about a future with him.

Maybe I was wrong to fall in love with Lucas.

Wait, did I just say I was in *love* with Lucas Valentino? Where had that come from?

"Let's go inside," he stated after a moment, turning around and walking inside without waiting for me to follow.

I caught onto his angered state, and my heart sank, forcing me to turn back to the city I missed so much.

Had I really fallen in love with my captor?

Somewhere along the lines of him treating me like a real person and not his prisoner, I had allowed Lucas into my heart.

I choked back the tears that threatened to well up in my eyes. There was no use crying over it now. It wasn't like I would be able to change what my heart was feeling.

But the real question was: did I want this?

I thought I did.

I wanted to be Lucas's sunshine, but in order for that to happen, he had to let me in.

And tonight, he'd given me just a glimpse before slamming that door in my face again.

# Chapter 45
# Lucas

*I pushed open the door to the building, my heart hammering in my chest. I didn't know why I felt this need to get inside, but something was wrong.*

*Something was fucking* wrong.

*Not bothering to take the elevator, I took the stairs instead, somehow climbing the flights with ease to my penthouse, finding it far too easy to get inside.*

*Where were my fucking guards?*

*Where was Leda?*

*The uncomfortable twist in my chest tightened, and I hurried to push open the stairwell door, finding the normally locked door open.*

*No.*

*I raced through the penthouse to my bedroom, where she should have been, but the bed was empty.*

*"Leda!" I shouted, fear clawing at my throat as I hurried back out into the main room.*

*The terrace doors were open.*

*"Leda?" I asked as I approached the doors, stepping outside. The wind whipped at my coat, and the sky was dark with pregnant storm clouds. I knew she preferred*

*to be on the terrace, and some of my anxiety lessened at the thought of it.*

*She was out there. I was sure of it.*

*Rounding the corner, my heart calmed in my chest when I saw her standing on the railing. I wasn't sure how she could be doing that. Her long black nightgown billowed around her body, and when she looked back at me, there was sadness in her eyes.*

*"What are you doing, Leda?" I reached out my hand. "Come back here."*

*She shook her head. "I can't. I can't be with a monster any longer."*

*They were the words I'd been waiting to hear from her mouth, but I had never thought they would hurt so fucking much.*

*"Please, Leda. Get down and we can talk about this," I pleaded, taking a step closer to her and trying to figure out how to get her safely back on the ground without killing us both. "Please, don't do this."*

*She let out a sob. "I have to, don't you see? This is the only way."*

*"Leda, please," I begged desperately. "Don't. Don't do this to me."*

*"Goodbye, Lucas," she said, and jumped.*

I jolted awake, my heart pounding against my rib cage and a cold sweat covering my body. The dream. It felt far too fucking real.

I knew it was just a dream. Leda's body was pressed up against mine, her long hair tickling my bare chest as she slept on, unaware of what my mind made me see.

Fuck.

I blew out a breath, letting my hand slowly sift through her silky strands. We'd been at the penthouse for four days now while I'd been trying to remind the boys in the Battery who their real boss was.

Adrian was moving fast, far faster than I expected, and even after I left from the meeting, I had a sneaking suspicion that my position was much weaker than I thought it was.

I was fucking sick of it. I should have had that bastard killed the moment I became Don. Instead, I gave in to a moment of mercy and let him live. Now, he went from a thorn at my side to a snake at my heel.

I would have liked to say that most of my days were spent focusing on business, but with Leda around, I found it hard to stray from her for too long.

I had tried it once, heading to one of the clubs for a drink, and found it an utterly unpleasant experience.

The club had been too noisy, the air too stuffy. And the women—hell, I had scared most of them off the moment they approached the table. Before I had had no problems having one or two join me, but none of them were Leda, and that was the problem.

None of them.

Disentangling myself from her body, I rose from the bed and found my loafers. I slid them on and walked out of the bedroom for some air.

Leda was in my fucking blood. She was all I thought about when I wasn't with her and all that I wanted whenever I came through the door at night. I wanted her smile, her laugh, and the way she fucked me right to sleep at night.

I felt at peace around her, and that scared the shit out of me.

After pulling a water bottle out of the fridge, I walked out onto the same offending terrace from my nightmare, glad to find it empty. A storm battered the city tonight, the rain matching my dark mood.

I didn't like this feeling Leda invoked in me. I didn't like her infiltrating my walls and making me care about her.

She was supposed to be my trophy, my triumph over Carmine. She was supposed to be my tool that brought the war to remove Adrian from my side without dirtying my own hands.

She wasn't supposed to become an obsession like this.

Now I couldn't even concentrate on work because of her, because of what she had done to me.

She made me want to be a better man, something different than what I had built for myself in my mind. She made me want to fight for her smile.

I wanted her fucking love.

"No," I barked into the storm. I didn't deserve her fucking love. I had bought her for reasons that should have made her hate me. I had wanted to use her and then cast her aside, a broken, used shell of a woman, to piss off Carmine.

Love had never been part of the bargain, but Leda was making me fall for her. She was making me feel things I couldn't afford, not with this shit with Adrian hanging over my head.

I couldn't afford to lose my credibility now. I couldn't afford to show my weakness, especially when that weakness was Leda.

## Chapter 46
## Lucas

I didn't sleep after my nightmare.

Quietly I dressed and called Rocco to come get me as soon as the sun started to lighten the sky. "Where to, Don?" he asked the moment I climbed in the waiting car.

"We need to make more rounds," I told him, gripping my phone tightly. "Make sure that Leda is watched today."

Rocco arched a brow but said nothing, typing out my message on his cell phone. "Yes, Don."

We ended up on the other side of the city, in the outer boroughs where I had spent far too much of my time. When people said that the city never slept, they were talking about Manhattan. In the outer boroughs, people were just starting to wake for the day. Halal cart vendors were firing up their grills, and New Yorkers rushed to catch whatever train or bus that was already fifteen minutes late.

I didn't have to tell Rocco where to start. He knew exactly where to send the driver, and my expression grew hard as I stepped out of the car, buttoning my suit coat.

"He's not here," Rocco said as he joined me. "He sends his regrets."

Fucking Adrian.

I had demanded a face to face with him days ago, but he kept eluding me with one excuse after another.

He knew I was in the city and was with Leda, hence the need to have tight security around her. I couldn't take the chance of him doing something stupid when it came to her.

"Well who the fuck is?" I asked.

"A few of the Battery boys who weren't there in the last meet and greet," Rocco replied. "They should be soon. You're up early this morning, Don."

"No rest for the weary," I told him. There was no trace of humor in my words. I wasn't going to tell him the real reason I had been unable to go back to bed.

And as much as it would have been nice to burrow next to Leda's warm body and forget the shit inside my head for a while, there were truly pressing matters at hand that I needed to take care of.

"You mean you like to torture me instead," Rocco groaned. "We are in the city, boss. There are temptations, and a man has needs."

Rocco's words brought a mirthless smile to my lips. "You knew the hazards of the job when you took it."

"Yeah," he grumbled. "Sometimes those aren't worth it. I don't get shot at nearly as much as you claimed I would be."

I cleared my throat before he could see my smile. "I'll be sure to change that."

Despite my early morning, the rest of the day went smoothly. If the capos had their opinions about me, they wisely kept them to themselves as I visited one site after another, keeping my questions about status reports and the like, and reading the expressions of the men who answered me.

I wasn't blind to Adrian's influence though. The capos in charge of the Battery were definitely restive. And despite the fact that I was their fucking Don, there was more than just unease when I showed up in person before them.

There was resentment.

*Too fucking bad. I make the decisions, not Adrian, nor any other prick. Cosimo gave the Mafia to* me. *Nobody else.*

The final capo I met with paled when I reminded him of that. "I mean no disrespect, Don," he stammered, swallowing hard. "I'm just trying to follow orders."

I leaned in and gave him a grim smile. "You're following the wrong fucking orders. Next time that Adrian gives you an order, you check with me or Rocco before you do it."

"Yes, Don," he stated, his eyes darting to Rocco, who just grinned at him.

I stood and straightened my coat, showing him that he hadn't ruffled me on the outside. Inside, I was seething that Adrian was trying to ruin me at every turn.

When we walked out, Rocco swore. "Still don't understand why you didn't let me kill him when you had the chance."

"Can't cry over spilt milk now," I grunted as we climbed into the car. "I thought I'd show him the olive branch, tell him no hard feelings."

That had been a fucking mistake. And right at that moment, the hard truth stared me in the face.

If I kept Leda around, I would be making another one.

## Chapter 47
## Lucas

It was nearing nightfall by the time the car pulled back up to the penthouse building. "She's been inside all day," Rocco said before I even asked. This had been the first mention of Leda between us all day.

Not that she was ever far from my thoughts. Hell, I had missed her every moment of the day, wondering what she was doing and if she was thinking about me. Thank fuck I hadn't left her a cell phone, or else it would have been too difficult not to text her.

"Go get some booze and sleep," I told him. "You deserve it."

Rocco snorted. "What I deserve is a vacation, but that's only after this shit with Adrian is over."

Yeah, I knew the feeling.

I rode up the elevator alone, leaving the guards on the main level as I tried to steel myself against seeing Leda again. She was just a woman, for fuck's sake, my prisoner.

And here I was, letting her stay in my penthouse, sleep in my bed, and treating her like she was my girlfriend.

I slumped against the elevator wall, and thrust my hand through my hair. This shit had to stop. She was affecting me in ways I couldn't control, ways that could get me killed if I wasn't careful.

Leda could become the weakness that Adrian or any other enemies could hold over my head. A Don's greatest weakness was the people that he cared about. Men who wouldn't break under the worst kind of torture came undone at the thought of their loved ones being hurt.

That wasn't in my cards. That couldn't be in my cards.

When the doors opened, I slid a mask of indifference over my face as I walked in. The smells of garlic and basil hit me almost immediately. Leda was standing at the stove. And fuck me if my cock didn't rise to attention at the sight of her wearing my clothes, her long hair tied in a simple braid down her back. Music played from a distant speaker, and she was tapping her bare foot to the beat.

I could've almost pretended like I was coming home.

For a moment, I watched her, feeling the odd sensation in my chest of what it would be like with Leda as something more permanent in my life. She was a Mafia Don's daughter, so my world wasn't entirely alien to her. It wouldn't totally crush her.

It hadn't yet.

She was tough, far tougher than I ever gave her credit for. And that was what I was so taken by.

But to let her in—completely in—would be disastrous. I wasn't the type of man she needed. I wasn't the type of man she should take care of.

I wasn't the type of man she deserved. She was too good and wholesome. I was the complete opposite.

She called me a monster in my nightmare. And she was right.

I was never meant to have anyone care for me. Least of all someone as good as her.

Leda turned suddenly, and instead of the wariness that had been in her eyes before, there was a brightness that sent my heart slamming.

"Hey!" she said cheerfully, coming toward me. "You're home. I didn't hear you come in. I hope you don't mind, but I had this thought to cook us a meal tonight. It's my grandmother's recipe."

I just stood there, unable to speak, inside me was a war between my brain and my heart. Between what I wanted and what I needed. The two directions tugged at me. It felt like the walls were closing in, like I didn't even know who I was anymore.

I couldn't be with her. I would never deserve her. She had no idea just what she let into her fucking bed.

Her expression was happy, happy to see me, the fucking guy that ruined her life by purchasing her and forcing her to be with him. It would have been better off had she hated me all along.

Then it would be easier to do what needed to be done right at this moment. Leda wouldn't understand. She'd think that I was just protecting myself from loving her, when the truth was that I was trying to protect her from loving someone like me.

So, I made a decision, one that was already hurting me before I let the words out. "You are a prisoner here, Leda," I growled. "Not some fucking guest."

Her steps slowed to a stop and her smile slipped, causing the damn ache in my chest to increase. "I just thought—"

I stepped closer, forcing myself to put on the mask that I had worn so often before meeting her, the one that would keep me from being hurt by anyone.

"You thought wrong," I said, my heart breaking as I watched hurt and confusion flicker over her lovely face. "I don't want your fucking food."

This had to be the right thing to do. It had to be.

Then why did I feel like a total asshole for doing it?

I fucked over a lot of people in my day as Don, and even more people as the enforcer that Cosimo had molded me into, but never had it felt this shitty.

I finally felt like the monster that was stole the princess and then broke her fucking heart.

And for the first time in my life, I hated myself in a way that I never thought possible.

## Chapter 48
## Leda

I stared at Lucas, not believing at how he was acting. All day I had thought about doing something nice for him until I finally settled on cooking him a dish that was so near and dear to my heart. Just to show him how much I appreciated the way he was treating me.

I didn't feel like a prisoner in this penthouse or in his arms for the last few days.

He wasn't the enemy any longer. Somewhere the lines had blurred for me, and now I was seeing him as something far more than the man who had stolen my life from me.

I felt like someone who was cherished by him. From the way he touched me, the way he held me at night against his chest, I thought that this might have been the turning point in how we saw each other. I was starting to feel like this might actually have been a good thing happening between us.

Until now.

Clearly, Lucas had had a bad day. It was written all over his face when he had first entered the penthouse, and I just thought that I could turn it around.

He had never reacted this way before, and frankly, it pissed me off a little.

Lucas brushed past me, heading for the bar. I followed him, my arms wrapped tightly around my waist.

"Bad days suck," I said softly. "But you know, it does feel good to talk it out."

I wanted him to know that I was here for him, that he couldn't shock me with anything he would say. Lucas's business didn't scare me, but the way he was reacting right now did.

His face was unreadable as he poured himself a glass of whiskey. "This isn't a fucking relationship where I come home and unload all my secrets on you, Leda. I think the last few days made you forget our arrangement."

That hurt. It wasn't just the tone of his voice but the words he said in general.

"Why are you being like this?" I asked hesitantly.

I hadn't tried to run, but the way he was acting, maybe I should have. Apparently, I had been too exemplary of a prisoner in these past few days.

*That,* a nasty little voice in my head replied. *Or his true nature was starting to come out.*

No. I didn't believe it. I refused to believe it.

Ever since we had that one moment back at his house upstate, he showed me a side that I wanted to see. There were moments when he could be caring, when he was willing to open himself up. Even if for a little bit. And from that moment, all I had wanted to do for him was show him that I appreciated that. Lucas could have easily followed through with whatever plan he had the night he had bought me, but he hadn't, and that was the side I wanted from him.

The same side that had my stupid little heart falling in love with him despite everything he had done to me.

Despite reality.

"What did I do wrong?" I asked.

Lucas didn't even bother looking at me as he threw back the drink, and slammed the glass down on the wood hard enough to crack it.

"You? Nothing."

I couldn't hold back my own bitter laugh.

"That's very hard to believe. You come home like the world owes you something and the first thing you do is insult me when I did something nice for you!"

I hated the way that my voice cracked at the words. I hated that he was affecting me more than I wanted it to. I had been *happy* to cook him a meal. I *wanted* to show him that there was more to me than the label everyone threw at me. Mafia Princess. Spoiled brat. Carmine's daughter.

I was a real person, dammit. A real person with real feelings, and he was crushing them little by little with this.

He turned then, and I tried to find some ounce of softness in his eyes, some notion that he was doing this for a reason, but found none.

Gone was the man that I had laughed with in bed last night when I had found a ticklish spot just above the elaborate tattoo on his rib cage. In his place stood the monster who bought me. A crack ran along my heart.

"Something nice?" He said coldly. "I *bought* you, Leda. I bought you and used you. I've *been* using you as part of my plans. You should consider yourself fucking lucky that I haven't tossed you to the rest of the wolves that want a piece of a D'Agostino."

His eyes raked over my body, and a smirk appeared on his lips. "Even if they are used goods."

If his cruel rejection of my cooking when he walked in was a hammer pounding at my heart. Those last words were the final blow that shattered them.

To think that I woke up this morning ready tell him that I loved him. That thought had come out of the blue, and I was stupid enough to think that he actually cared about me. I was so stupid, so stupid to believe every one of his lies. A boat ride, some Chinese food, and then a couple of night in his penthouse, and I was ready to believe that he actually gave a shit about me.

I had been duped again. All because of the last name I carried, the fucking father who had ruined my life.

Lucas shook his head, as if he couldn't believe that I had fallen for this. "Did you really think that I cared about you?"

I stumbled back as if he had slapped me. I almost wished he had. At least that would hurt less.

"Shut up," I hurled back at him. "Why are you telling me all of this?" I asked, when what I wanted to ask was: *why are you breaking my heart?*

A cold smile crossed his lips. "Because I am a fucking monster, Leda! You of all people should understand that."

He wasn't wrong. Most of the Dons didn't care about anything but their business, how much money they could bring in, and who they could take over in the process. I had seen my father do just that repeatedly.

I thought Lucas would be different. Until now.

"You say that," I forced out, perilously close to tears. "But I've seen your actions, Lucas. You're not a monster! Not to me."

He growled and moved away, and grabbed the glass.

"Well then you're wrong!"

I couldn't fight back the tears anymore. My vision blurred and I took a shuddering breath.

"Then why am I still fucking you every night? Why do you even bother putting me in your bed, Lucas? Tell me why you kiss me, why you hold me!" I stopped there, not wanting to divulge to him that I thought he was falling in love with me.

Had I been wrong about him all along? It didn't feel like Lucas had been putting on an act at all.

When his cold eyes met mine, I knew he could see the tears streaming down my cheeks. I hated to show him that weakness, but he was ripping my heart apart and making me wonder what I had gotten myself into in the first place.

"I don't think you are cold-hearted," I continued. "I've seen the worst of the worst, Lucas, and you aren't it. Please. Please don't do this."

Lucas pushed away from the bar suddenly, and I found myself backing up as he advanced on me, his face hard as stone. No matter what I did, what I said, it wasn't getting through to him, and for the first time since meeting Lucas, I felt real fear race through my veins.

I wasn't stupid. I knew what he was capable of. I just never thought it would be something I would see.

His eyes were soulless, devoid of emotion, and I swallowed.

"What are you going to do to me?" I challenged, refusing to back down. "Hit me? Choke me? Isn't that what you Dons do? Push your weight around and wait for the rest of us to bend to your will?"

Lucas paused, and for the first time, I saw his jaw clench, the barest hint of emotion that he had shown from the very second he had walked into his penthouse tonight and decided to give me the third degree.

I had done nothing to deserve any of this, and I was tired of being a doormat to all things Mafia, my father and Lucas included.

"Get out." I sobbed, not bothering to wipe away the tears on my cheeks. "Just get out!"

I was about half a second away from losing it.

"It's my fucking house!" he yelled, and reached for me.

I cringed as his hand hovered around my throat, and knew that I had pushed him too far.

What did it matter anyway? He had already told me that he didn't care about me, and the moment he turned me out on the street, I would just get picked up by some other Don trying to make a name for himself. I was never going to have the life I wanted or see my nephew, my brother, or anyone else ever again.

Lucas shook his head and dropped his hand. "No, this isn't worth it."

His words were barely a whisper, but I heard them anyway, watching as he walked away from me, his broad shoulders tense under his coat. It wasn't until the door slammed behind him that I let my legs give out, sliding against the island that had been holding me up and to the cold tile floor.

What had just happened? Where had this all gone south?

A sob wracked me, and I threw my arms around my knees, drawing them up against my chest and letting the tears come.

I had been stupid, so stupid to think that he actually cared about me. That he might return the feelings I had.

What was I going to do now? I was still his prisoner. Lucas had made that abundantly clear. I had nowhere to go, and the moment I did actually escape, my father would be hauling me off to the husband he had picked out for me. It would be the death of my happiness.

I wiped my eyes. Happiness. That seemed like such a foreign word now. I had dared to hope that Lucas could be my happiness, that we might have built something together.

Instead, all he had done was prove to me just how much he could crush my heart, along with any hopes of a future. From the way I was hurting, I might as well do him a favor and jump off the terrace so he wouldn't have to clean up his mess when he returned.

But he didn't return that night. I didn't bother to clean up the food in the kitchen, and sat there watching the door warily for hours until I realized that he wasn't coming back.

He left me in this prison, alone and confused, but mostly devastated at the way he had flung his careless words in my face. All he had done was remind me that I had been an utter fool to trust my heart with a Don and not expect to be burned as a result.

I wanted to hate him.

Instead, I curled up in his bed, between the sheets that still smelled of Lucas, and cried myself to sleep.

## Chapter 49
## Lucas

It took two bottles of whiskey before I admitted to myself that I made a mistake with Leda.

Rocco was the one who dragged me out of the bar I had forced him to take me to, muttering the entire time about lovesick fools and Dons that were too stubborn for their own good.

Somehow we ended in his apartment on the Lower East Side, a fucking hole in the wall since he spent most of his time watching after me.

"Here you go," he said as he dumped me on the sofa. "Something tells me she doesn't want you back in your own fucking house tonight."

I rubbed a hand over my face wearily. The liquor dulled my senses to the point where I couldn't see straight. Normally I wasn't one to be out of control like this, but fuck, the pain that I had felt lying to Leda hadn't gone away like it was supposed to.

In fact, it had only intensified the longer I was away from her. I had hurt her, hurt her for no fucking reason at all.

Well, not no reason. I had hurt her because I couldn't stand to look at myself in the mirror and know that she had made me fall in love with her.

"Fuck," I growled, leaning back against the sofa.

Rocco chuckled as he lowered himself into the leather recliner, clasping his hands loosely between his legs. "So, you figured it out."

I eyed him. "What?"

"That you care for her."

"This wasn't the plan," I said after a few minutes, closing my eyes so I didn't have to see the truth slapping me in the face. "She wasn't supposed to be like this. She was supposed to be a spoiled princess that I could just throw away once I was done with her. This shit is not fair."

"Well," Rocco decided. "You could just stay away for a few days. I can have the guys take care of her."

"Don't fucking touch her," I interrupted, my voice laced with steel. I would rip their heads off if they laid one finger on Leda. She was mine.

"Look, I'm just trying to help," Rocco snorted. "But if you don't want her gone, then why the hell are you sitting here in my fucking living room, drunk off your ass instead of back home apologizing?"

*Because I was an asshole and a monster.* Because I thought I could destroy her and keep my fucking heart safe from being hurt.

Because she had gotten too close for comfort for me. Leda had broken down the walls. Seeing her in my penthouse tonight, being domestic as fuck, had started to make me want other things for my future. Things that didn't involve the Mafia.

Right now, the Mafia could burn in hell for all I cared. Adrian could have it all. All I wanted was Leda.

"Get some sleep," Rocco said gruffly.

I cracked open an eye, and saw that he hadn't moved from his spot in the chair. His gun was visible on his thigh. "What are you going to do?" I asked. "Watch over me while I sleep?"

Rocco shrugged his shoulders. "Yeah, boss, I am. That's my job, remember?"

Well, hell. Now I felt like shit for that too. At least I was batting a thousand for ruining people's days.

## Chapter 50
## Lucas

The next day, after a few aspirins and a visit to the yacht so I could shower and change clothes, I dove into my work. I knew that no matter what I did, it wasn't going to help me forget the tortured look on Leda's face before she kicked me out of my own fucking penthouse. I had to channel that feeling into something productive.

There was one more capo that I had been told was spouting some shit about my role as Don, and as much as I didn't want to make the tension any tighter within the Mafia, I couldn't allow him to continue to disrespect me like that.

I had to make an example. Let them know that I wasn't fucking around.

So, Rocco and I paid him a visit at his home in Bushwick. "You sure you want to do this?" Rocco asked in a low voice as we walked up the stairs of the brick building that housed the man's apartment. "I can take him to one of the shops: give him the old one-two, maybe work the body, and carve up his face. You know. The usual."

I shook my head, and cracked my knuckles absent-mindedly. "Yeah, I'm sure."

"Why do I get the feeling you're going to be the death of me?"

We climbed the rest of the way until we came to the apartment, and I pounded on the door. The smell of piss and garbage lingered in the hallway. Somewhere down the hall, a dog barked, followed by a baby crying before both were quieted by their respective owners. You'd think that someone as well paid as one of my own capos would have the dignity of living in a better place.

When I heard the locks flip, Rocco withdrew his gun and held it at his side in case we were greeted with the same cold steel. I knew that he would push me out of the line of fire if there was a hint of danger, and even take a bullet if he had to.

The door flung open, and it only took a matter of minutes for the man to realize who was beating down his door so early in the morning.

His eyes widened, but before his mouth could open, we were pushing into the apartment. "D-don Valentino," he stuttered. "To what do I owe this pleasure of your visit?"

I gave him a cruel grin, stripping off my dark coat. "Enzo, I think you know why I am here."

He nervously ran a hand through his blond hair, his eyes on Rocco's gun. "I-I don't know, Don, I swear it."

I made a tutting sound and rolled up the sleeves of my dress shirt casually. "Now, Enzo. What have I told you about lying?"

"That lying only brings trouble," he bit out, some of his surprise fading.

"That's right," I answered as Rocco locked the door. Enzo swallowed visibly. Poor bastard probably thought I was just here for a talk, nothing more.

It couldn't be further from the truth. "I don't like being lied to," I told him, my fists balling at my sides. "Nor do I like my own fucking men talking behind my back about mutiny."

"Don Valentino, please," Enzo started in, holding up his hands nervously. "I don't know what you're talking about."

I chuckled darkly. "Is that so?"

"Yeah. Look, it was just some drunk talk." He gave a feeble smile. "You know how it is. Put a couple of drinks in me and I can't shut the fuck up about anything and everything. My mother always said my mouth was going to get me in trouble."

"Well," I answered, taking a step forward and placing a hand on his shoulder. "She was right."

He didn't even have time to react as I drove my fist into his solar plexus. My next blow landed on his nose, and I felt the satisfying crack of bone under my knuckles before blood started to rush out onto Enzo's face.

"Fuck!" He screamed, attempting to defend himself.

I didn't give him the chance and landed one punch after another until he was crumpled on the dirty tile floor. It wasn't until Enzo quit moving that I stopped and looked at the blood pooling under his body.

"Now?" Rocco asked.

I stepped back, grabbing the blanket from the back of the couch and wiping my bloody fists on it. "Yeah, now."

Rocco took my place and put two bullets in Enzo's head, the silencer muffling the noise. Enzo's mother was right. His dumb fucking mouth definitely got him in trouble.

After we left the apartment, Rocco called in the cleaning crew so that they could dispose of the body, and I spent the rest of my day in my office in one of the buildings that Cosimo had owned on 8$^{th}$ Street for the sake of owning it. He could have rented it out to tenants, considering the price of real estate in the concrete jungle, but he had told me that he preferred the solitude of an entirely empty building.

I hadn't understood it until recently.

Pushing away from the desk, I stood up and walked over to the bank of windows that overlooked Washington Square Park. I was going to have to face Leda sooner or later, figure out how the hell I was going to explain my actions in a way that would make sense to her.

The truth was: I was fucking terrified about what I felt for Leda. She was the one weakness I couldn't afford but couldn't live without.

I hated it. If word got out, Leda would be turned into a pawn to get to me, just like I had done to her father. She could be bargained for or even killed just because it would be a convenient way to hurt me.

And if she died because of me, I'd never forgive myself.

I ran a hand through my hair, and contemplated my next move. I would have to tread carefully with this tonight if I wanted to walk out with my balls intact after she got done laying into me.

Hell, I deserved her anger. I deserved her hating me for what I had done to her, for the lies I had told her. For breaking her heart so callously after she worked so hard to make me happy.

Leda deserved a hell of a lot better than me, but as much as I didn't want to admit it to anyone, I hoped she hadn't given up on me.

I waited until darkness fell before I made my way to the penthouse, and forced the driver to stop by a florist so I could pick up some flowers for Leda. Rocco snorted when I slid back into the car, shaking his head.

"I hope you hid a few diamonds in there too," he said. "Because you are going to need them."

I clenched the bouquet tightly in my hand. "Diamonds are next on the list."

He grinned. "They better be."

When I finally reached the penthouse, I realized that maybe Rocco wasn't wrong after all about the diamonds. The living room was dark, but I could see Leda's outline on the terrace, staring out over the city. Quietly I crossed the room and walked outside, where the wind tugged at my hair. "Leda."

She turned, her eyes falling on the flowers. "Really, Lucas? You think that I'm going to be swayed by cheap-ass flowers?"

Okay, first of all, these flowers weren't cheap. But that wasn't the point.

She was spoiling for a fight.

"You're right," I maintained my own composure. I had caused this anger in her, this hurt, and it was my job to diffuse it and smooth this over so she wouldn't be looking at me like she wanted to hurl me over the terrace.

I threw the flowers onto the nearby lounger. "This was a stupid idea."

Leda wrapped her arms around her waist. "What the hell do you want?"

Killing a man had been easier than this.

"I lied to you," I started, figuring it was easier if she knew that up front. "Everything I said yesterday was a lie."

Leda's hard expression didn't change. "Why?" she challenged.

There was hurt in her voice. And I hated to hear it because I knew I caused it. She was going to force me to say it, and I could only hope that once I did, my cock would be buried in her before the night was over. That we'd wake up in each other's arms, and all of this was just some bad nightmare.

"I care about you, Leda."

She scoffed and dropped her arms. She wore a crop-top sweatshirt that gave me an ample view of her flat stomach, and a pair of yoga pants that molded to her ass so tightly that she might as well be wearing nothing at all. Her hair was in a messy bun, and her face was withdrawn and pale. I wanted to see her smile for me, to give me that look that sent my blood roaring to my ears and my cock.

I wanted her to be happy again.

"You don't know the meaning of caring," she was saying as she went to move past me.

I reached out and grabbed her arm, forcing her to meet my gaze. "Don't do this."

"Do what?" she asked, pursing her lips. "Don't give you the time of day? Fine, I won't."

Tamping down my sudden flare of anger, I didn't let her go. "I don't think you heard what I said."

"Oh, I heard you!" she exploded, pushing her finger into my chest. "I heard you just fine! You care about me. Big deal! It's not going to fix this, Lucas!"

"Don't you fucking walk away from me!" I raged at her.

Her eyes widened, and a cold boulder settled into my stomach. Those weren't the words I wanted to tell her. I wanted to tell her that I was falling for her, that she made me feel in ways I've never felt before. But somehow, those words couldn't come forward. Somehow, I could only keep hurting her.

"I'm sorry." Loosening my grip on her arm, I cleared my throat. "I fucking lost control."

Her gaze narrowed. "Is that all you have to say? That you lost control?"

My teeth clamped together. "You don't understand. I'm a Don. I can't lose control."

I always had to be in control. I had learned long ago to be in control of every aspect of my life. Because if I was, no one else could be. But with Leda, everything she did took that control out of my hands. She could ask me to jump off the Brooklyn Bridge right now, and I would seriously consider it.

I cared that much about her.

Leda let out a bitter laugh, her gorgeous eyes flashing with anger and tears.

"You know what, fuck you!" She exclaimed. "Why can't you just admit something for once and not worry about your fucking title or how you need to be in control? Why can't you be honest with me?"

The anger curled in my stomach. "Careful," I warned her, grinding my jaw.

"Or what?" she asked angrily, her finger stabbing against my chest. "Tell me, Lucas! What the fuck are you going to do? Are you going to throw me over the terrace?"

I narrowed my eyes. Did she really fucking think that I was going to kill her?

"Or are you going to fuck me to teach me a lesson?" she challenged. "Are you going to show me what a *Don* truly is like?"

My cock roared to life as I grabbed her around the waist and pushed her against the wall, trapping her underneath my body. "Is that what you want, Leda?" I asked harshly, feeling the excitement override the anger. "Do you want me to fuck you to show you what a Don is really like?"

She pushed at my shoulders hard, but I refused to budge. Instead, I covered her mouth with mine. This wasn't a kiss full of passion but one colored with anger. My lips bruised hers and Leda let out a muffled cry, her hands batting at my shoulders. But slowly, slowly I felt her kiss me back, confusing the hell out of me.

Blood pounded at my ears. I wanted to be buried inside her so much that I could taste it. The thought of being with her overrode any fears I had that she was going to wipe her hands of me because of my actions the night before.

She wanted me. I could *taste* it in her angry kiss. I could feel the passion vibrating through her body.

She wanted this just as much as I did.

Tearing away from her lips, I gripped her thighs, prying them open. "Take those off."

"No," she told me, lifting her chin. There was defiance in her gaze, and it only drove me crazy with need. With a growl, I gripped the fabric and ripped the yoga pants open. The scent of her arousal hung heavy in the air, and a shiver of need rushed through my head. My ears were practically ringing, and the only thing I cared about was to bury myself inside of her.

With my free hand, I unleashed my throbbing cock. Leda squirmed under me futilely as I hauled her upright. My knees pinned her thighs against the wall and my cock pushed into her soaking wet cunt.

"Fuck," I groaned as I pushed myself deeper, expecting her to return the favor.

"I hate you!" she shrieked instead, clawing at my shirt. "I fucking hate you!"

I pulled out a little before I slammed back into her, feeling her body quiver in response. My hand came up against her throat, and this time, I closed my fingers enough to feel her pulse quicken.

"Tell me how much you hate me," I whispered against her neck, biting the tender flesh there.

"I hate you!" she strained, this time with a sob as I continued to thrust. "I fucking hate you! You fucking bastard!"

"Yeah, just like that," I snarled, drilling into her. "I can *feel* how fucking wet you are. You want this, Leda. I know you fucking want this."

Her nails raked down my back, drawing painful scratches through the shirt, but I didn't care. Nothing short of a bullet to my head was going to stop me from fucking her until my point was made

Leda screamed as her pussy contracted around my cock, an orgasm ripping through her. Tears ran down the edges of her eyes, smearing her mascara. I covered her mouth with my hand so that the neighbors wouldn't think I was killing her. My heart pounded at my throat while my hips continued to thrust with reckless abandon.

I would break her down, inch by inch, one orgasm after the next until there was nothing left.

That was what I did. I was taking back my control.

Except, I wasn't.

The sense of control was slipping with every scrape of her fingernails against my shirt, the way that she writhed under my thrusts, screaming against my hand on her mouth.

But I saw in her teary eyes what she wanted, and I was giving it to her.

Fuck, I was in love with this woman.

My own orgasm hit me hard and fast as I poured myself into her tight warmth, shouting her name repeatedly until there was nothing left. My knees weakened, and I collapsed with Leda in my arms onto the floor. Leda struggled against my embrace, but I refused to let go as my cock continued to twitch inside of her. I didn't give a shit what she was going to do next. She could kill me now for all I cared.

But she didn't.

No, the minx's hand went for my softening cock. The fury in her eyes was unmistakable.

"Is this what you fucking wanted?" She hissed, her fingers gliding over the wet skin until I was hard again. She jerked my cock with a cold fury, drawing equal shares pain and pleasure as tears continued to run down her eyes.

"You're not fucking done, Lucas Valentino. Not by a long shot. You want to fuck? Fine, let's fuck."

## Chapter 51
## Leda

I wanted to hate him.

Lucas was panting before me, his eyes wary, and I wanted to take my hand off his cock and walk away. He had cut me deep with his words the other night. And the fact that he thought that he could just walk back into the penthouse with flowers and I would fall into his arms pissed me off to no degree.

I was tired of being used. I was tired of him thinking that his words could sway me to his side again. He was hiding something, something that wouldn't let him fully commit. I thought he might make a real fucking apology, instead, it was just more of the same fucking bullshit.

The same fucking excuse. Oh, he was a Don. Oh, he lost control.

*No, fuck you.*

*Fuck you for stomping all over my heart. Fuck you and your flowers. Fuck you for thinking your dick is the fucking magic pill to make it all go away.*

Right now, I wanted him to suffer. And there was only one way I knew how.

"Leda," he growled, his eyes finding mine. "What are you doing?"

"Didn't you want to fuck?" I snarled through gritted teeth, my heart racing. When he had pushed me against the wall, I thought I was about die. Then he ripped my yoga pants open, and fucked me like I was just his property.

The way that he kept fucking me no matter how hard I struggled under him. No matter how hard I cursed him.

I hated to admit that it had turned me on more than anything else we'd done.

And now I had him in the palm of my hand.

"Shut your fucking mouth." I pushed at his shoulders.

I didn't care that we were outside or that if anyone heard my screams. *Let them hear me scream. Let them think he's raping me. Or killing me.*

To my surprise, he obliged, and I mounted his now-hard cock, shuddering as his familiar presence filled me again.

He was growling something as his hands reached up to grab my hips. I didn't want to think about what he was saying. Sex was the only constant with us, the only thing that didn't require feelings or talking, for that matter.

I pushed his hands away.

The message was clear.

*Fuck you. This is for me. Not for you.*

So, I rode him, rough and fast. I heard a sharp intake of his breath before I felt his hands reach up to grab my breasts cruelly. He felt it, too, the *need* for both of us to hurt each other.

Not only physically. I wanted to punish him for every tear that I had shed over his cruel, hateful words, every lie that had crossed his lips, and he wanted to punish me for making him feel like he was anything other than a Don who had to be in control.

We were quite the pair.

I picked up my pace, and felt another orgasm making its way from deep within my core. The way he squeezed at my tits. The way he matched me, stroke by stroke. It was too much.

*Fuck you! Fuck you! Fuck you!*

When the orgasm hit, it fucking *hit*. It swept through me like a hurricane raking at the coast. I couldn't suppress the shriek of pleasure rising from my mouth even if I tried. I squeezed my eyes shut.

His hand moved up to cover my mouth. Without thinking, I bit his finger.

Lucas roared underneath me and I felt a sharp sting on my cheek.

Stunned, I stopped moving, and my eyes flew open at the realization that Lucas had slapped me.

I liked it.

I liked him.

I hated him.

I loved him.

The initial shock turned into anger. My hand reached up and felt something wet and when I pulled away, I saw blood. I looked down again and the finger I bit was bleeding.

Without thinking, I slapped him back. The sting of his face on my palm probably hurt me more than I could hurt his stupidly handsome face.

His eyes hardened and his look turned feral. His hand returned to my hips and I screamed as he thrust roughly into me, rattling my teeth as he made me bounce atop of him.

"You want it rough, you bitch?" he asked, his hands guiding me up and down on his hard cock. "You want to take control? Fucking do it! Show me that you deserve to take control!"

The words went in one ear and out the other. I knew how he felt about me from the way he fucked me.

This was nothing more than a game between us. One of us was going to win, and neither of us was about to give up. This was crazy, but I wanted more.

I wanted him to hurt.

I wanted him to feel the pain. When his hands tried to move from my hips to my breast, I grabbed them and pinned it at his side.

"No! You don't get to fucking touch me like that!"

Lucas's eyes flashed with something more than just sexual heat, and he tried to wrench free from my grip. Anger gave me a strength I never knew I had.

I kept him pinned while I rode him like he was the last man on earth, teasing him while torturing myself to the endless waves of pleasure that threatened to overwhelm me.

It wasn't going to be like the others. It was going to be more.

The heat curled in my stomach, and I watched Lucas's jaw clench, seeing the warring struggle he had going on inside him. "Leda," he warned, moving his hand a fraction of an inch underneath mine. This was likely killing him, not having any way to take control, and it made me want to draw this out as long as I could.

I liked Lucas like this, nothing like the strong, proud don I knew him to be.

I wanted him under me. At my mercy.

"You will come like this," I seethed as I rocked against his hard cock. "Or not at all."

He swore, sweat dotting his forehead, and my arms started to strain against his. Though I wasn't holding him hard, he was following my commands.

He was letting me take control, and something broke loose inside me. Lucas trusted me, and while it should have been a victory, I felt like it was something akin to sadness instead.

"You bastard," I whispered, letting my guard down for a moment as my world swam behind a veil of tears. "You fucking bastard!"

Lucas's hard eyes found mine. "Look at you," he answered roughly, withdrawing himself the best he could with me sitting on top before he was thrusting into me again. "Mine."

Oh God. I was his, completely and fully. It made me elated and angry, torn and content.

"Fuck you! I'll never be yours."

His lips curved into a smug smile, and I felt myself start to lose control. "Yes, you fucking will be, Leda, even if you don't know it yet."

I shifted my hips suddenly, hating the way his words made me feel. He wasn't wrong. I was going to lose myself to him.

"That's it," he urged, matching his hips to my rhythm. "Show me how much you belong to me. Take it out on me. You fucking love this, don't you?"

The word *love* shot through me like a bolt of lightning, and for a moment, I felt it in his voice, in the way he was giving it to me as much as I was taking it. Grunting, I closed my eyes and decided that I had tortured us both enough.

So, I let go, crying out his name as I flooded him with my orgasm. His raw cry followed a moment later, pouring into me for the second time tonight. For a moment, I felt him touch my soul, tainting it with his touch.

It angered me, knowing that no matter what Lucas did to me, I was deeply, irrevocably in love with him.

He could ruin me, and I would love him still.

Did it make me weak? I didn't know.

Angry with myself, I pushed off his body suddenly, not caring that his seed was running down my thigh. This had gotten out of control. I was supposed to hurt him, but somehow I was the one suffering for it.

My heart ached in my chest, but it wasn't the only thing.

"Get out." I sobbed.

Lucas pushed up to a sitting position, his expression hard. "What?"

"Get the fuck out!" I yelled, my voice breaking.

I didn't want to fall apart in front of him, but this was too much.

What we had done was too much.

His jaw clenched, but Lucas rose to his feet and tucked his cock back in his pants, zipping them up in jerky movements that made me flinch that he could hurt himself. He was a hot mess, his clothing wrinkled from my attack on his body, and he looked nothing like the cool, calm man I once knew.

If nothing else, he looked just as confused as I felt.

"This isn't over between us," he said softly, raking a hand through his hair. "But I will give you this one night, Leda. After that, I'm not walking out again."

I couldn't even look at him right now. My body was shaking from what we had just done, and I knew he was doing the same.

Something had passed between us tonight, something that was hard to process, and right now, I didn't want him here. I wanted to be alone.

"Just leave," I said tiredly, biting my lip and looking out over the city. "Please."

I felt Lucas draw close to me, and his lips brushed my temple. It was a tender gesture, one that brought tears to my eyes.

But before I could say anything, he was gone, and the terrace door closed a moment later.

# Chapter 52
## Leda

I didn't say anything as he walked back into the penthouse, waiting until it was clear that he had left before I slumped against the wall, tears falling on my cheeks. There was no doubt about it. I fell for my captor, the man who should be my sworn enemy.

I shouldn't want him to come back and wrap me in those strong arms of his, to soothe this horrible ache inside me that I knew he caused.

I hated him and hated myself for letting this spiral out of control like it had. Maybe if it hadn't done so, I wouldn't have just lost the last piece of my heart that I had been holding onto.

I angrily wiped at the tears with my hands, leaving my torn yoga pants on the floor as I stripped off the remainder of my clothing and slid into the hot tub, hissing as my sore body collided with the hot water. I tried not to think about where Lucas would be staying the night again, much like I had thought about last night, or if he was going to be safe.

Of course he was safe. He had his guards, but my heart still worried, and I hated it.

Reaching up, I touched the cheek he had slapped. Normally I would have been appalled by his slap. But this was different.

There had been a look of horror on Lucas's face when I looked down immediately after the slap. That look told me that he hadn't done it in any other manner other than losing momentary control. I doubted he would raise a hand to me again unless I asked him to.

And the kiss he left on my temple afterwards. There was still affection in him. Deep down, I knew he cared for me. Maybe it wasn't love like normal people had, but it was his own fucked up way of telling me he loved me. I knew that.

It elated me and saddened me both at the same time. Mainly because I knew I never had all of Lucas. There was a piece of him that he was holding back, one that was likely the culprit for the past twenty-four hours.

So, what was I going to do about it?

The stars twinkled in the sky overhead as I leaned back, sliding my entire body into the hot tub. That was the problem. I didn't know what I was going to do with Lucas, with any of this. What if, after tonight, Lucas turned around and gave me over to my father as he had planned?

What if he decided that I wasn't worth the trouble?

My heart, my entire existence, wouldn't be able to take it.

"Oh God," I whispered, closing my eyes against the new onslaught of tears. I didn't belong here.

I didn't belong anywhere.

Everything was still up in the air regarding not only this precarious situation I found myself in with Lucas, but also the small chance that he might not want me around. And that meant I would be turned back over to my father.

No. No, I couldn't let that happen.

By now my father must have known what was going on, what Lucas had done, and more importantly, what he had done to me. I was soiled goods, no longer the good little Mafia daughter that would have been a prize catch for her handpicked husband.

He would likely kill me after he killed Lucas first. The thought caused me to swallow hard. I had to protect the Don that had bought me.

Lucas didn't know who he was up against in my father. Even from behind the iron bars, Carmine D'Agostino was dangerous.

I couldn't let anything happen to Lucas, which meant I had to fight like hell to stay in his life. This had only been the beginning of something between us. It had to be.

The storm of thoughts that swirled in me when he slapped me returned, and I confronted the ugly reality before me: I was in love with him.

"Ugh," I groaned, pushing myself out of the hot tub and grabbing one of the nearby towels already laid out.

I needed to pull myself together for when Lucas did come back, because he had promised that he would. This wasn't over between us.

Not by a long shot.

## Chapter 53
## Lucas

After another shitty night on the yacht alone, I woke with a clearer understanding of my feelings for Leda.

I was falling for her, if not already in love with her. The thought was terrifying. But the way that we had acted toward each other last night had only cemented that reality.

Too bad I wasn't able to tell her the truth.

As I nursed my hangover, I thought about everything that had happened in the last twenty-four hours. Nothing yet from Adrian about Enzo's death. That had been a rash act. It was an escalation, and only time would tell if it was truly necessary. I had fired the first shot—figuratively and literally—in the war that would rip apart the Cavazzo Mafia.

It would accelerate Adrian's plans to seize control.

I needed to focus on what mattered most. The longer I held onto Leda, the less likely the two of us would survive the coming storm.

Rubbing a hand over my face, I stared at myself in the bathroom mirror. I looked and felt like total shit. The man in the mirror who returned my stare was a man hell-bent on recovering what was lost to him, but at a loss on how to do so.

I wanted to go back in time and take back every second of the other night when I thought it was a good idea to hurt Leda in a pathetic attempt to push her away.

And last night…

I looked down at my finger. The wound left by her teeth was angry and red. It started to scab over, but it was a reminder of just how far either of us was willing to go to hurt each other.

How far I went.

I took a deep shuddering breath and closed my eyes, only to immediately open them as the room started to spin.

She made me lose control. And in that single moment of weakness, I had put my hands on her in a way that I never thought I would.

The moment she bit me, reason went out the window and I reacted on instinct. *Retaliate*.

I hadn't meant to slap her, and once I did, there would be no going back.

The thing was: she *liked* it. No matter how much she cursed me, I knew that deep down, she craved it. It was the same dark streak that I saw in Leda the first time I made her submit. The same dark streak that liked the violence and rough sex that most shied away from.

I wasn't the only one who lost control last night.

She had been like a wildcat, and gave everything to me. Though I had walked away last night, physically sated, I woke this morning with a gaping hole in my heart that I knew only she could fill.

The truth was: I wanted her completely, heart and soul. I wanted there to be no doubt that she was mine.

But I couldn't figure out how to fucking keep her.

"Fuck," I muttered before splashing water on my face to clear my head.

Life hadn't been this complicated before she became a part of it. I shouldn't have made that decision when I saw her on the auction block. She was supposed to be a tool. Instead, she stole my heart.

Love wasn't something I had bargained for. It wasn't something that I wanted to feel. Feelings were a weakness in my world, and the very thought of having a weakness meant that I couldn't be a Don effectively.

Cosimo had been clear on that very point the last time we had discussed the meaning of power. He eschewed all weakness, and tossed aside anything that could have been used against him. Yes, he had had dalliances and illegitimate children, but the man lived and breathed the Mafia.

Which in turn, I was supposed to do the same.

But now, I realized just how fucking lonely of an existence all of this would be.

But what choice did I have? If I couldn't hold my title as Don, I would have no means of defending myself or Leda. I had a dilemma on my hands, a choice to make. And no matter which one I picked, I would lose the other.

I didn't want to push Leda away. I tried, and realized the pain was worse than anything else in the world. It was hell sleeping on this yacht without her, with the only consolation being the knowledge that she was safe in my penthouse.

I hadn't resorted to watching the live security feeds of my place yet. But another night alone, and I might be turning them on.

A knock outside of my bedroom door demanded my attention and I took a deep breath, swallowed two Advils to deal with the pounding headache, and grabbed my suit coat from the bed where I had laid it earlier.

I was all business when I opened the door, and found Rocco standing there.

"What?"

"Emil is here," Rocco said dryly. "He says he needs to talk to you."

I shrugged on my coat, adjusting the cuffs. "Then by all means, let's talk."

If Emil was here, something was wrong, and my gut twisted at the thought. I would bet this yacht that it was something I wasn't going to like.

Rocco showed me to the upper level of the yacht, where Emil stood at the railing. Another summer storm was brewing in the distance over New York harbor, and the air felt heavy with the threat of rain.

"Emil," I greeted him.

"Don," he replied as he turned to me and dipped his head. "I went to the penthouse, but the guards said you were here."

"This couldn't have been a phone call?" I asked.

"I figured it was best to tell you this news in person."

*Well, fuck.* "All right," I said. "What do you have to tell me?"

Emil's jaw clenched. "Someone has been in the vault."

I felt a chill cut through me. The vault was just a name for a locked storehouse deep in the city that I kept a small surplus of money and weapons in. It was my last-resort stash, in case I needed some reserves in a deal or bribe. The cache was also meant to be an emergency fund.

"How much was taken?" I asked lightly.

Emil swallowed. "All of it."

"Are you sure?"

Emil nodded. "I went there myself to check. There's nothing left."

I turned away from the railing, my fists clenched tightly. I wanted to hit something. The vault wasn't just money. It had plenty of weapons too.

*Adrian.* I immediately thought. *It had to be Adrian. He knew I caught onto his little operation and now he was hitting me where it hurt the most.*

Well, almost where it hurt the most.

"The cameras were disabled," Emil continued. "And the memory wiped from the access panel. Whoever did it was thorough. The discs were burnt to a crisp and sitting on a pile of magnets. No way to recover them."

His voice trailed off as I stared at the city in the distance. A streak of lightning flashed in the distance. War was coming. I was sure of it.

"Who else knows?" I asked.

"Just the three of us," Emil stated. "And whoever pulled the shit. I haven't made my rounds yet, but if I had to guess, I'd say Adrian and the boys in the Battery as well."

So it was going to be like that. Maybe I should've taken Rocco's advice from the get-go. Cruelty rather than leniency.

"That's not all."

I turned to face him. "What?"

He didn't flinch at my hard words. "Three of our spots in the Lower East were hit last night right as they were closing. Cash drawers were taken. Two guards killed."

Fuck me. Adrian was moving fast. I turned and put my fist through the nearest window, the glass cutting my knuckles on impact. I barely felt the pinprick of the cuts as the glass slid through my skin. Bitterness ran through me. In just a few days while I was distracted by Leda, Adrian had managed to take advantage of my absence.

My plans were falling apart at the seams, and there seemed to be nothing I could do.

*No.* I refused to give up. Not now. I might not have been the pick Adrian and the traitors wanted to take Cosimo's place, but the old man wanted me there. No one was going to stop me.

"Double the guards," I said, not bothering to stop the steady flow of blood dripping from my fist. "And put out the word. From this moment on, Adrian is now *persona non grata*. If anyone, and I fucking mean anyone, is caught working on his orders, they'll answer to me personally."

"Yes, Don," Emil said. "I'll put the word out. Anything else?"

"Get a list of who's still loyal. Tell the Lower East capos to be ready for war."

*I want Adrian's head on a platter.* I thought bitterly. *I want all of the traitor capos dead, and their bodies hanging off the Brooklyn Bridge.*

He had pushed me too far, or maybe I had let him get away with shit that I should have stopped months ago. I wanted peace, but trying to keep the peace was proving to be nothing more than a losing battle.

Rocco held out a towel to me. I took it and nodded in gratitude. "That'll be all. Get to it. We don't have much time."

"Yes, Don."

Emil took his leave, and I was alone on the deck of the yacht with Rocco. I couldn't help but glance at the city towards the direction of my penthouse. Anger dissolved into something else, something akin to weariness.

I knew I wasn't the Don that these fuckers wanted. But now that I was in the position, I wasn't about to lose it. Adrian thought he could just run his fucking mouth, and replace me at the first sign of weakness?

No, he just kicked the hornet's nest.

I wanted to kill him. I wanted to put him in a shallow grave and piss on his corpse. There would be no turning back now.

"Let's go." I said to Rocco.

"Where?"

"City. We're going to sit down with Adrian and talk terms of his surrender."

## Chapter 54
## Lucas

As Rocco drove me into the city, my cell rang. I looked down at the caller ID and felt my blood pressure spike.

*You little shit.*

"Don Valentino," Adrian said cheerily when I answered. "I trust you got my message?"

"Yeah, I got your fucking message," I growled as the car weaved through the crowded streets of Manhattan. "Funny thing. I was just about to give *you* a call. We need to talk. Face to face."

I wasn't surprised when he chuckled into the phone. "Of course, Don. I move at your command. But I just wanted to say that I did warn you about what would happen if you didn't get rid of the D'Agostino bitch."

*You shut your fucking mouth.* My fist balled.

"What I do in my personal life is none of your business."

"None of my business?" Adrian asked. "I warned you that you brought down the wrath of Carmine D'Agostino down on our collective heads the same day you bought her. But you didn't listen. And now, I hear that Enzo's been murdered, places in the Lower East were hit, and God knows what else happened since then. Carmine is pissed, and he won't stop until you bleed."

*Carmine? Or you?*

"Are you trying to tell me that I'm not doing my fucking job?" I asked hotly, hating that he could easily get under my skin in a short time.

"I'm telling you that there are consequences to your actions, Don." Adrian replied smoothly. "That's all. Me and the boys down at the Battery are worried. I mean, if we were going up against Carmine's son, I'd be less worried. But word on the street is the old man is back in the driver seat. So forgive me for taking some… precautions."

He was baiting me again. By now he knew I would have been briefed on the robbery and the attacks on my own businesses. Instead of waiting for me to bring them up, he was front-running it. As for the "precautions" he was talking about…

He might as well have admitted to me that he was stealing. I refrained from saying what I really wanted to say.

It wasn't the right time, not yet.

"I think you need to start choosing," Adrian continued. "Between loyalty to the *family* and that bitch you are hanging onto. The Mafia needs a leader in this time of crisis. Wouldn't you agree?"

A leader? The Mafia was barely hanging on because he refused to acknowledge me as the true Don, and if Adrian continued to press his claims, the whole ship could go down from his tantrum. All this talk of loyalty, and family was just hot air.

I definitely should have killed him when I had the chance.

"Look, it's simple," he said. "You give the boys a sign that you're willing to do what's right for the Mafia. Put her back on the block and let someone else buy the used goods. It will show that you are as ruthless and pragmatic as my uncle was. Get rid of her, and Carmine will back off. Get rid of her, and we'll all go back to being one big happy family getting stinking filthy rich.

"Isn't that what you want?" He pressed me. "To be a ruthless Don, respected by all?"

I did want to be a ruthless Don. But not if it came at the cost of giving up Leda.

"Think about it," Adrian said after a moment. "I would hate for something else to happen to our family. These next few days are about to get *wild*."

He ended the call, and I tucked the phone back into my pocket, ignoring Rocco's probing stare in the rearview mirror. I was in no mood to tell him the thoughts running through my mind.

Adrian wasn't wrong, and that was the truth that hurt the most of all. If I wanted to stay on as Don, I *had* to get rid of Leda. The division within the Cavazzo Mafia had its roots in half of the capos believing me to be some usurper. But the fear of retaliation from Carmine because I bought Leda was the water that allowed this division to grow.

*What other choice do I have?*

My stomach was in fucking knots at what I had to do next. I couldn't lose the Mafia. I wasn't anything without the family, and I had worked too fucking hard to get to where I was. The control was slipping through my fingers and the hole in my heart widened.

Leda had only been in my life for a short time, and in that time, I had somehow fallen heads over heels for her. But I couldn't pick her over the Mafia even if I wanted to. Not at this point with my back pressed against the wall. In the time that I spent with her, I had left my flank wide open.

And Adrian exploited it.

I underestimated him, and now I was about to pay the price for it.

It was a shit move to ignore business for the one person who gave me happiness, but business was what kept me alive. Between my heart and my life, I had no other choice.

I steeled myself against the overwhelming guilt and self-loathing that assaulted me. Hadn't I *just* resolved that I wasn't going to give her up? Didn't I already decide that she was worth fighting for?

*That was before you put yourself in this shitty position.* Cosimo's voice echoed in my ears. *You let a distraction take your eyes off the prize.*

The choice was clear.

I already broke her heart.

What I was about to do next would make her hate me.

But not as much as I would hate myself.

## Chapter 55
## Leda

Lucas found me seated on the sofa, my legs curled under me as I flipped through the channels on the massive TV. I was going through the motions and not paying attention to anything in particular. I hadn't slept well, tossing and turning alone in his massive bed with dreams of the things that we had done replaying in my mind.

Dreading the moment when he inevitably returned.

And now, he was here.

I felt my pulse start to race when he closed the door. My heart ached at the sight of him in his suit, his hair windblown from the storm that raged on outside.

It was perfect for both our moods.

"Leda," he finally said, hands in his pockets. "How are you?"

"Fine," I told him. My body was raw and sore from last night, and my cheek still smarted from his slap. But other than that, I was physically fine.

My heart on the other hand…

But I didn't want to talk to him about that.

Lucas eyed me for a few moments before he walked over and joined me on the sofa, leaning back against the cushions as he sank in.

I wanted to move over and curl against his side but stayed in my place, not sure what to say to him, really. Lucas had put me on an emotional roller coaster the last few days, and I wasn't sure if I was about to take another turn.

I wasn't sure if my heart could handle another turn.

"I'm sorry," he said quietly, his jaw clenched as he looked at me. "I'm sorry about last night and the night before that. I know you don't want to believe me, but I am, Leda. I never wanted to hurt you like that."

I felt the sting of emotion in my nose, and fought to keep tears from welling in my eyes.

"You probably fucking hate me for what I did," Lucas continued. "But you need to know that I'm terrified of losing you."

Clearing my throat, I forced back the tears. "I'm not going anywhere," I told him. It was the honest truth. No matter what went on between us, I didn't want to leave.

I didn't want to leave him. I wanted there to be something for us in the future, something that both of us could find peace in.

Lucas let out a ragged breath and turned his face away from me.

"You will."

I doubted it, but there was conflict in the expression on his face that I wasn't able to decipher. Something was wrong.

"Why?" I asked softly, hoping that my prying wasn't going to scare him away again.

He shook his head and I moved off the couch, walking over to stand in front of him.

"Lucas, talk to me."

His eyes followed my every move as I straddled him, clasping my hands to either side of his face. Up close, I could see the exhaustion in his blood-shot eyes, and my heart clenched just a bit tighter.

Lucas was still, barely breathing as I ran my fingers over his gorgeous features, from the high forehead to the tip of his chin, pressing my lips in random places on his face. My teeth scraped the underside of his jaw, and he groaned.

"Leda," he breathed, his breath fanning over my cheek. "Please don't do this. Not now"

"Lucas," I said against his skin, my hands sliding down to his shoulders. "I want to."

I wanted to just love him. My feelings had become pretty clear over the past few days, and no matter how much I really didn't want to love him, my heart knew what it wanted.

It wanted Lucas.

My fingers found the lapels of his suit coat, and I pushed at it. "Take it off."

Lucas awkwardly got his coat off with me seated on his lap, and worked on the buttons of his shirt. My heartbeat picked up as I feasted on his broad chest.

"You're beautiful," I told him.

And he was, scars and all. From the broad shoulders to the tattoo that licked up the side of his rib cage. I ran my hands over his biceps, and when I reached his forearms, Lucas shook his head.

"I'm not," he growled. "There's nothing beautiful about me, Leda. Nothing."

My hand found his belt. "I disagree."

A sad smile came to his lips, and I shook off the feeling of foreboding that had settled in my gut. Lucas wasn't being the flirty comeback guy I grew to know. He was seriously concerned about something. Something he wasn't ready to tell me.

Something that I was too afraid to ask.

So, I pressed my lips to his, threading one of my hands in his thick, soft hair as the other worked on the waistband of his trousers. To my surprise, Lucas didn't take over the kiss. Instead, he allowed me to guide him into what would happen next.

He did hiss in my mouth when I finally succeeded in getting his pants undone. My hand reached for his hard cock, and pulled it out into the open.

"Leda," he breathed against my lips as I traced him lightly. "Let me touch you."

"Not yet," I murmured, kissing him hard before sliding off his lap onto the floor in front of him. Lucas's nostrils flared when he realized what I was about to do, but he didn't stop me. He continued to allow me to touch him however I wanted, with my hands, my mouth, and my body.

I tasted him and he pulled me away from his cock carefully, his hand in my hair.

"Please," he whispered, his normally hard expression replaced with something that almost bordered on tenderness. "My turn."

My entire body flushed with heat as I backed away, and Lucas rose from the sofa, pushing me lightly on the shoulders so I would lie on the sofa's soft cushions. I shuddered as he pulled down the joggers I had on, a curse escaping his lips when he realized I didn't have any underwear on.

"You're so fucking beautiful," he said.

I knew he could see how wet I was, how I trembled as his hands slid up my calves to my knees before trailing across my thighs. When his lips met my skin, I let out a gentle moan, arching my hips toward him so that he would hurry up and sate the ache begging for release.

When his lips touched my inner thigh, my legs fell open in a silent plea. "That's it," Lucas breathed against my mound. "Open for me, my love."

*My love.* I couldn't process the words because his tongue was delving between my folds, and my thoughts scattered. Lucas licked me like I was a feast he had been waiting on all day, stroking my clit with his tongue until I sobbed his name, the pressure almost too intense for me to deal with.

When he inserted his finger, I lost it, my body putty to his touch. I was barely aware of Lucas pulling away from me, shedding his shoes and trousers before sliding between my thighs.

"You are fucking gorgeous like that," he rasped, his eyes roving over my naked lower half. "Your skin flushed and ready for me to fuck you."

I squirmed under his intense stare. "Then what are you waiting for, Lucas?"

He shook his head. "Nothing. Just admiring the view for a little bit longer."

There was something almost sad about his expression, and I realized I had never seen Lucas like this. "Lucas?"

He shook out of the look, pushed my legs open, and positioned himself. "Let me love you."

I gasped as he pushed inside me, and a tear came to my eye. This felt *right*. "Oh," I breathed. "Lucas."

My eyes closed, and I was only aware of him inside me. His hands were clenching my hips, but not in the possessive way that I knew him. They felt gentle, like he was holding something delicate. In that singular moment, I felt complete.

This was us. The way Lucas made me feel was everything.

I opened my eyes and found Lucas looking down at me, sweat dotting his forehead as he moved within me slowly, as if he were savoring every moment. One of Lucas's hands pushed up the sweatshirt to bare my naked breasts, his hand trailing up to touch me. A thrill of pleasure shot through me, and I gasped as I clenched around his cock, angling my hips higher so that he could touch the very core of my body.

"Leda," Lucas ground out before he crushed his lips against mine and took my breath away.

He picked up the pace as we explored each other's mouths. Our limbs and bodies tangled into a hot sweaty knot. I reached up to caress him. Bit by bit, his pace became more erratic. He tried to slow down, as if he wanted the moment to last just a little bit longer. But he had already crossed over the edge. A moment later, there was a guttural groan that escaped his perfect mouth. His body slid against mine as he collapsed into me.

I gasped, not from the weight but from the way I felt. From the way we felt.

This was making love.

When Lucas finally rolled off me, I looked up at the ceiling with a stupid grin on my face. I felt like I had just run a marathon. Not physically, but emotionally.

It wasn't a bad feeling.

Rising on my elbows, I watched as Lucas's naked form gathered his clothing, his nearly perfect ass on full display.

"Lucas, I—" I wanted to tell him that I loved him, but when he turned back to look at me, there was an unmistakable sadness in his expression.

"Get dressed," he stated. "We have to go."

"Okay," I swallowed, pushing myself off the sofa. "Are you all right?"

He grasped me by the waist as I reached for my joggers, and pulled me against his body, facing away from him.

"I will be," he said, brushing his lips over the side of my neck. "Please remember this time between us, Leda. Please."

My knees weakened. "I won't forget it, I swear."

His kiss was quick before he let me go. I sucked in a breath, already missing his touch.

I might remember his words, but the worry didn't ease in my stomach.

## Chapter 56
## Leda

After changing into a pair of tight leather pants and an off-the-shoulder top just in case I needed to make an impression, I walked out of the bedroom to find Lucas standing before the windows. He had a glass of whiskey in his hand.

For a moment I just stared at him, my heart thudding something fierce at the love I had for him. It was crazy, of course, to think that I could love the man who had bought me, the man who took my innocence, but I did love him.

I could feel it in my very soul. I wanted to protect him to the ends of the earth to keep him from being hurt. I wanted to heal the hurt in his heart.

And there were a lot of unresolved hurt. I needed to peel back the layers if he was ever going to open to me completely and without regret.

But it was something I was willing to do.

For him.

So, I walked up to him and wrapped my arms around his waist, placing my head on his back so that I could hear his heartbeat beneath the layers of clothing.

"I love you," I said softly, my voice barely above a whisper. "I don't know why I do, but I do, and I'm willing to do whatever it takes to keep you, Lucas." I felt like he needed to hear me say it.

Lucas shuddered in my arms, surprising me before he was pulling away. "Come," he said softly, refusing to meet my gaze. "We're late."

I swallowed, dropping my arms. It was okay. Whatever was worrying him was going to be just fine. I wouldn't let him go at it alone.

There was a car waiting when we exited the building and I climbed in, Lucas following me. His second-in-command Rocco was sitting in the passenger seat and gave me a small nod before the car pulled off.

Lucas reached over and pulled me against him, wrapping his arm around my waist so that I would be pressed against his side. Inhaling his scent, I allowed my head to rest on his shoulder, my thoughts going a million miles an hour about where he was taking us.

This new Lucas—worried and reserved—wasn't the man I was used to. And if he was worried, then I should be as well.

What if he was taking me to my father? Surely not. If he was going to do it, I would think that Lucas would have already done it by now.

Besides, he had told me he loved me, right? From the way he held me, I came to the conclusion that he had no intention of having me go anywhere else but right next to him.

Especially now that he was pressing his lips into my hair, drinking in my scent like I was doing with his. Closing my eyes, I tried to remember this feeling, just in case it was my last.

I must have drifted off because of Lucas's body warmth because the next time I opened my eyes, the car had stopped. Lucas was still holding onto me.

"Where are we?" I asked. "Are we here?"

"Leda, I—" Lucas started, sliding his arm away from me. "I'm so sorry."

Puzzled, I tried to catch his eye, but all he did was open the door and climb out, leaving it open for me to follow. When I stepped out, it took me a moment to realize where I was and I pushed down the panic rising in my throat.

No. No. *No!*

He wouldn't take me back here. He couldn't.

Now it all made sense. The way he was acting, the final love declaration.

He broke my heart all over again.

And this time, there wouldn't be any pieces left to put back together.

## Chapter 57
## Lucas

This was too fucking hard.

I clenched my jaw tightly, not wanting to look back at Leda now. I heard the gasp of recognition. She knew where we were, and all I really wanted to do was push her back into the car and drive off.

But as my fucking heart wanted to do one thing, my brain reminded me that this was the only choice I had.

I hated it. I hated myself.

*I'm sorry, Leda. I'm so fucking sorry.*

"Lucas?"

Turning, I found Leda staring at me, her face pale. "What are we doing here?" she whispered.

"Leda, I—" I started, not sure what to tell her.

How could I tell her that she was the most important thing in my life, but I had to give her up? How could I even *look* at her right now, knowing I was about to hand her off to another fucking Don?

My hand clenched in a fist. Leda was mine. But I couldn't keep her right now. No matter how much I wanted to.

"Lucas, why are we here?" Leda's head shook slightly. "Lucas, please. Why are we here?"

I could hear the unmistakable panic in her voice tugging at my heartstrings.

I closed the distance between us, fighting everything I had not to touch her. Because I knew that the moment I touched her, I wouldn't be able to do what was necessary.

"Tell me this is some sick, twisted joke," she continued. "Tell me that you are going to tell me to get back in the car, Lucas.

"Tell me that this isn't happening!"

"I'm sorry," I told her, every word a dagger stabbing into both our hearts. "I have to."

Leda's eyes widened, and she took a few steps back.

"No, please don't do this. Whatever I did, I won't do it again. Please don't put me back there. Please!"

The terror in her voice was real, and I hated it. I couldn't comfort her. Hell, I didn't know what she was about to face out there or who would be the one to take her. I couldn't tell her that this was tearing me in two, that I hated this more than anything else in the world. I didn't want to give her up.

Some would call me a coward, and maybe I was.

"You didn't do anything wrong."

Tears sparkled in her beautiful eyes. "You lied!" she cried. "You said you would protect me!

"You said you loved me!"

*I did. I do.*

That was what she didn't understand, and I didn't expect her to, but I loved her to the point of it physically hurting. Adrian wasn't going to stop, and he was demanding for me to make a point with Leda, to save the Mafia.

Without that, Adrian would destroy me. And it wouldn't matter then if Leda was with me or not. Her death would be nearly guaranteed.

"I'm so sorry, Leda," I told her. "I truly am."

I nodded at Rocco. I couldn't bring myself to touch her again.

Rocco gently grabbed her by the shoulder, and she physically tried to fight him.

"Let's go, girl," he stated, grabbing her wrists and placing the zip tie there.

She called my name, called for me to save her, to take her away from here. Instead, I turned away. I had to turn away. Her voice was breaking my own heart. Her despair was ripping out my very soul.

By the time I got to the door, I had composed myself, sliding behind the mask of indifference. This shit better work, or I was going to tear Adrian's limbs from his body.

"Good evening, Don Valentino," the auctioneer stated when I reached the double doors leading to the auction room. "I'm surprised to see you bringing your purchase back yourself."

"I have a special interest in this one," I replied evenly. "To see where she goes, of course."

The auctioneer didn't even bat an eye. "Of course. You know the rules, Don Valentino."

I held up my arms and allowed the wand to be dragged over my body, ignoring the way that the bouncer at the door patted me down. No weapons were allowed in the auction room. Otherwise, it would be the perfect place to carry out a hit or to get rid of an enemy.

As much as I hated to go in blind, what they didn't realize was that I was just as dangerous with my bare hands as I was with any weapon. Cosimo had molded me into an enforcer that needed neither steel nor bullets to kill someone. Those very skills would be used tonight.

"He's clean." the bouncer grunted and stepped back.

"Well then," the auctioneer replied, tapping her red nail against her tablet. "All I need is your thumb, Don Valentino."

I pressed my thumb to the screen, and watched for the green light.

When it happened, the auctioneer stepped back with a satisfied nod. "Go right on in. Enjoy your night."

I pushed the door open and stepped into the velvet opulence that was the auction house. Every don was given admittance as long as he followed the rules. Cosimo had left me his card to show on my first visit. The last time I was here was when Leda had gone up for auction.

And now I was back, about to watch her go up on that block again. I didn't know how I was going to handle it.

There were curved black sofas in the greeting room, but I bypassed them, ignoring the looks as I walked through.

"Something to drink, Don Valentino?" the bartender asked by way of greeting.

"Lagavulin, neat. Make it a double," I said. I wanted to forget everything that had happened from the time I climbed out of the car to now, but there wasn't enough alcohol in the entire fucking world for that to happen.

For the rest of my life, I would be haunted by Leda's devastated face and her desperate screams for me to save her. And the knowledge that I just watched as she was let go.

The bartender pushed the scotch in front of me and I took it in my hand, throwing it back in one swift gulp, not bothering to savor the taste. The liquor burned a fiery path down my throat, and I relished in it. Even if it wouldn't do anything to dull the pain, it sure was going to help me forget it for a while.

"Don Valentino."

I turned to find Don Salasito behind me, curiosity in his gaze. He wasn't much older than I was. But unlike me, he had gotten the title like many of the others here: through the death of his father. I really didn't like the fucker. His smile was too oily and his eyes roamed where they shouldn't. But he hadn't done anything to wrong me. Not yet. So I tolerated him.

"Don Salasito," I said.

"Are the rumors true?" He asked , motioning for a drink. "Did you bring the D'Agostino bitch back to the auction block?"

I clenched my hand to keep from wiping the grin from his face with my fist. "I guess you will have to wait like everyone else."

He chuckled as the vodka was pushed in front of him. "Frankly, I was surprised to hear she was still alive given your, well, your reputation. Tired of her already? What was she like? Tell me all the details. She looked like she can suck a mean dick."

*Fuck you.*

Scowling, I watched as the asshole picked up his drink. It would be so easy for me to smash the glass into his face, and draw a thin red line across his throat.

"That's none of your fucking business."

"Watch your mouth, Valentino.," The smile dropped from his face and all pretense of friendly banter disappeared. His hand clenched around his glass. "I've heard that your *family* isn't as strong as it once was. And don't think I forgot what you *really* are. You'll be back to turning old tricks real fucking soon."

I didn't react to his words. "Good to see you, too Salasito."

He didn't have a chance to respond.

The doors opened and captured the attention of everyone in the room. "The auction will begin momentarily."

It was time. I followed the crowd into the room and took my customary stance in the back of, crossing my arms over my chest. I fucking hated everything and everyone in this room right now.

It wasn't long before the auctioneer took her place, smiling at the crowd.

"First up, one that has been here before with us, and we are pleased to see her again."

I swallowed hard as Leda was pushed out onto the stage, wearing a black silk negligee. It took all I had not to rush the stage and cover her with my coat.

Her eyes were searching the room. Was she looking for me? Would she hate me when she saw me? Fuck. She looked terrified, and this was all my fault. My stomach twisted in knots as the buzz about the room started to build again.

"Leda D'Agostino," the auctioneer stated, a cruel smile on her lips. "The bidding will begin at five million."

Far more than they had started out with the first time. There was a bite immediately, but I ignored the bid, watching Leda's face as she scanned the sea of faces before her. I didn't want her to see me. I didn't want to see the hope fade from her eyes when she did.

It was one of the main reasons I had stuck to the shadows of the back of the room.

"Eight million."

The voice caught my attention, and I frowned, searching the room myself now. *What the fuck?*

I had to be hearing things.

"Eight million going once!" the auctioneer called out. "Eight million going twice!"

I finally found the source of the voice, my blood raging. Adrian met my eyes and smirked, giving me a nod as the auctioneer indicated that Leda had been sold.

To him.

I pushed my way through the crowd and grabbed him by the hem of his shirt. "What the fuck are you doing here?" I seethed, keeping my voice low.

"I heard you put her back up on the auction block tonight," he replied, crossing his arms over his chest. "I had to make sure you had actually done it."

"You don't have eight million," I growled as the next auction started.

"Oh, I don't?" he challenged, a glint in his eye. "You know. Oddly enough, I suddenly came into quite a bit of extra money, you see. Just enough to buy Leda D'Agostino to make sure she doesn't end up in your bed again. You see, I had the good grace to ask her father for permission first." He leaned in, brushing imaginary lint from my shoulder. "So all of this? Done with the old man's blessing."

I didn't reply, stepping back so that I wouldn't be tempted to do something to him like bash his face in. "You lay a finger on her, and I will fucking kill you."

Adrian smirked. "She's mine now, Don. Surely you will respect that."

He didn't wait for my answer, walking away to pay his fees and gather his prize.

"Calm down," Rocco grabbed my arm. "You don't want to make a scene. Not right now."

"That fucking bastard," I seethed, my eyes still on the spot where Adrian had vanished to. "He played me like a fucking fiddle."

He wanted what I had. Not just the title.

Everything.

"You can't go after him," Rocco cautioned. "Not here."

He told me that giving up Leda meant peace within the Mafia. The fucker played me.

"Come on," Rocco was saying. "It's over. We gotta go."

But I couldn't, and he knew that. I had fucked this up. I had put Leda on that auction block because I thought it was the only option I had. Instead, I betrayed the one person I loved more than anything in the world.

And now, all I wanted was to get Leda back.

"Shit," Rocco swore. "You are going to do something that I am going to regret, aren't you?"

I ground out my jaw. "I have to."

"Like I said before," Rocco sighed. "You are going to be the death of me."

# Chapter 58
# Leda
*Moments Before*

"Let me go!" I yelled, trying to pull myself out of Rocco's grip as he marched me back into the one place I had hoped I would never see again.

"Listen, I don't know why he's doing this," the second-in-command said softly, for my ears only. "But he's got a damn good reason, so just be patient, all right?"

I didn't want to hear anything he had to say. Lucas lied to me. He had brought me back to the place where it all started, and I highly doubted that this time I would be looking at him at the end of the night.

The same old woman from what felt like a lifetime ago met us at the door. The disapproving glare on her face was the same as it had been. "You know the drill," she replied, throwing a small scrap of clothing at me. "Come on. You're late already."

This time I didn't argue with her, numb to the fact that I was going through this again. My clothing fell onto the floor in a tangled heap, and I slid on the thin, trying to keep myself together as I did so. Once I was dressed, she nodded. "Come."

I walked the familiar path to the stage, my feet barely making a sound on the cold floor. The auctioneer gave me a passing smirk, but I held my head high. Screw them all. It didn't matter. So what if Lucas had ripped out my heart and fed it to the room full of sharks?

So what if I had believed that he could be my future?

So what if I had thought that he was different?

He wasn't.

Lucas was just like the rest of them, and I should have known better than to trust him in the first place.

The lights were blinding as I stepped up onto the stage, barely able to make out the shapes of people beyond them. Was Lucas out there, watching this with a smirk on his face, knowing that he had won? I really wished I could see him now, so that he could see the anger in my eyes.

How much I hated him.

"First up, one that has been here before with us, and we are pleased to see her again," the auctioneer stated, catching my attention. "Leda D'Agostino. We will start the bidding at five million dollars."

The number didn't even faze me. Five million dollars. I had gone for twenty to Lucas.

A hysterical laugh bubbled up inside me, and I had to force myself to keep it down. Maybe if I broke down on stage, they wouldn't want me.

Probably not.

They wanted me for my name. Not how mentally stable I was.

I clamped my lips tightly together as the auctioneer droned on behind me, the bids coming quickly. Unlike before, I kept my head held high.

I was still Leda D'Agostino, a survivor for all those that thought they could destroy me. Whoever got me this time was going to find someone defiant, someone who wasn't going to just lie down and take it.

I scanned the room, hoping to catch a glimpse of Lucas. Not because I wanted him to be my savior, but because I wanted him to see just how much I hated him.

I wasn't going to open myself to anything or anyone ever again. Lucas had taught me a valuable lesson, and that lesson was never to trust anyone again.

"Eight million going once!" the auctioneer called out. "Eight million going twice! Sold for eight million!"

There were jeers, and the murmur rose, but I was already turning away, not caring who had bought me this time. It really didn't matter anyway.

I was alone in this fight.

But I didn't get far. The auctioneer stopped me as I passed, and before I knew it, there was a guard at my elbow, grabbing at my arm.

"Let's go, bitch," he said, tugging me away from the stage and back the way I had come. We passed the room that I had been undressed in, walking further down the corridor until I lost track of where we had turned. I briefly thought about asking him to let me go, telling him that I could pay him handsomely for it, but where would I go?

I wasn't safe anywhere, not with my father still alive and now an enemy of Lucas Valentino.

That had to be the only thought, after all. He had to hate me, not love me. Otherwise he would never have allowed me to be put on display like that, to be bought by some unknown person for their own personal enjoyment.

A person in love didn't do that. People in love didn't hurt each other.

They sure as hell didn't turn their backs on the person they loved. I had been prepared to do whatever it took to keep him safe.

Now, I wanted to kill him myself.

The grip on my arm tightened and I winced. My feet were cold against the wood floor, but hey, I had been here before.

I knew what was going to happen next, and this time, I wasn't so sure I would like the outcome.

The guard escorting me pushed me into a room, one that was different than the first one. "Don't cause any trouble," he growled before shutting the door.

I let out a crazed laugh, looking at the bed and extraordinarily little else in the room. Cause trouble? I was going to go insane, more like it.

Lucas had put me back up on the auction block. I still was having a hard time processing the fact, not to mention why he would do so in the first place.

Had his words meant nothing?

Had this all been a sick, twisted dream? I felt like it must have been. I felt like at any moment I was going to wake up and tell Lucas how crazy this was. That it was all just a sick nightmare.

But the cold air on my skin was real. The shiver in my body was real.

This wasn't a nightmare.

This was real, and the pain was real.

I hated the pain. I thought I had felt it all, but the way that Lucas had coldly walked away from me, letting his second-in-command take me to the same old woman who had forced me to dress like this…

He said he loved me, but then he did this? No wonder he had acted the way he had in the penthouse.

Lucas was saying goodbye. He knew all along that he was going to bring me here tonight. Yet he still allowed me to touch him—allowed me to think that we were making love. He gave me a single happy memory, and then cruelly ripped it all away.

A sob escaped me suddenly, and I clamped my hand over my mouth, forcing the rest to remain. It wasn't time to break down. Not yet. Not until I knew who bought me this time. I needed to find out if I was going to survive.

I refused to be a pawn any longer. I was going to put up the fight of a lifetime, one that would give me what I needed most.

I needed my freedom.

Or I would die trying.

Either way, I never wanted to see Lucas Valentino again.

Just thinking about his name hurt, but I forced it away. There would be time, if I could get out of here, to mourn the loss of the fleeting happiness I thought I had found with Lucas.

And plan his demise. One thing was for certain. Lucas had better stay far away from me in the future, or the next time I saw him, he might get a knife to the gut for what he had put me through. This wasn't love. I didn't know what his reasoning was behind it, but it wasn't going to be good enough.

I just hoped that it had been worth it for him.

Steeling myself against any further thoughts about Lucas, I did the same thing as before and looked for something I could use to defend myself against whoever was going to come through that door. There were no sheets on the bed. The bed frame itself was iron and bolted to the ground.

Aside from the black negligee I was wearing, I had nothing else.

Stupidly, I tried the door. It was locked from the outside. If I got out of this alive, I was going to go somewhere that no one could ever find me. I would change my name and just disappear.

Stepping away from the door, I ignored the bare mattress and chose to stand in the furthest corner instead. Maybe I would get lucky and my new owner would be old so that I could rush past him when he entered the room and find my way out of this hellhole.

Or maybe no one would come at all. Maybe this was Lucas's perverse game, one where he got his kicks by putting me up there repeatedly so he could purchase me.

At least I would know what to expect.

I hated this feeling. The anxiety for what was going to happen next was awful, but not as awful as feeling betrayed by the way that Lucas had walked away earlier.

It was like I didn't even matter to him.

It wasn't the same act he had put on back at the penthouse, but none of that mattered any longer. Right now, I was focused on making it through the next moment.

And after that, I was going to erase Lucas from my brain, my heart, and my body.

The door opened, and my hopes died as a guy around Lucas's age walked in, a smirk on his face. The door shut almost immediately, and I pressed myself against the wall, not bothering to move from my spot.

"Leda D'Agostino," he replied, his voice full of malice. "You are every bit like your father described."

I clenched my jaw, choosing not to respond. Maybe if I irritated him enough, he would leave me alone.

"You know," he continued, clearly not caring about my actions. "I've dreamed of this moment for quite some time. And I have to admit. You're no disappointment."

I didn't blink, hiding my fear from him. What the fuck was he talking about?

"And as much as I would have loved being the first man you fuck," he said after a moment, stripping off his coat. "It seems that the *whore* got to you first."

The whore? What was he talking about?

"That fucker," the stranger seethed. "A whore who thinks he was a Don. It should have been *me*. Not him. It was my uncle's legacy, and that senile old man just gave it away." His grin turned into a snarl. "But that doesn't matter right now, does it, Leda? You and I? We're going to have a *lot* of fun."

"Don't come any closer," I finally said, hoping that my voice was steady.

He laughed and stepped closer. "Did you tell him the same thing? Right before he fucked you bloody and raw? I promise you, I'm twice the man that whore is. Valentino will be nothing more than a smear in your thoughts when I finish with you."

His words were chilling, and I felt the first frisson of fear snake through me. Unless I was able to somehow get away from him and out of this room, I wasn't going to survive him. It was his snake-like eyes. Where Lucas showed me a degree of warmth, there was nothing of that sort in this man.

And the fact that he had a personal vendetta against Lucas made things even more complicated.

"Take off your fucking clothes," he sneered, reaching for the waistband of his pants. "I want to see what eight million looks like."

"No," I said bravely.

The back of his hand slapped me across the face. Hard. The coppery taste of blood filled my mouth. He laughed and flexed his hand. "That wasn't a request, you fucking cunt."

I didn't have much of a choice. Fighting back tears, I slid the thin straps off my shoulders and let the whisper of fabric slide down my body, not bothering to cover up any of my parts. I didn't want to give him any more excuses to hurt me.

"Oh very good, I can see why he was infatuated with you." He raped me with his eyes. I felt dirty and wanted to cower away from his gaze.

"On your knees. And open your mouth," he said after a moment, grabbing himself through the front of his pants. "Like a good little whore."

"You put that thing in my mouth and I'll bite it off." I shot back behind gritted teeth.

"What did you say?"

"I'll bite your fucking dick off."

He moved faster than I had anticipated, and pain bloomed in my stomach as his fist collided with my solar plexus. I fell to my knees. Nausea climbed my throat, and for a moment, I saw stars. The pain was overwhelming. He grabbed a fistful of my hair and yanked me up to meet his eyes. I saw the gleam of satisfaction in them.

"Open your fucking mouth," he said.

I spat in his face instead.

"You fucking cunt." He snarled.

Without warning, fingers wrapped around my throat and began to tighten. I clawed at his face, at his wrists, at whatever I could reach. But he refused to let go. I kicked out uselessly and only found empty air.

As my world started turning black, real fear shot through me. This wasn't a fight I was going to win. Tears threatened, and I forced them back, hating that I felt this way.

I was giving up. I had no options, no way out of this.

Nobody was coming to save me.

## Chapter 59
## Lucas

The auctioneer was the first person that crossed my path. "Don Valentino," she said smoothly, no hint of concern in her eyes. "I'm afraid you made no purchases this evening, so I can't let you go any further."

Rocco murmured something like a curse behind me.

"I'm afraid," I seethed, "that you will let me pass, or you will find yourself out of a job, madam."

She clearly was made of sterner stuff than most, likely because she dealt with assholes like me for a living. She didn't flinch at my harsh tone.

"You know the rules, Don Valentino. I can't change them, not even for you. Besides, you put the girl up. She's no longer yours."

Wrong answer.

Leda was mine; she was going to be mine for the rest of my miserable fucking life. I had made a mistake, a shitty one, but I was in the business of fixing my mistakes.

I grabbed the auctioneer by the neck and shoved her hard into the wall. The first flicker of fear crossed over her face as the façade of invincibility shattered before her eyes.

"What are you doing?" Rocco asked in a low voice. He knew the ramifications of what I was about to do and the shitstorm we would have to deal with later.

"Where is she?" I asked, keeping firm pressure on her neck. "Where did you put her?"

The auctioneer licked her lips, her eyes taking on a maniacal look. "What are you willing to do, Don Valentino?" she rasped. "Are you going to kill me? If you do, you will never find her."

I leaned in. "I will burn this fucking place down with you inside if you don't show me where Leda is." I solidified my request by tightening my hold, and she winced.

"Down the hall," she finally forced out. "To the right."

I let her go, her body crumpling to the floor as I started to move up the hallway. If Adrian was still in that room, he was going to be a dead man.

A hoarse cry went up behind us, and Rocco stopped. "I'll handle this. Buy you some time," he said urgently. "Go!"

"Start the car," I answered in a near growl. "We will be leaving as soon as I get Leda."

Rocco nodded and took off in the opposite direction of the hallway, leaving me to move forward. The sounds behind the doors as I passed them only sickened me further. I was going to burn this place down one way or the other.

I took a right at the end of the hallway and drew up short when a bouncer crossed my path.

"Out of the fucking way," I told him.

"Yeah, that's not going to happen." He grinned and I returned that grin with one of my own.

So be it.

With a roar, I was on him before he even realized I could move that quickly. Using the narrow corridor as leverage, I pivoted around him, pulling him down to the ground in a chokehold. As his body went limp, I gave his neck a hard twist. There was a sickening crunch, and it was all over. Without a second look back, I was already on my feet.

I hoped I wasn't too late. Fucking Adrian. He had planned this all along to get his hands on Leda, on the Mafia, and God knows what else.

He knew that I would give her up for the sake of the Mafia. He knew exactly which buttons to press. He knew I would fight for the title above all else.

What a fucking fool I had been.

A scream echoed in the air, and every hair on my body stood at attention.

Leda.

"No," I breathed as I followed the source, reaching the door that held her within. Wasting no time, I planted my boot into the wood and kicked hard, feeling the locks give way under the force of my kick.

I saw him first, standing over a kneeling, naked Leda with his hands wrapped around her neck. He was killing her.

I had put her in this fucking position, and I would spend a lifetime making it up to her.

Well, however long we had left.

"Get the fuck away from her," I snarled, catching Adrian's attention.

Adrian chuckled and let Leda go, causing her to slump to the floor. I saw the barest flash of metal in his hand and realized that he pulled out a knife, somehow smuggled into a place that was supposed to be weapons-free.

It didn't matter. I didn't need a knife to defend myself.

"Well, well," he said. "You made it, Lucas. I was wondering if you would be able to walk away."

"You fucking played me," I seethed as I removed my coat, throwing it in the general direction of Leda so she could put it on. "No more."

"You're so right," he replied, his eyes gleaming. "Because after tonight, I will be Don, you will be lying in a pool of your own blood, and I will fuck your bitch in front of your corpse."

I smirked, beckoning him forward. "Let's test that prediction then, shall we?"

Adrian's expression darkened and he charged at me, the knife extended. I moved quickly to avoid being slashed, kicking at his right leg so that I could get him on the ground. Grappling was where I was best at in hand-to-hand combat.

Adrian regained his footing nearly immediately and we clashed again, his knife slicing my upper bicep. I grimaced but caught him under his chin with the heel of my hand. His head snapped back as we both stumbled away from each other.

"Well played," Adrian laughed, looking at the tip of his knife. "Looks like I drew first blood."

I straightened my shirt like there wasn't a line of blood on my arm. "But I'll have the last laugh."

"I wouldn't have it any other way," he responded.

I narrowed my gaze and looked for a weakness in his stance, knowing that he had the same training I did, from the same person. We blocked each other's hits, my eyes ever watching where the knife was. He knew where to sever tendons, and if he did so, I would be helpless to fight back.

I wasn't about to go down like that.

The knife bit into my side and I hissed, knowing that cut was a little deeper than the one on my arm. It was a game Adrian was playing. Death by a thousand cuts. My shirt was growing sticky with blood, and by the look on Adrian's face, he knew that he just had to drag out the process.

Well, I wasn't going to let him win tonight.

I didn't even glance over to see how Leda was as I came at him with my fists raised, landing a few blows before feeling another sting on my upper thigh.

"What's wrong, whore? Looking a little slow there," Adrian taunted. His own face was a blooming red from my punches. His mouth was bloodied, and he was starting to favor his left side.

I, on the other hand, was dripping blood all over the floor from the various cuts Adrian had inflicted. I had to stop this shit now.

With a growl, I charged him, catching Adrian off guard as I did so. We crashed against the wall, the movement jarring my body, but it was enough to loosen Adrian's grip on the knife, sending it clattering to the floor.

Adrian's grin dimmed as he realized that he was now unarmed.

I kneed him hard in his balls and he doubled over. The moment was all I needed to grab the knife off the floor. In a flash, I plunged the knife into his thigh and pulled it back out. A spurt of blood emerged from the open wound.

It would have to do for now. I was growing weak, and if we didn't leave now, it would be too late.

Adrian bellowed with pain and rage as I hurried over to Leda. She had wrapped my coat around her naked form, her entire body quivering.

"Let's go," I told her urgently as Adrian tried to pull the knife out of his bloodied hand. "We have to go now."

"Lucas," she breathed, standing. "You're—"

"Don't fucking worry about me," I panted, hating that I had to be this way with her right now. My vision was starting to get blurry, and I was afraid that I would pass out if I didn't concentrate. "We don't have much time."

Luckily she heard the urgency in my voice, and together we started toward the door.

"This isn't the end!" Adrian yelled behind us.

I knew it wasn't and hoped that he would come after me. It would give me a chance to finish what I had started.

"This way," Leda finally said, leading me away from the way I had come in my disorientation. "It's the way they brought me in."

My heart twisted at her words, and if we got out of this mess alive, I would be begging her forgiveness.

Right now, I could barely feel my own legs. I felt like I was drunk, but it was just blood loss.

I stumbled into the hallway, and Leda let out a cry, tucking her arm around my waist to keep me upright. "Come on, Lucas!" She urged, propelling me forward. "It's not too much further. Just a little while longer."

"I'm sorry," I rasped, shaking my head to clear the sudden cobwebs. "I'm so fucking sorry." I wanted her to know that I hated every minute of what I had subjected her to, that it would be one of my biggest regrets.

"Apologize later," she responded, coming to a shut door. It only took a few tries to get it open, and the cold night air rushed in when we crossed over the threshold, not far from the entrance of the underground club.

"Goddamn it." Rocco swore the moment we rounded the small exterior building. "We got to go."

I let him take my weight, and he dumped me in the back seat, with Leda scrambling inside before the car was moving, tearing down the road. "Tell me what to do," Leda was saying, her hands roaming over my skin. "Tell me what to do, Lucas."

I opened my eyes, seeing her frantic gaze meeting mine. "Stop the bleeding."

She nodded and pulled the shirt out of my pants, tearing the fabric at the bottom. She balled up the fabric against my thigh and my rib cage. I groaned against the sudden pain, but now that I was lying down, my vision was clearer.

The problem was: we were still in danger.

Leda's face hovered over mine, pale in the dim lighting. "Why?" she asked tearfully. "Tell me the truth, Lucas."

Swallowing, I didn't turn away from her intense gaze. "I thought I had to choose. And I chose wrong."

Her eyes widened, but she didn't say anything, realizing what I was saying. It had been either her or the Mafia, but I couldn't have both.

Now that I had her, I made my choice, a choice that I couldn't go back on.

Because it was the right choice.

"Oh, Lucas," she said softly, some of the anger fleeing from her face. "Why didn't you just tell me?"

Yeah, I didn't know that answer either.

We fell silent the rest of the way to the docks, and by the time we pulled up to the yacht, the bleeding had slowed. Leda climbed out first, but it was Rocco that helped me out of the car.

"You look like shit," he said, grimacing as we made our way down the dock to the yacht.

"I know," I said instead, stepping down into the boat. "Get this thing out into the water quickly. Adrian will be coming."

Rocco frowned, but he nodded, and I grabbed ahold of the railing to steady myself, my body still weak from the blood loss. What I would like to do was to get Leda into bed and sleep for fucking days, but now wasn't the time.

I felt the engines start under my feet and continued to move inward, finding Leda standing right inside the outdoor living room area where I had had my discussions with Emil this morning. She was shivering in my coat, her hair blowing around her head.

I gritted my teeth. "You need clothes," I bit out. "Go to the bedroom and find some."

Leda turned to me, and there were tears on her cheeks. "Tell me that you love me," she whispered, her arms wrapped around herself tightly. "Because if you don't, I'm not coming with you."

"Leda," I growled. "This *isn't* the time."

Didn't she understand what I had just done? I just declared war with my own Mafia.

"No!" she shouted. "This *is* the time! You put me back on that block, Lucas! After you promised to take care of me. You were ready to give me up to those, those *animals*. He was going to kill me!" She marched toward me, not caring that I had just been in the fight of my life.

"So tell me that you love me. Because if you don't, I will jump from this boat."

"Fuck," I swore, reaching with my free hand to cup the back of her neck. "You have no idea, Leda, no fucking idea."

Her lips pressed into a thin line, and I sighed, pulling her closer.

"I love you," I growled. "Or else I wouldn't have come back for you."

It was true. I wouldn't have been able to leave that place without her by my side.

Leda was meant to be with me.

She rested her palm against my chest. "Alright. I'll come with you for now. Where are we going?"

I pulled away from Leda's touch, and cleared my throat. "Back upstate," I told her. "I can protect you better upstate."

Leda opened her mouth, but I placed my hand on her cheek, rubbing my bloodied thumb over her delicate skin. "I promise, Leda. I promise that I'm going to protect you. I know that my words may not mean anything to you now but it's all I have to offer. You are the only thing that matters right now, and I'll never let you go."

Her lips parted, but I was already hobbling away as the yacht started to pull out of the harbor. This was far from over.

## Chapter 60
## Leda

I didn't know what to think as Lucas hobbled away, blood sticking to his dress shirt. I had half a mind to go after him again. He had come. He had rescued me from that asshole who had purchased me, but at what cost?

Lucas had been specific in why he had put me up on the block to begin with.

The Mafia forced him to choose. And his first choice had been the Mafia instead of me. I could understand the decision. I could rationalize it. Hell, I grew up in a Mafia family. Without his family behind him, Lucas was just a man.

But that didn't make things hurt any less.

*But he came back.*

He had changed his mind, and ultimately his choice was me.

God, why did this have to be so confusing?

Blowing out a breath, I shuffled to the bedroom, shivering in his coat the entire way. When Lucas had busted down the door tonight, I knew that he knew he made a mistake. Everything he did up to that moment told me that he wasn't completely convinced he was doing the right thing.

And now, as we pulled away from New York on his yacht, I felt that he actually cared for me.

I yanked open the door to the bedroom that Lucas and I had shared and stepped into the warmth, stripping off his bloodied suit coat as I did. I wanted a bath, a long, hot bath to make me forget those cruel fingers on my throat. But given the urgency of the situation, there wasn't a lot of time to do anything other than hope that we could get somewhere safe.

Lucas was worried. I could see it on his face, feel it in his touch, and hear it in his words.

He was going to need me.

Quickly, I pulled out a warm pair of pants and a long-sleeved shirt, pairing it with a sweater while the yacht sliced through the water. I slipped on a pair of fur-lined boots, and I gathered my hair up in a ponytail to keep it out of my face the best I could.

Once I was warm, I made my way to the top deck, watching as the city disappeared in the distance. Thank God. I was done with this place for a while.

There was one thing I still needed to confront Lucas about, and it was the comments that the asshole had made about him.

*A whore who thinks he was a Don.*

It made no sense what he had said. I knew that Lucas's rise to his title wasn't the traditional route apparently.

But what did those words mean? Was that what Lucas refused to tell me?

And was it true that he lost all loyalty with his Mafia for me?

A secret thrill went through me at the thought. Maybe it was real. All of it. Maybe he did really care for me like he claimed. He made a mistake, but in the end, he chose me.

The object of my thoughts rounded the corner at that moment, and he stopped when he saw me.

He, too, had cleaned up, throwing on another long-sleeved shirt that wasn't smeared with his blood. He still looked pale, but I knew it was going to be a hard time to get him to slow down right now.

He believed we were in danger, and until we were safe, he wasn't going to listen to a word I said. "Tell me you bandaged the cuts," I finally said instead.

"Rocco did," Lucas replied, rolling his shoulders. His eyes looked at my neck, and I wondered if there were bruises there. "I'm so sorry, Leda."

It would take months for me to forget what that other man nearly did to me.

I wouldn't so quickly forget the way that Lucas had done to me either, but I felt safer with him right now. Despite everything he had done to me, I could still love him.

"Another time," I answered.

Lucas nodded, and turned back to look at the inky black water of the Hudson. The skyscrapers were moving past us.

"He's going to come after me," he said after a moment. "And when he does, I need for you to do everything I say, Leda. Promise me."

I swallowed hard. "Tell me that you will let me fight, Lucas." I was so tired of being the victim.

I wanted to show them all that I wasn't a wilting flower, that I could defend myself without their help.

That I wasn't weak like they all thought.

# Epilogue
# Lucas

I heard Leda's words, but they barely registered. Let her fight? I couldn't put her in danger like that. Whenever Leda was around, I couldn't think straight because I was worried about her and her safety. I wanted her out of danger so that I wouldn't have to worry about her, but it had no bearing on how strong she was.

She was the strongest person I knew.

"Having you out there fucking terrifies me," I told her honestly, forcing myself to look at her. "You don't know what it would do to me if something happened to you."

She was the weakness that I couldn't leave exposed. But she was also something I couldn't lock away. "It's not an option for me, Leda. I need you safe."

"Then let me help!" she exploded, throwing up her hands. "You have to trust me that I can take care of myself, Lucas."

Closing the distance between us, I grasped her upper arms lightly. "I do," I said softly, my eyes searching hers. "I do, but I just got you back. I can't risk losing you. Not now."

"Lucas," she breathed, tears glimmering in her eyes.

I couldn't help it. I pressed my lips against hers, wanting desperately to show her how much she meant to me, as well as the concern threading through my veins.

She didn't pull away from me, participating in the kiss like I had hoped she would, showing me that I hadn't screwed this up after all.

When we broke free, I pressed my forehead to hers, catching my breath.

"Please," I begged her. "Don't make me worry about you, Leda. If you are out there, I won't be able to focus."

I couldn't have her in the middle of the action and not seek her out. Besides, I wouldn't put it past Adrian to try and take her, considering I just stole her from him. He would be out to prove a point to me and to everyone else, which would make him reckless.

Dangerous.

"Fine," she finally said. "I will do what you say, but if you do anything like you did tonight, I will kill you myself."

Smiling, I nuzzled her cheek with my nose. "Never again. I will never give you up." And that was the truth. It fucking killed me to do it the first time. I never wanted to feel like that again.

Leda sighed, wrapping her arms around my waist and holding me against her. "We really have to work on this thing between us, Lucas. This isn't how normal people act."

I crushed her against me, burying my nose in her hair and drinking in her citrusy scent. "Darling, there's nothing normal about us."

She was a Mafia princess, one that was forever linked to an asshole hell-bent on making his comeback. I wasn't even from Mafia blood—in a position of rapidly cooling power with a Mafia that was far from stable.

I was a bastard, both ruthless and rotten to the core.

Yet Leda had found a way to love me. If I had been a better man, I wouldn't have pushed her away. But I did, and both of us suffered because of it.

Leda lifted her head, her beautiful eyes meeting mine. "Let's just say we have some work to do."

I smiled. This was why I loved her. This was why she was clearly the other half of my soul, the better part of me that I didn't know I needed.

Leda was everything.

"Boss."

I broke away from Leda and found Rocco standing behind me. "What?"

"He's got jet-skis," he said.

Adrian was coming for vengeance. And he brought an army with him.

"Find the guns," I told him, all warmth fleeing from my body. "We are going to need them."

Rocco nodded, and I turned back to Leda.

"They won't take us," I told her urgently, framing her face with my hands.

She trembled against my touch, and I wanted to soothe her worries, but there was nothing I could say to help her. This was reality.

"We will get through this." I promised.

"I know," she whispered, panic in her eyes now. "Please don't die."

I brushed off her concern. Hell, yeah, I was hurting, but it wasn't anything I hadn't felt before in my lifetime. Rocco had given me some pain meds to take the edge off, and luckily only the cut on my thigh had been deep enough for a few hasty stitches. I would be fine, and I had to ensure that she was going to be as well.

But die? Not yet.

"You are going into the hold." I took her arm and led her toward the set of stairs that would put her in the bowels of the ship, away from the gunfire. It was the safest place, unless the ship was sinking.

Leda fell quiet as we walked down there, and I opened the door, turning on the light as I did so. "There are some things already in place," I said. "Food, water, and some blankets."

She turned to face me, and I saw the worry clearly written on her face. "Stay," she urged. "You aren't in any condition to fight."

I wanted to stay with her, but that would be wrong. I was the Don. And it was time for me to law down the law for the mutinous members of my own Mafia.

"You'll be safe here." I drew out the gun I had tucked into my waistband after a change of clothes and handed it to her. "Here."

Leda took the gun, turning it over in her hand with a practiced gaze. I had no doubts that she knew how to use it, but didn't want to imagine a situation when she would need to.

"Lucas." She started.

"I have to go," I interrupted, brushing my lips over her forehead. There was so much I wanted to say to her, but there wasn't any time. If we were lucky, we would have time later on for me to explain my actions.

"I love you," she cried out as I turned to the door. "Promise me you'll come back."

I kept moving, emotion clogging my throat, and shut the door behind me. It felt good to know that she didn't wish for my death, but I still didn't deserve her love. I had fucked her over repeatedly, yet Leda still found it in her heart to love me.

It was something to sort out later, when we had a chance to.

Once I was up top again, I fished out my cell phone and dialed Emil's number.

"A little busy, boss. Shit's kind of fucked right now!" Emil said immediately.

I could hear gunfire in the background as Emil spoke.

This was a full-on fucking coup.

"Un-fuck it and do it fast!" I told him as I strode toward the back of the yacht. "Grab who you can and meet me upstate. We have a war on our hands."

"Yes, Don," he answered. "Working on it."

I ended the call and tucked the phone back into my pocket, reaching the back of the yacht. In the distance I could see the bob of lights, still too far to fire at and hit a target.

Rocco joined me a moment later, handing me one of the AK-47s we had on the yacht. He held another in his hands. "Well," he stated. "You did say the war was coming."

"Yeah," I bit out.

"And Leda?" he asked.

"In the hold," I replied. "If something happens, you go get her and get the hell out of here."

"My job is to protect you," Rocco grumbled as he racked the rifle.

"And her," I said. "She is to be protected at all costs."

Rocco blew out a breath. "Fine, whatever. I will make sure that she's safe."

I nodded and turned back to the moment at hand, feeling the familiar warmth of anticipatory violence welling up in my belly. I had been here before. Hell, this was where I was most comfortable.

This was the first time, though, that I had had someone else to fight for. In the past, the Mafia had been what I fought for—the most important thing in my life.

Now it was Leda.

The Mafia had turned its back on me. Well, some of the Mafia. No more of this cloak and dagger bullshit. At least now, all the cards were on the table. Things were clearer now. Black and white instead of the different shades of gray.

"So what's the plan?" Rocco asked, breaking me out of my thoughts.

I shrugged. "There's not much to it. Shoot at anything that moves until we get to the house."

Rocco scoffed. "You do realize we are on the back of a fucking yacht, and they are on jet-skis. This boat can only go so fast. They're going to catch up."

I clapped him on the shoulder. "Then shoot straight."

"Remember what I said before?" Rocco asked, a smile playing on his lips.

"That I was going to be the death of you?" I grinned despite the tension in my body.

"Yeah, that."

"Only one way to find out, right?"

He might be right. This might be the fight that neither of us could win.

I checked the magazine and clicked the safety off the AK.

But I would do it to keep Leda safe.

### End of BOOK 1

Leda and Lucas' story continues in Book 2 – *Merciless King* – paperback and hardcover coming in October 2021